EAGLE

BIRDS OF FLIGHT – BOOK THREE

J. M. ERICKSON

Eagle: Birds of Flight—Book Three (2nd Revision)

Editor: Suzanne M. Owen

Cover design: Cathy Helms
Avalon Graphics, LLC
http://www.avalongraphics.org

Layout and eBook conversion done by eB Format
http://www.ebformat.com

Publisher: J. M. Erickson
Blog - https://www.jmeindieblog.com
Publisher website - http://www.jmericksonindiewriter.net

ISBN (MOBI Format): 978-1-942708-36-0
ISBN (ePub Format): 978-1-942708-37-7
ISBN (Softcover): 978-1-942708-38-4

Printed in the United States of America

Praise for *Eagle: Birds of Flight*

"...Well-written characters will grip you from start to finish as they experience chapter after chapter of action pack adventures...This novel hold a brilliantly executed plot line with multi-dimensional characters that will have you hanging on the edge of your seat..." - *Readers' Favorite*

"...the story just builds and builds layer upon layer. I do give the author credit for actually making a story that is intelligent and makes you think, and has a psychological cat and mouse edge to it...." - *Indie Book Reviewers*

"Readers looking for a new hero to follow after exhausting Bond and Bourne will gravitate toward the professional, enigmatic Burns, and the trouble that seems to follow him without rest." - *US Review of Books*

"...the story is first rate, the characters are developed professionally, the plots are clear and hold true throughout the book, and the settings for the scenes are spot on in regard to the little things..." - *Pacific Book Reviews*

"Erickson really pulled me in with this one and kept me flipping the pages as fast as I could take in the words. All of the characters are very well developed and you keep wanting to find out what is happening with each of them." - *Readers' Favorite*

Other Works by J. M. Erickson

Action/Adventure Thrillers

Albatross: Birds of Flight—Book One
Raven: Birds of Flight—Book Two
Eagle: Birds of Flight—Book Three
Falcon: Birds of Flight—Book Four
Flight of the Black Swan

Action/Adventure Science Fiction

Future Prometheus I: Emergence & Evolution—Novellas I & II
Future Prometheus II: Revolution, Successions & Resurrections—Novellas III, IV & V
Intelligent Design: Revelations
Intelligent Design: Apocalypse
The Prince: Lucifer's Origins
Future Prometheus: The Series
Intelligent Design: Revelations to Apocalypse
Rogue Event: Novella
To See Behind Walls
Time is for Dragonflies and Angels

He clasps the crag with crooked hands;
Close to the sun in lonely lands,
Ring'd with the azure world, he stands.

The wrinkled sea beneath him crawls;
He watches from his mountain walls,
And like a thunderbolt he falls.

The Eagle: A Fragment,
Lord Alfred Tennyson, 1851

Prologue

"Novum principium" – "New beginning"

"God damn it!" Alica Wise yelled at herself for the fourth time, having missed her exit to the auxiliary control room. As her car narrowly missed other vehicles fleeing the Merrimack Valley, she knew that every minute the Foreign Intelligence Agency's operation center was offline was another minute her country was at risk of attack.

It's already under attack! Bombs, fires, cyber attacks. How is he doing all this? He has to have help, she thought. *Maybe he's got his old support team back? Martinez and Perez have been gone as long as Burns has, even longer!*

With the operations center's backup system still dark, that could only mean trouble.

"How the hell could you be so stupid!" she continued to berate herself. Finally she arrived and her car vaulted into the parking lot after narrowly missing an ambulance going in the opposite direction.

Stopping her car right at the private bank's front door, Wise jumped out with her semi-automatic weapon poised to shoot as she cautiously entered the building. Even as she took a whiff of air and knew the smell of discharged gunpowder, she was more disturbed by the silence in the entire building. Before climbing upstairs to the auxiliary control room, she peered into the now-empty bank.

Odd. There's always someone here. If there was a gun fight, I bet it cleared out pretty quick. She looked left and right and saw that it was clear. Silent and still the environment was unnerving. After seconds of scanning she focused back upstairs as perspiration began to form on her brow. For early May, it was still warm, but she knew it was the stress more than the temperature that was making her sweat.

As she ascended the stairs, walking on the edges closest to the walls so as to reduce the wood creaking sound, she slowly approached the opening to the foyer above.

How the hell did I end up here? He couldn't this alone.

Wise felt her grip tighten on the gun handle. She had been working on another case when word came in on the Regional FBI's command center being breached, and then her own operations center falling dark under the same cyber attack. Then she heard that Anthony Maxwell, a seasoned operative, was KIA in addition to bombs at a hospital, office center, and town offices near a school. All this resulted in her being re-deployed to cover the route for the manager, Jillian Davis, to make it to this very place. If she hadn't missed the exit requiring her to back track against the traffic, she might have been able to do her job. What unnerved her most was getting a re-routed, two-way radio transmission from the chairman himself, warning her that all the mayhem looked like Alexander J. Burns's work.

Burns? He went MIA almost five years ago. With Maxwell dead and the Operation Center breached, it does make sense; he's the only guy who could do it. Get your head back in the game!

Shaking her thoughts to the present, Wise refocused as she looked around the corner to see if the area was secured. At first she wondered if she was in the right place, because it was deathly quiet, and the area was a shambles. The auxiliary control room door was wide open and there was paramedic material all around the floor, with chairs and the desk toppled over.

"What the hell...?" she said. She surveyed the scene. Looking over the trashed desk she saw the first guard, who was missing his shirt, with his hand raised, handcuffed to a chair rail. To his right was another guard, fully attired, and beyond him a dark-haired woman similarly handcuffed, who clearly had been in some kind of altercation based on the bruising, blood, and dishevelment.

"Shit!"

Wise felt for the woman's pulse. The light, long green jacket and features clearly matched Davis's description.

Well. You're alive, for what it's worth.

Feeling suddenly vulnerable, she jumped up and ran into the open door with her gun ready to look for the external hard drives she had hoped would be in place. She found nothing she was looking for in the deceptively larger than expected vault, including the cache of weapons, money, blank official documents, and code books--all were gone.

Slamming her hand against the dark monitor she yelled out, "Fucking Burns! How did you find it! How did you do this?"

Feeling her heart beating faster, she suddenly turned to find a hard line in the room, only to see that the two phones were yanked from the wall.

Shaking her head in disbelief, she marveled at how Burns and his crew had created some kind of computer virus that affected the majority of cell phones, making hardline telephones king again. The media was calling the virus "Albatross."

That's a stupid name.

Frustrated, Wise marched out of the room and was trying to avoid the medical debris strewn on the floor to find a working phone. As she descended the stairs to the bank, she stopped for a moment and retraced her steps back to the side of the desk where she found a discarded, large paramedic kit still open. While she was peering closely at it and then at the floor, her mind flashed back as she remembered the ambulance she nearly hit on the way here.

"What paramedic leaves their gear at the scene?" she said to herself. The answer came in milliseconds. She turned and ran at full speed down the stairs to find a working phone.

"Stupid, stupid, stupid!" she kept saying as she stabbed out the numbers of her boss's private line. It took only one ring before the chairman answered.

"Report" was his only greeting.

"Auxiliary control room breached. Davis and guards are alive but down."

"He didn't kill them?" he asked. Wise couldn't tell if he was disappointed or surprised.

"All appeared to be alive. All material in the vault, external drives included, are gone. Repeat, all external drives are gone. I May have a lead. An ambulance leaving the scene."

"Direction?" Eric Daniels asked.

"East, toward the expressway. I'm guessing north, but you never know with Burns."

"You have no idea. Pursue. Cratty is on her way to secure the scene. Go now."

"Webber?" she asked. She was truly concerned that Burns might have somehow killed her boss, Director Thomas Webber, as he was nowhere to be found during this crisis. From the tone of Chairman Daniels's voice, it was evident that death might be preferable to the consequence of being on vacation during a national crisis.

"He's still MIA. Go now, Wise. No time. Every second missed is another second that compromises foreign operations and gives the terrorists the advantage."

Wise simply hung up the phone and ran to her car. She jumped into the car, put the keys in the ignition, and her car was moving before her door slammed shut.

"Damn it!" she said as she tried to find the fastest way to the highway. "You gotta five-minute jump on me. You can't be far!"

Wise kept hitting the steering wheel every time she thought about her opportunity of catching a ghost slipping between her fingers. She had heard about Alexander J. Burns for years, ever since he disappeared from surveillance nearly five years ago. There had been reports of periodic sightings, as well as chatter about some group he put together to strike back at his old boss.

Scanning the roads for any sign of an ambulance, Wise kept wondering, *what the hell did they do to you to piss you off, Burns? Where are you?*

~

Alexander J. Burns sat quietly on the newly appointed marble seat inside a well-maintained mausoleum that held his beloved Samantha.

Looking back over their time together, the planning phases of finding the Operations Center, and living together as a family on the Rhode Island/Massachusetts border, were easily his fondest memories.

"Two years already," he said to himself.

He didn't expect an answer from her vault. It was just that when he visited, which was infrequently, he liked to talk to her. *Two years already since you've been gone.*

"It's getting close, Sam," he started to say, changing the subject from those painful memories of her death. "In addition to Cougar and her guys, Daniels finally made his move with sending someone in to do recon. He must have gotten tired of all the Senate hearings and just wanted to do it his way. The woman he sent is good, very good. I've only caught glimpse of her – small, athletic, always with a hat and dark clothes, usually in a crowd. If it wasn't for the team she was with, I never would have noticed. Cougar has some skills, too; she noticed, and her guys are watching them. Cougar's guys used to work with Welch. You would have liked Welch. She's a Marine like Helms."

Shifting his weight to take in the entire width of the small mausoleum, Burns was ambivalent about the other three empty vaults with names already in place.

"You know, I appreciate David's planning and the deal he got for a family package, but I really didn't believe him when he said 'It will be like old times. Hiding and hanging out together in Rhode Island.'" Looking around, he appreciated the mix of Orthodox Christian and Catholic stained glass and icons, and was impressed with how the groundskeepers kept the place clean, refreshed with daily flowers, candles, and incense.

Looking at the names plates under each vault, Burns smiled at David's inclusion of their code names for middle names: David "Coleridge" Caulfield, Rebecca "Tiny" Littleton, Alexander "Falcon" Burns, and Samantha "Raven" Littleton. To further personalize the crypt, Becky had put frames for pictures of each of them. When he would look at Samantha's pictures it made it much easier to talk to her. Both David and Becky put most of the money from the government to good use in the residential home Samantha attended when she was young.

Apparently, they had some extra to find this little gem. Cumberland Hill, no less.

He turned his attention back to Samantha's vault; he looked at her picture again. It was one of the rare times when she was smiling. *Something David and Emma were doing, I bet.*

"I miss you, Sam," he said quietly in the silent room.

Burns's mind wandered as he thought how glad he was that there were only four vaults, and not one for Emma.

It just wouldn't be right to have a place for a little girl.

Thinking of her, he realized he had some news about Emma. Digging into his pocket to retrieve his smart phone, he started his side of the conversation.

"It's strange to think that Emma has a sister out there. Helms tells me that one of his people, Janeson, spent quite a bit of time researching to find her," he said. He brought up a couple of documents on his cell as he continued. "Helms and Andersen do know what they're doing, I have to say. They know how to get people to work well with each other ... kind of the way you and David started our team." Taking a deep breath, Burns tried again to think of the present rather than on the past.

"Okay, Sam. I know you never had any interest in poems, but keep in mind these are from Emma."

After a moment of searching, he found the four he wanted to read.

He looked at his watch and noted the time.

"I'm sorry, Sam, but I can only stay for a couple of hours. Cougar gets upset when I'm MIA, even though I left her a message. Okay. Here are the better ones. If you forget about the grammar, they are pretty intense in emotion."

As Burns absently looked for Emma's work, his mind wandered back two years to Samantha's death. It was still painful to remember. He found himself more haunted by his past, as faces and names of people he had killed seemed to be surfacing more--an entire lifetime of death. It was strange to feel as if he was healing from Samantha's death as other people's deaths, people he didn't even know, seemed to weigh heavily on him.

Maybe it's my praying that's making it worse? Maybe my thinking about it so much is the problem, he thought. *Regret and remorse don't even capture the feelings.*

It was true that the more he prayed the more regrets he had for his past actions. Shaking his head out of the distraction, Burns refocused on his task as he found what he was looking for.

Clearing his throat while looking at Samantha's picture one more time, Burns started to read...only to stop a little way in.

A clap of thunder came out of the north and he could hear rain hitting the stained glass and roof. Taking in all of the sounds, smells, and Samantha's smiling image, Burns continued reading to her. After another moment, he stopped again.

Getting up, he realized that he had left his high-maintenance dog in the car, and that she was terribly afraid of lightning.

"Sorry, Sam. I'll be right back. You know Roxie. If I don't bring her in, she'll make a mess of the truck."

Pulling his sweatshirt hood over his head, he called back before exiting,

"I'll be right back."

~

Eric Daniels woke up before dawn, stirred by dreams of his early days when he was the operations center's director for Foreign Intelligence Agency.

My God, that was nearly twenty years ago. Long before Maxwell, Foley, Wise, Webber, and Burns showed up.

Getting up early in the morning was the new normal habit, as he was spending more time reading, exercising, and preparing for the future. Under other circumstances he must have looked like any other middle-aged man taking a break in life: camping and communing with nature just outside of Mackenzie, British Columbia. He had originally planned on camping more southwest of his present location, by Burns Lake, but the irony was simply too much for him to endure. Even though it was late May, the evenings were cold but the days were comfortable. Daniels chose to stay off the beaten track and keep a low profile deep in the woods far from people. At the same time he needed some elevation to make sure he obtained some cell phone coverage and maybe capture someone's wifi signals.

He straightened his back and stretched out as he shook off the sleep from his eyes and the cobwebs in his head.

"I really do miss wine." Long ago, he used to feel much worse in the morning, as he would consume at least two to three glasses of wine a night. Since his exodus from civilization, he had few provisions and wine was at the bottom of the list of needs.

It's good wine, though. But only one bottle for ten days at a time, he thought as he slowly built his morning fire for coffee and eggs.

He had plenty of freeze-dried food and military meals ready to eat but he decided that today was going to be special, allowing for a special morning meal.

Daniels took in the emerging morning light as it broke through the canopy of trees, and enjoyed the smells of coffee filling the immediate space. He cooked his eggs and noticed that the sounds he was generating seemed so abrupt that he tried to finish as fast as possible. He had become so used to the sounds of silence, wind, rain, and leaves that his cooking seemed more like a racket than usual. Even the thunder and lightning storm that had passed through last night seemed quiet compared to the noise he was making.

Happy to be finished making his eggs, he allowed them to cool as his coffee completed brewing. Cooking, camping, leaving his apartment, leaving his books, getting back at Burns; it was all about risk now, Daniels thought. He smiled as he remembered an old proverb of Asian descent he heard:

"'One cannot refuse to eat just because there is a chance of being choked'... it's gotta be a Chinese proverb," he said. It had been one of his favorites when he was chairman, not too long ago.

"When I used to be somebody," he said with a chuckle.

He turned his internal engine down considerably in the past several months not to rush, but rather to deliberately think, enjoy, and immerse himself in the moment.

I should have done this earlier, he thought to himself as he ventured a taste of his eggs. *I shouldn't have had to have everything taken away from me to do this.*

He tried not to think about how Burns had destroyed everything. How Burns had somehow returned from the dead years ago and in a matter of months destroyed his agency, his reputation and legacy, and compromised the safety of every US citizen.

He destroyed everything. Why? Over a woman! Because you were hurt! You were soldier, Burns! You took an oath to protect the United States. What about that? What about me? What about your loyalty to me and your team?

Daniels found himself always getting angry when he thought about Burns. But when he thought of the "others" his mind always ran rampant.

And those other bastards who are rewarding your treason! What the hell? Helms? Davis? Cratty? The President? Welch? What about my years of service? No reward for me. Let's give the traitors a house, why don't we? How about beachfront property in Spain?

He immediately pulled his thoughts out from the depths of hate to focus on his breathing. It always helped to focus on breathing as a way of getting out of his angry thoughts and his loss.

"Breathe ... Eric .... Breathe ..." he chanted slowly.

Daniels returned to the present and squatted down to eat his eggs and enjoy them.

Good thing I didn't stay by Burns Lake.

After taking his time, he poured himself a cup of coffee and blew on it to cool it down.

The first cup of the day is still the best.

As he held his cup, he continued stretching while looking about his simple camp, readying himself to start the day's chores he once took for granted--things that others did for him or took minutes to do were now part of a day's duty. Daniels breathed in the air and could tell it was going to be a warm day. He was glad for not being in "exercise mode" today, as he was planning to be busy coordinating "the missions" for the next forty-eight hours, or longer if necessary.

"Anyway, I'm tired."

Daniels had good reason to be tired: he had lost twenty more pounds in three months with his regimen of daily running, swimming, calisthenics, and karate kata. The thought that he should have lost weight changed his ways and doing it "old school" had pervaded his thoughts for weeks. While he was pleased with his revived muscles, endurance, and stamina, it was so boring to do hours of exercise and mundane activities. Further, though he was armed, he did not practice shooting as a result of not wanting to draw attention to himself.

Maybe some of my hair will grow back, he thought as he took stock of his physical metamorphosis.

If it hadn't been for his Shakespeare collection he had saved from his apartment and a set of Milton's works he picked up at the US-Canadian border, he was positive he would have gone raving mad with rage, boredom, and enmity.

He smiled for a moment when a line from Milton seemed to be fitting. He searched his memory, but it came to the forefront of his mind with little effort as he spoke aloud: "Never can true reconcilement grow where wounds of deadly hate have pierced so deep ...."

Wow. Do I hate Burns that much? Do I hate them all?

With eyes narrowing, and reflecting deeply on what was originally a rhetorical question, he found his answer quicker than expected: *Yes. Yes, I do.*

Daniels busied himself with setting up a folding table and chair in addition to two laptops, a tablet, and several cell phones. He also produced several wifi boosters and searched to find a number of internet signals he could piggyback on. While he was sure there were relatively few people camping close to his vicinity, he was positive there had to be a number of bored, type-A personalities, or teenagers who could not be completely out of contact with the world. It took twenty-five minutes to find three signals that would support his leaching.

He had three sets of color-coded notebooks which he now opened to specific pages and carefully marked off key points in each notebook.

Once done, he took a moment to look at his watch and did a mental calculation of the time in Spain and New Hampshire.

Almost time, he thought as he stood up to pour another cup of coffee and take in the sights and smells of his immediate environs before he buried himself in his work.

"Scanning really. Waiting. Keeping the lines open and making timed calls. Not exactly directing the action."

Daniels recalled the "old days" when he could be in the middle of every operation, set objectives, and maintain constant contact.

The old days weren't that long ago, really. Getting rid of my middle name and finally having people forget it, that was really long ago. It was at times like these when he had all the time in the world that he would focus on the more mundane and idiosyncratic thoughts.

What were you thinking, Mom, when you picked that name? Dad was Greek, but really ... do you know how many fights I got into over that? And the women didn't find it cute, either!

Daniels stopped for a moment and tried to refocus.

Oh boy, too much time to think again.

He began new efforts to focus, and was glad he had coordinated future calls, and would have to search the Internet for police scans and other law enforcement or media coverage for events that should unfold in a matter of hours.

That should keep me busy--or at least distracted.

Yet another Milton line seemed to fit the bill with regard to capturing the moment:

"They also serve who only stand and wait."

Daniels smiled and reflected on his situation.

So is this the way it's going to be? Shakespeare and Milton quotes?

Burns was never good at them. He should have done more reading. No one really reads anymore. I'm sure Glenn wouldn't have a clue if I rambled off some quotes. Who would?

His mind went back to his former manager, Jeff Glenn, and truly wondered if he was up to for such a big job.

He shook his head and tried to drop his negative thinking before it took a hold of him again.

Jesus, between Webber and Glenn, they couldn't even fire Cratty! How the hell is he going to control his team and pull this mission off?

Daniels shook his head again as a way of breaking up his dark thoughts, and made his way back into his tent to retrieve an MP3 player. He searched the menu and finally found one of his favorite collections of jazz.

"Yes ... this will help."

About thirty more minutes of this and I will be good to go, he thought. As he listened he came to a startling conclusion:

It doesn't matter if Glenn can do it or not. He has to. No choice.

Daniels smiled again. *Life is simpler now.*

~

Former Operations Manager Jeffrey Glenn, would have preferred a nice, quiet federal cell in Virginia than where he was at the moment.

Maybe pick up a trade. I always wanted to learn how to make watches. Now that would have been fascinating, he mused while standing on a flat roof above a vacant, half-constructed building over a narrow street. Looking at the empty condominiums, he thought their location was actually nice.

Fishing for his well-used sunscreen tube, he made a mental note to pick up more, as his third tube in as many days was beginning to run dry. As he watched the well-tanned, dark men around him, he shook his head as he calculated how many days of life were shaved off their lives as a result of ultraviolet rays. With both parents gone, from cancer, he did not plan to follow suit as a result of cigarettes, too much sun, or lack of medical exams.

Just a couple of medical tests, sunscreen, and smoking cessation could have kept them here longer to see us and their granddaughter.

He squeezed the lotion out of its tube and liberally applied more lotion to his face.

Under profoundly different circumstances, he might have enjoyed Torrox Costa, Spain, but the mission he was on threatened civilians and former colleagues. The only thing positive about this mission was that he was to play only logistics.

Lucky me. Logistics for a bunch of monkeys. No. I would have better luck with monkeys than these idiots.

Glenn looked around at his accomplices and then busied himself with reviewing the road three stories down as his "team" was making preparations to hit a convoy of VIPs in about an hour.

Team ... this "team" required constant review of keeping time, how to fire a rocket launcher ... point in the direction you need and shoot ... Jesus. Give me monkeys, please.

Looking at them as a group, he felt his jaw line hurt and face scowl as he looked down at his feet to expose his neck to put more sunscreen on.

What do they call me? Blanco hombre? White man?

Glenn knew that the days of working with a trained team was over. Ever since Burns compromised the Foreign Intelligence Agency and then revealed its secrets, his days as manager in an elite, clandestine, armed federal agency was over. He had been able to salvage his career and was cleared of all charges, but he and many other members were radioactive to their sister agencies, who wanted nothing to do with them. Instead, he now worked with third-rate hired guns of the Panelli family from the East Coast in the US. He had done some limited business with two family heads, a brother and sister named Angelo and Regina, but it was, fortunately, brief. As organized crime goes, the Panelli family was second-rate to a more sophisticated organization run by John Murphy. But that didn't mean that the Panelli family was happy with its position, and hitting this convoy was part of the plan to raise their standing.

He shook his head, trying to figure out if there had been another way he could have escaped this moment. If he had made a different decision, maybe he wouldn't be here now.

Shit, he thought. *No. There wasn't any other way.*

Glenn knew he had looks, intelligence, and a pretty good sense of right and wrong. Unfortunately, he had very bad luck at the tables, horses, and nearly every game of chance. His income had fed a gambling addiction, and once in a while he was able to take "some money" from evidence room, and confiscated property. All was well until he had lost nearly everything before his last assignment, the one that went after Burns that got his boss, Webber, killed.

Well, I guess there's a silver lining to every cloud.

He remembered what a piece of work his former boss was, and how he put himself ahead of his team.

That cost us sixteen agents' lives in Kea and the fall of a great agency ... what an asshole.

Glenn shook his head. *How did I get here ... easy. I was stupid.*

It was when Glenn was packing to fall off the grid that he got a couriered package filled with money, about seventy-thousand dollars with the proposal to receive more for "short contract work." The signature on the package was familiar and the call sign was legendary: "Eagle."

I could have just handed it back and gone to Cratty. I'm sure she would have helped. Why do I always second-guess myself? I needed the money, damn it. Anger swelled in his stomach.

Once he had used the money to pay off some debts, another package arrived with one-hundred thousand dollars more and tickets to Boston.

When he arrived and talked to the Panellis, he was positive the money wasn't worth it. But then they handed him another fifty-thousand dollars, and he took it. With his debts paid off and with the expectation that he was "just logistics" and an advisor, he took the job.

At least the money went to some good.

His sister and niece were in Germany alone, as her live-in boyfriend and father of the child had left them both. Glenn had planned on seeing them, but needed to take care of his debts. She was strapped for money, and now he was able to use his money for good. Hearing his sister's cries of joy as the money was wired to her was just priceless.

Hmmm. I also stopped gambling. No desire. Another good thing from this mess. So that's all I need to do is sell my soul to a mobster and the devil. Just great. Couldn't do gambler's anonymous or get treatment could you, dumb ass. Had to complicate things with getting into bed with Daniels and Panellis. Just dumb, Jeffery.

Glenn looked up at the scene of the ambush, his faint smile faded to a thin lined scowl, reflecting his not feeling as if he was lucky today.

He looked at his watch and scoped out his team, who were preparing for their assault. *You pay peanuts and you get monkeys.* He looked at one of the hired help.

He had gone over the plan repeatedly with the monkeys for weeks at some awful bar in tavern: *two support cars with the VIP car in the middle; the support car in the rear is on our team, and the front support car can be taken out with an SUV; block the VIP and show that you have a heavy weapon pointed at their car and they will give up ... how simple can it be!*

Glenn had all the routes, times, weapons, and more than enough people on the inside to make this work. Still, there were some additions in his cache of weapons and gear he received for the mission that he was really surprised at.

Maybe it was a mistake. Why do you need a rocket launcher? The guns alone and being boxed in should be enough to persuade anyone to get out of their car. Glenn had continued to think about the excessive firepower since he first saw the weapon.

Although there was a better choke point in the road for an ambush further down the road, he decided he wanted more isolation. His present location had three- and four-story condominiums that were in varying degrees of construction. They were supposed to be luxury apartments near the shore. That was, until the economy crashed and Spain followed Greece over its economic cliff. While the exterior shells and the majority of the basic interiors of the buildings were done, construction halted entirely, leaving a somewhat desolate small patch of street that the VIP convoy had to go through.

He smiled as he was hoping that his business would be concluded soon and he could just slip away to Germany.

When they captured the VIP, he planned to walk away. *It's Panelli and Daniels's problem,* he thought as he reviewed his exit strategy for the thousandth time.

Tangiers. It's a long drive out of here but I bet I can get there for the late-day ferry.

Glenn had been searching for months as to why he still felt loyal to Daniels. Having met the chairman two times, it wasn't a personal connection; it was more the association with the agency. It was his agency and Daniels was the agency.

Loyalty by proxy? Stick to logistics and leave the psychology to someone else His thoughts immediately went to his target. One target was the psychologist who helped Burns.

Helped Burns? Helped him do what? Become a traitor? Yeah ... I think I'll stay out of therapy.

Glenn watched his team deploy. *Two men on the end of the street, the SUV out of view well down the street, and the guy with the rocket launcher right next to him. Two additional guys that will block the retreat. They'll be boxed in.*

As he scanned the team's positioning, Glenn's anxiety increased as he listened to some unusual conversations from the monkeys. They had taken to talking in their own language, and seemed to be smiling a lot more, which made him nervous. As a result, Glenn had modified his plan. First he planned to make sure the VIPs were put in the monkeys' SUV and en route out of the scene, but then he decided that once he saw the VIPs were boxed in their car and he relieved his team member of the rocket launcher so that he could join and assist his comrades, Glenn planned on just walking away. He couldn't fool himself that it was just paranoia that made him want nothing to do with interfacing with the VIPs and their bodyguards. He was positive that the female VIP, Rebecca Littleton, would recognize him from their last meeting in Boston Bay, and Denise Cratty and her team would know him for sure from Operations Center, Bravo. He just couldn't endure that guilt and shame, or to look over his shoulder all his life.

Glenn had another disturbing thought: he hoped that the VIPs were all adults. There was speculation that there was a child, a girl named Emma, who might be with them. But he had been assured by Daniels via cell phone that she was typically home-schooled and not likely to be with the VIPs for safety reasons.

But anything can happen. Is Daniels always right? He missed on the whole Burns case. People make changes and alter plans, he reasoned. *And then there are the monkeys who are running the show.*

Yeah, I got good reasons for being paranoid, he thought.

As if to confirm his worst fears, members of his team seemed to smile more as they looked back at him.

"What are you assholes up to?" he asked himself as he took out a tube of sunscreen to apply to his face and hands.

Suddenly aware of time, he looked at his watch. 2:00 p.m. was rapidly approaching, and still no word from the inside team that would be following the VIPs' car. From what he knew, the psychologist worked as an elementary school teacher and would be heading home between 1:00 p.m. to 3:00 p.m. He was typically met for lunch by his wife.

"All we have to do is waiting," Glenn said to his smiling accomplice.

Yeah right, Smiley ... you assholes are up to something.

Chapter 1

"Secunda vita" – "Second life"

Burns stifled a yawn and found himself drifting from the conversation that was supposed to help him better understand himself. He had visited with Samantha for three hours and then drove through a thunder and lightning storm so that he could get home and be ready for his morning appointment. At the moment he was not paying attention to his therapist when she asked him what must have seemed like a simple question. Existentially, he was remembering how he had changed his life; yet again he yearned to be something he had forgotten to be: normal.

On his way back to the United States from Spain, he made a decision to put an end to the real threat of his former agency. In order to do that, he needed to become visible.

If I do this, Daniels might leave Emma alone. He might leave them all alone and come to me.

Upon deplaning, he made a point to walk in plain view. He remained vigilant, but he had to fight all his impulses to refrain from slipping incognito. From that point on, he became visible to all. His first step was to find a place to live, and after a week he had found an apartment in the small urban town far north into New Hampshire. The town of Waterford was nice, he thought, even though it had a lot of people in a small area, with a beautiful backdrop of the White Mountains. Originally he had found a nice small house to rent, but it was too isolated, and it was also in the town of Littleton. He couldn't think of living in a town that shared Samantha's name.

Once he found a place to live, he picked his bank, a place to shop for food and clothes, and a "regular" place to eat breakfast and lunch, and a tavern ostensibly to drink. The drinking part would be a little difficult, as he no longer liked the taste and effects of alcohol.

I guess the cover story will be a veteran who is on the wagon, he conjured up. *Should be easy to pull off.*

Most importantly, he made an effort to get to know the locals.

Gotta use all natural resources. The townies are the best ones.

There were times when he would watch the townies and feel some envy as they went to and fro in their daily tasks, spend time with their families, and hoped for the future.

Could that be me? Could that really ever be me?

To enhance his visibility, he decided to become an interior house painter so that he appeared employed. After seeing customers, buying supplies, and then eventually finding his way home, Burns experienced true loneliness.

He remembered thinking that this part of being normal wasn't good at all. Sounds of the clock, water going through the pipes, creaks from the wind, all conspired to reinforce how empty his home was, with plenty of room to add. After three weeks, he decided to take on a pet. He originally thought a cat would be good, except that he hated cats. Samantha did too, but she was partial to small dogs, he remembered. Also, he would have to take the dog out, which would give him yet another opportunity to see who might be watching. Still sitting in the office as his therapist seemed to be talking, he smiled as he thought of Roxie. She had been so good, waiting for him in the truck until it started to rain. He had to bring her in when he was visiting Samantha the day before. *Good thing she likes dogs.*

Finding a dog was not as easy as he had thought. The scrutiny the animal rescue team subjected the adopting pet owners to was more rigorous than his psychological testing he did annually when he was in the field. However, their efforts yielded a pretty good match: a high-strung, high-maintenance cockapoo dog was recommended. Something to do with "her needing a strong yet caring alpha male to heal" was the rationale for the match. To her credit, she was hypoallergenic, prickly, and had a name that Burns liked: Roxie. She was also cute, which proved to be important, as she howled the first week until he finally gave up and let the creature sleep in his room. She decided that the bottom of Burns's bed was adequate. His home was not empty anymore, and her addition made him feel less lonely, since Roxie simply followed him everywhere. She preferred closed-in spaces, so the cab of his truck was also fine for her when he took her to work. He had to get a tent for her as the days became warmer, as it would be too hot in the truck. The most striking effect of all was that she made him laugh and smile; she had adorable eyes and was also playful with him. With other people, he had to warn them to not pat. She was not friendly to others.

Clearly you got some trust issues, he was thinking when his therapist asked him a question.

"Mr. Tennyson? Did you hear me?" Dr. Cohen asked.

Burns had to remember that his last name was "Tennyson."

"I'm sorry. I was distracted. What did you ask me?"

Dr. Beatrice Cohen shook her head slightly and placed her pen on her pad of paper. She was an attractive, petite woman who wore bright make-up. Though stylish and fashionable, especially for the local color of flannel and camouflage, she stuck out like a New York socialite who made a wrong turn to Vermont during hunting season. Moreover she wore her clothes too tight.

That's gotta mean something.

It had taken him a while to find someone who was trained and good at cognitive-behavioral therapy. Fortunately David Caulfield had given him a short and long list of questions to ask to determine abilities.

The big thing he wanted help with from a therapist were ways to deal with the ever-present hole in his heart around Sam, and the numbing of other feelings such as hate, love, vengeance, joy--all the emotions he had felt when Samantha was alive.

"It's as if I'm stuck. Frozen in time when it was safer to feel nothing than to really feel that she was gone," he had told David earlier.

"You might need to let go before you can move on," he counseled.

How does he know this shit? Burns often wondered.

While Dr. Cohen did not fit the stereotype of a therapist who had her own personal issues in check, she did know her clinical stuff.

But she also did a poor job of keeping her feelings in check, as it was easy to tell when she was annoyed, especially in the morning, evidently before her third cup of coffee. Even though it was 9:00 a.m., she was not that bad.

Maybe I caught a break today. David wasn't kidding when he said that therapist had issues and were the worst in dealing with them. Burns tried to focus less on her problems and more on his. Getting out of his head was difficult sometimes.

Dr. Cohen leaned back in her chair from behind her desk. She was stretching a bit, which she also did when she was annoyed.

"I asked whether you had ever trusted any woman in your life before you met Samantha.

Burns's scalp began to itch as he fiddled with his necklace. It was the same necklace with the cross that Samantha had held when she died. The image of her dying with her asking him to pray was still too hard to talk about.

"I don't think so. The accident seems to have wiped out all of those personal memories," was his short answer.

"So she is, by default, the only woman you ever trusted. Maybe even loved. That is quite a loss, wouldn't you say?"

Burns looked at her to try to figure out why he did not like her very much. While she was often right in her assessment, her style was very different from David's. David was older and more confident, while significantly more nurturing.

She really does love hearing her voice and being right. David never had an interest in being right; he wanted to do the right thing for the patient no matter what ... even if it meant his own life. I wonder if Dr. Cohen would do that.

But she was right. Before David, Samantha, and Becky, he had trusted no one. Actually, he had to revise that thought.

"You are right Dr. Cohen. Though I do have a recollection of a woman I used to work with whom I did trust to some degree, but nowhere near to Samantha."

Dr. Cohen seemed to get excited, and pressed on with more questions.

"Where is she now? Do you still talk to her?"

Burns felt guilt in remembering his old colleague from several years ago, Deborah Foley.

She never should have been sent out on that mission. What was Daniels thinking? He wasn't thinking of her. He never did. Maxwell, me, Foley. We were all tools.

"No. She died in a shooting in the line of duty," Burns summed up. His scalp itched more and the itching now traveled to his hands as well.

Dr. Cohen sat back in her chair again and wrote a note. Then she took her glasses off after she put her pen down. It was a habit Burns knew too well, since she always performed this specific array of behaviors when she was going to make a clinical point.

Here we go. Another pronouncement, really?

"So the only woman you think you had trusted before Samantha also died a violent death?"

Burns found he was without words. He had to admit it; Dr. Cohen was right. *Again.*

Resistant to giving her credit, he thought, *Even a blind dog finds a bone once in a while.*

Dr. Cohen jumped at the silence: "You see, Mr. Tennyson. When you let your guard down and trust women, they die. That might make you very reluctant to trust a woman. Even men, for that matter."

While it might have been a distraction, Burns constantly had difficulty trying not to compare Dr. Cohen's approach to David Caulfield's.

You see, David would have let the silence sit. He would have let me fill it in and answer it ... Now why did I pick "Tennyson" as a last name? Oh yeah. Bait for Daniels. He loved to read ... all the classics, Burns remembered. More distraction, but he had to give her credit when she was right.

"When you put it that way, I guess you are right."

Dr. Cohen took another deep swig of her coffee and then noticed the time.

"I'm sorry, Mr. Tennyson, but it looks like our time is up. Same time next week?" she asked.

"Absolutely," Burns responded convincingly.

As always, he stood up first and extended his hand to shake hers, and left.

As he entered the waiting room, he noticed a small, athletically built woman who had dark hair and dark-brown eyes. She smiled at him as he walked by to exit the room. He made sure to smile back.

He immediately pulled up visual pictures of the clients he would see leaving and waiting for Dr. Cohen, and she was not one of them. She was new--she looked very familiar, but out of context. As he racked his brain, he saw Roxie getting excited to see him. Part of their routine when he finished therapy was to take her out to go to the bathroom and complain about Dr. Cohen. It was when he was picking up Roxie's fecal matter that he remembered where he had seen the woman before.

"She's a bank teller, Roxie," he said. "Yes ... she changed her hair and is taking a more direct approach. I guess Daniels gave her the word to move things faster, don't you think, Roxanne?"

Roxie looked at him attentively as she always did when he talked to her: her dark eyes widened a little bit and her tail wagged as if she completely understood every word.

"You see. You get me. You understand. Am I truly that difficult to comprehend?" he said as he rubbed her ears with both hands.

As Burns bent over to rub Roxie, he checked his truck out to see if there was anything attached to its undercarriage. He then lifted the hood to "check the oil" and make sure nothing else was there. Somehow having his truck explode seemed anticlimactic.

No way Daniels would authorize a straight kill. He's got to prove his superiority.

Satisfied that his truck was not rigged to explode, he and Roxie entered the cab and he began to drive away.

As he drove he saw that his tail was with him, as he had been under surveillance for several months. While initially he had been alarmed and planned to make his move, he soon realized that the tail was being clear and that they wanted to be seen. It took less than a minute to figure out who it was. He smiled as he watched the car move sloppily behind another car. For sure, it was not the small, athletic woman he had just seen in Dr. Cohen's waiting room.

Burns turned to Roxie, as if she had asked a question.

"Yup. Davis is with us. And I bet she and her buddies noticed the teller in Dr. Cohen's office too." He turned to Roxie and saw his very attentive dog listening as she always did.

And Dr. Cohen says it's difficult for me to trust women.

He stopped at a light and waved to a young woman pushing a baby in a stroller. He felt his smile fade as the memory of a crying baby in a van he had used as a weapon to kill a terrorist flooded back. There had been three civilian deaths before, but it was the baby's mother's death that stuck. Deb Foley had been killed in a fire fight just before he caused the accident that resulted in the mother's death.

It started then ... the memories, he thought as he sat at the green light. Feeling shame, angst, and guilt, he found himself uttering another prayer. This was the new norm over the last two years; when a memory of his past behaviors emerged, he prayed for forgiveness. As a horn honked behind him, he snapped out of his trance and waved to two women in the car behind him. Another smile emerged as the young woman looking to be the same age as Emma made a face as they drove away. Shaking his head, he started to speculate about what Emma's sister was like.

~

David Caulfield felt the warm afternoon sun on his face as he stood near an open window in the teachers' lounge, sipping warm afternoon coffee. Typically he would be having tea, but his sleeping had been far from normal the past week. Why exactly, he was not sure.

"Maybe it's guilt over my sins." He closed his blind eyes toward the sun, more out of habit than necessity. Years after he set his house to explode in Kea, trapping and killing sixteen federal officers in the process, he found himself constantly tired and far from rested. The small joys he had-- listening to Becky sleep, hearing Emma sing, catching

Becky laughing with Cratty or one of her girls--were wonderful...with a backdrop of pain, remorse, and guilt over being the instrument of death for sixteen souls. Taking another sip, David smiled at how Alex had somehow used prayer to heal and to seemingly move on with his life.

If you've got guilt, you hide it well, Alex, he thought. *Still, you see God as kind, benevolent father. I wish I did. I might pray more myself.*

Shifting his weight from one foot to another as he continued to soak up the sun, David smiled at his more recent discussion with Becky about God. While they were worlds apart in upbringing, once again they found a common ground. In the case of God, both he and Becky saw him as a very busy, short-tempered omnipotent being responsible for running the world, and not to be bothered with "small" prayers.

"If you got cancer or you have a dying relative, then you can pray. But pray for 'being happy,' 'finding love,' or 'losing weight,' God's more likely to give you cancer just to give you a real reason to pray," Becky told him weeks ago.

Blunt, as always. Still, I have to say, she's got a good point. But maybe that's why the international spy and assassin is happier than me? He has an all-powerful ally while I have a God that's just too damn busy. And if I piss Him off, that could be a bigger problem.

Still, putting logic and reason aside, David found that when he did actually pray selected prayers Burns had suggested, he felt better too. The guilt and fear subsided, while hope for the future grew. When he did pray, he prayed for others, living and dead.

We all are human. We all make mistakes. Redemption? I hope. I wish I could take mine back. I can at least remember those who need help and those who passed.

David felt his Braille watch to see when he should be getting ready. Emma was finishing up with assisting teaching as he waited for Cratty's team to make sure all the kids were gone before they moved out. Cratty and Ramsey had been particularly vigilant about security, and that meant everything went with "all deliberate speed."

Hmm. Maybe fifteen more minutes. By then it should be 3:30, he thought as he put his coffee down and rubbed his face with both hands. *I just can't wait to get home and sleep.*

"You know, Alex, if you were here you would know what to do."
David felt for his cup again and returned to feeling the sun: it took
about five minutes of careful review before the thought finally
crystallized in his head. As if to confirm his thinking, David said the
quote out loud as if the mere act would solidify the thought:

"It is a far, far better thing that I do, than I have ever done; it is a
far, far better rest that I go to than I have ever known."

Charles Dickens. A Tale of Two Cities. *You see, Alex? You would
have gotten that.*

Smiling, he closed his eyes yet again and waited.

Chapter 2

"Ex malo bonum" – "Good out of evil"

John Daniel Murphy sat quietly with his granddaughter, Rosemarie Flores, in a very ordinary, Spartan conference room of the Federal Bureau of Investigation in Boston. He was not used to waiting for anyone, let alone waiting for fifteen minutes. While the receptionist was pleasant enough to offer both of them either water or coffee, waiting was something he did not care for. Often he looked forward to times spent alone with Rosemarie; she was finishing her junior year in a college preparatory high school from Connecticut, and was often busy with school and homework. Murphy's relationship with his granddaughter was very close, as the girl's father, his son, had been killed many years ago in a drive-by shooting associated with their family business. That business, organized crime, had its obvious hazards. He had never really recovered from that loss, and as a result he tried to spend as much time as he could with his granddaughter even though that was often complicated by her mother, Lucila, who was very overprotective, and did not like sharing her daughter with him.

Early in his life, Murphy had met a lot of people in his line of work and had been personally involved in a number of decisions that left a lot of people dead, or worse. Unfortunately, his son followed suit in his treatment of others--but in addition, he enjoyed his women. Rosemarie was the older of the two girls he discovered after his son was killed. The youngest, illegitimate granddaughter was the reason both of them were there today. Although Rosemarie's mother was alive, she had a great many psychological issues that made her want to stay at home and not venture out. It took a while to find out that Lucila, who used to be one of his most productive girls in turning tricks, had also fallen in love with his son. When he died, she retreated further into her home, rarely going out. But when it came to setting up visits to have relationship with his granddaughter, Lucila was the most difficult person to deal with, to say the least. It might have been easier to just kill her and be done with it, but he found it an unpleasant thought most of the time. A new sense of morality pulled at him when he became a grandfather.

When Rosemarie was seven years old, she did most of the explaining to her mother, which helped Murphy get to know and love her as his own daughter. After some time, Lucila allowed Rosemarie to go out and attend school. But it meant that Murphy had to supply money and people to assist in taking care of them both. When they moved to Maryland, Murphy bought the house down the road from the elementary school and middle school. He made sure food was delivered and furniture purchased, and that there were at least three hired caretakers to be there for Lucila. When Rosemarie was accepted at an elite private college preparatory high school in Connecticut, he did the same thing. With Lucila's needs met, requiring her never to leave her home again, Rosemarie spent more time away at school at events, and with him than at home. In the past year, as controlling as Lucila could be, she was satisfied with calls from Rosemarie. While the thought of just disposing her reared its ugly head and brought him some pleasure, the idea of hurting Rosemarie's mother made that all but impossible.

She's gotta be on medication or something. How can a person stay in the house all day?

Rosemarie was the only living memory of his only son. She had his dark hair, nose, and chin. She also had his laugh and some mannerisms. When he was with her, it reminded him of when his son had been young and innocent. Whenever he got the opportunity, he spent time with her.

This was the first time Rosemarie had been at a very high- level meeting. Since the death of Murphy's son, he had her kept out of all meetings that would shape the family business future. While counterintuitive to most parents, Murphy's greatest regret was that his son learned the family trade directly from him and then paid for it with his life.

Murphy felt a wave of pain in his heart.

Must be the guilt.

To avoid the same fate as his son, Murphy planned on having his granddaughter know nothing about the family business's specifics, which would open up more legitimate ventures, and hope, for her. He was greatly pleased that Rosemarie seemed much more interested in more conventional business--specifically, international banking. If she continued on the right trajectory, she would move toward more legitimate enterprises. That meant Rosemarie would have to eventually "part ways" from him and seemingly disown the family, if she were to ever break free of the family legacy.

My God! I can't even think about it! It's heartbreaking to think we won't spend any time together. But if I want her to live, I have to start the process now. I hate law enforcement rooms. So sterile. His gaze took in the conference room as he thought about Rosemarie's future and next steps to secure her future.

It was all part of the plan, he reminded himself. Today's meeting was absolutely critical--Rosemarie had to be there, as it involved her directly and her half-sister.

Of all the meetings to attend, this one has to be a hard one for the lass, he thought.

Still, Murphy hated waiting even more than the room, and especially alone with Rosemarie and none of his bodyguards. While his bodyguards were only forty feet down the hall, he felt naked waiting in the conference room. Since he had also made it clear to his lieutenants and his "number one" man, Robert "Bobby" Fitzpatrick, that he needed the Bureau to pass along a warning, he was sure that they too were feeling nervous.

Maybe they think I'm going to rat them out? Kind of stupid to do that and bring them along. Still, blood is thicker than water. Soon the wait will be over.

The door of the conference room opened and a young woman with her staff came in. While Murphy had heard a great deal about the director, John Helms, his deputy was more of a mystery.

All the money in the world and I got nothing on this woman, he mourned. *No leverage. No pull. No skeletons. Nothing. Except that her parents might live in Florida. There's something about Russia, though? Uncle? Why couldn't I get more intel on this girl?*

Murphy watched and stood up as Deputy Director Rachael Janeson, flanked by three of her staff members, entered the room. He stood up and was about to sit down when he was taken by surprise by the deputy's next action: she walked toward him and extended her hand to greet her guests. He was surprised by her extending her hand to shake his, since few people in law enforcement ever showed him that courtesy. He took it and was pleasantly surprised by the firm grip.

Maybe this will all work.

The deputy introduced her team, who maintained distance but nodded their acknowledgments while they remained standing, taking positions around him. Murphy introduced his granddaughter, who demonstrated her education by properly addressing the deputy director as "ma'am," and she went to shake hands with the other agents, who gracefully shook hers.

That's my girl. Good manners will get you far. Respect will get you further.

Then, when Murphy, Rosemarie, and Janeson took their seats, another unusual event occurred. Janeson took the seat to the immediate right of him within the less-than-comfortable, three-foot personal space rule, rather than taking the head of the conference room table.

Well, this is all strange ... I hate everything that is strange. And those blue eyes.

Murphy had never been in this situation before. He expected the other agents to remain standing, which they did. But the fact that Janeson did not need to sit at the head of the conference table to reinforce her authority in the meeting was remarkable.

"So, Mr. Murphy, what brings you here today?" Janeson asked.

He readily regrouped and began with a preface.

"For the record, you have already concluded that I am here without counsel and only in the presence of my granddaughter," he stated.

As he was expecting some kind of rant or questions, Murphy was again surprised by her less-than-expected answer,

"Duly noted."

There was a momentary silence. While expecting a bit more than a literal acknowledgment of the obvious, he shrugged his shoulders and bent over to get an envelope out of his briefcase. The three field agents-- Gilmore, Johnson, and apparently the "new gal" Dillon-- immediately put their hands on their hip holsters; the female agent opted for her shoulder holster which harnessed a very large-caliber semi-automatic gun.

"Wow, people," he said as he brought both hands back up to show he had nothing in his hands.

Murphy could see that Rosemarie sat perfectly still, watching everything but remaining poker-faced.

Now that's more of what I'm used to.

Similar to Rosemarie, the deputy director still sat calmly and quietly right next to him.

What is your story, Janeson?

"I'm getting an envelope out of my briefcase; your people were very good at searching me and my granddaughter. I half expected a full cavity search," he said.

"The deputy director asked us not to and we reluctantly accepted," one of the agents responded. Murphy made a mental note that the agent was Gilmore, and it was clear he wanted Murphy dead. With Gilmore and the other agents, he was feeling comfortable; the enmity was familiar.

They're readable. Predictable. You can see where they're coming from ... her ... not so much.

The deputy director was another story. If his concern wasn't so important, he would have wanted to spend more time trying to figure Janeson out.

Murphy continued, ever so slowly, to extract the large manila envelope and hand it carefully to Janeson. As he sat back, he began to explain his situation.

"I'm here because I'm very worried about my granddaughter. She is presently in Spain with her family. They are taking very good care of her, but I have information that leads me to believe that she is in danger."

He watched Janeson closely for any visual cues as she reviewed a number of black and white stills and a few color prints of a teenager, walking to school, being hugged by a very athletic, blonde woman and observed very closely by another woman, and doing other mundane duties. Murphy went on.

"Just to be clear, these pictures were taken two years ago. They were only taken for reconnaissance so that I was sure she was safe and well cared for by her family."

"And is she, Mr. Murphy"? Janeson asked as she passed the pictures to the other agents.

Who is this woman? No visible response at all to the pictures, and an odd question to boot.

The other agents demonstrated some evidence of recognition, especially the agent named Dillon.

As odd as she is, she is at least listening.

"Yes. As much as I hate to admit it, she has blossomed under their care, as well as the care of the US and Spanish governments. As you can see, I have known where she is, but have chosen to do nothing and leave her in their care. I would have been fine leaving things be, but I think she is in danger."

He watched for some kind of reaction but nothing seemed to register. Janeson simply stared back at him with her piercing blue eyes.

Now this is the part where you say "Danger? What danger?"

Finally, Janeson spoke, but again it was far from what he expected.

"You will need to elaborate on how all of this is related before I need to leave for another meeting. If you could do that rapidly, that would help me out in scheduling," Janeson said matter-of-factly.

Murphy stopped dead in his tracks, at a loss for words. He could not bear that she was rushing him.

"Are you fucking kidding me? Do you know who I am? I am trying to keep my granddaughter safe, and you want me to rush so that you can get to another meeting?" he fumed.

It was easy for him to see that all the agents tensed up. He really wanted to strike the woman, but Rosemarie was there and he was sure the two male agents would have loved to kill him right then and there.

No, that wouldn't be good for Rosemarie to see, he reminded himself. Again, he noted Rosemarie was still, but taking everything in without fear. *God, she is strong. Fearless*, he thought.

"Yes, Mr. Murphy. I know something about you," Janeson responded very coolly. To Murphy she seemed almost oblivious to his anger, which made him more angry and confused--two emotions he hated.

Almost the worst of emotions...except for maybe feeling helpless, he added to his mental list.

Janeson went on.

"You are John D. Murphy, III. You are suspected in at least thirteen murders; all gang-related. You reportedly move and sell drugs out of state. You have been implicated in a number of racketeering and prostitution charges, but there was never hard evidence to make the charges stick. Since the murder of your son, Joseph Daniel Murphy, thirteen years ago, you have shifted a number of your enterprises into legitimate businesses with the sole exceptions of reported gun running to Ireland and Greece. You have been 'at war' with other organized families in Boston as you have seemingly made it you life's work to keep 'your town' clean of drugs, illegal guns, and violent crime. Interestingly enough, you have been talking to various lobbyists to push for legislation to make prostitution legal, so I am guessing you see prostitution as 'better' than overt violence," the deputy director concluded.

Murphy was searching for words. He had difficulty focusing at the mention of his son's death. He also was shocked that this deputy had listed all of the allegations in front of Rosemarie. She knew he had a past, but neither ever talked about it. He was sure that Lucila told her things about him and his son, things a little girl shouldn't hear about her family. *But to hear it from a third party!*

He sighed and tried to find words.

Fortunately, Rosemarie was there to help out.

"My grandfather is worried that my half-sister is going to be kidnapped or worse by another family to gain leverage over my family's business," she said calmly.

Murphy looked as his granddaughter and felt sad and ashamed.

I can't even do this right. She had to ask for help for me. Why couldn't I've just said that without all the bullshit?

There was no noise, as the response from the young girl had not been expected. From his perspective, this Janeson seemed as if she was focused solely on the data and needed more. He had come back from his grief and went right to what he knew.

Okay. You want data? Here you go. I really don't want Rosemarie to hear this, but I've got to get my point across now.

"Two months ago, some of my men came across a meth lab in South Boston. As we were disposing of the material, the chemist wanted to bargain for his life. Since he felt set up by my competitors, he offered any information he could to get back. He had apparently spent time with one of the higher-ranking lieutenants of my competitors, the Panelli family, who was shooting his mouth off about how I would be packing up and leaving in a couple of weeks. He mentioned something about a former federal agent and me having 'some family in Spain.' The last part alarmed me, so I had a team assembled to do a couple of break-ins to find any information of what he might have been talking about. I received this late last night," Murphy concluded as he slowly and carefully extracted a single piece of paper that held a letterhead on a memorandum that had not been seen in years.

He handed the document to her, who read the document very carefully and then handed it to Dillon. Her reaction, unlike Janeson's, was clearly readable: *Fear. She'd be terrible at bluffing at poker if she needed to.* When Dillon saw the document, she seemed to blanch. Murphy shifted his focus back on Janeson who seemed to take that painfully obvious, non-verbal statement to confirm that the document might be original. *I guess there's a national threat brewing.*

Finally Murphy was feeling a bit more in control of the meeting.

"Mr. Murphy, I am guessing there are a number of your key 'staff' who are aware of this document," she pursued.

"Yes. I think they know that if they talk they will have to pay a steep price," Murphy concluded.

He watched as Janeson was quiet for a moment. She had been leaning slightly forward with her hands folded for the entire interview. But now she leaned back in her chair with steepled fingers, thinking.

He looked at Rosemarie, who finally did move and shrugged her shoulders, and watched Janeson ruminate for a long two minutes.

"All right, Mr. Murphy. You have my attention. I need you to do me a favor," Janeson said.

What? I have to do you a favor?

"You want a favor from me? I came here to give you gold to keep my granddaughter safe and you want me to do you a favor?" he said with great frustration.

"Mr. Murphy!" Janeson said.

Murphy could see that the sudden change in tone and volume caught everyone else off guard as well. Up until that moment, her voice had been low, even, and cordial. Now her raised voice was jolting as she demanded attention right then.

Okay ... you have my attention....

"I have two ways to make sure I ensure your granddaughter's safety. One is through unofficial, back channels that I would trust with my life, and the other is through official channels I am positive might be compromised. I need to talk to my unofficial contacts as soon as possible and to my boss, Director Helms, who is on assignment. He and his colleagues will want to talk to you directly. I will then have to talk directly with the security team leader so that she can tighten up her team. I need to do these things simultaneously. Finally, I have to inform the Bureau in DC. I hope you are picking up on the subtlety here when I say I am putting the Bureau in DC third on the list. As a result, my unofficial contacts will want to talk to you directly. If you go home and wait right now, we might be able to move people to a more secure place within ninety minutes. If I go to DC first, we will get movement in thirteen hours. Which one do you want?"

Murphy now understood why Janeson was in charge; she seemed to think on a multilevel tier that was based on data.

Well. All right. I feel pretty stupid.

He hated to admit it, but the deputy director was probably right. She did not wait for a response from Murphy.

"Mr. Gilmore, would you please escort Mr. Murphy and his ward to the front desk? Do you want a uniformed escort to get to your home?"

Murphy smiled.

She really does seem to run hot and cold. However, it's nice of her to offer an escort.

"I think I can get there with my guys; no problem," he said as he started to collect his brief case. But then he was caught off guard again by Janeson's sudden response.

"Thank you for coming in Mr. Murphy and sharing this critical information," Janeson said as she extended her hand again to shake it. She continued as she also shook Rosemarie's hand as well:

"We may be talking quite a bit over the next thirty-six hours, Mr. Murphy. So, if you would be able to leave your cell number with Mr. Gilmore, that will be helpful. I do plan to get a court order to track your cell number. You will not have privacy to conduct any business."

Murphy was genuinely puzzled by the deputy director. She kept treating him with respect and was actually being honest with him that she was planning to track his phone.

"Do you plan to eavesdrop as well?"

He already knew the answer was "yes." He just wanted to hear her say it.

Candor is so refreshing. Maybe I can read you. Honesty. Up front. No hidden agenda. Kind of nice. Really don't see it much in law enforcement.

"More likely, if I can get it. I am guessing that will be difficult, and I'd rather focus on protecting people than finding a cooperative judge," Janeson answered.

"Thank you for clarifying," Rosemarie replied.

"You are welcome."

Then the deputy director turned to Rosemarie.

"Miss? Do you have a phone?" she asked.

It was easy to see that his granddaughter was caught off guard by the question, but she did respond.

"Ah, yes," she said.

Murphy watched the deputy make eye contact with the agent Gilmore.

"Mr. Gilmore? Before Ms. Flores leaves, I want her phone to be loaded with a GPS and eavesdropping recorder as well."

Murphy was struck by how Rosemarie's face seemed suddenly struck with fear until he remembered she was a teenager.

"But what about my friends? We talk about stuff I don't want you guys to hear. Personal stuff."

Poor thing, he thought. With a smile he was about to tell Rosemarie that safety was more important than privacy at that moment, when the deputy director provided a solution.

"How about this, Ms. Flores? Mr. Gilmore will give you a very small, flip phone that holds a GPS and recording device that you need to keep with you, on your person, at all times. It won't be connected to your phone, but it will be on for three days until it needs to be recharged. Mr. Gilmore will show you how it works. But let me be clear. If you fail to take care of it and do not keep it with you, we will know. And I will be forced to bug and trace your phone. Nothing will be secret. Deal?"

Murphy smiled as he watched his granddaughter smile and agree. He thought it was funny that this woman was treating Rosemarie as if she was a twelve-year-old.

Not much experience with young adults, I see.

As both grandfather and granddaughter were walking out, he turned to ask another question. *This woman was so honest that maybe I can glean more information.*

"How do you know I am telling you the truth?" he asked.

Murphy watched as Janeson reflected again and then carefully outlined her thinking.

"First, I suspect that you have more important things, however illegal, than to come into the FBI regional office to present a farfetched story while exposing your credibility and safety with both your immediate associates and your competitors. Secondly, you produced a classified document with genuine Foreign Intelligence Agency Operation Center seal, and the code name 'Rising Phoenix,' which pertains to your granddaughter and her family. Third, the two people who took the telephoto pictures you showed me were identified by two former operation center field agents. They allowed your men to go back to you so as to back track their origin, which was your place of business. Finally, our sources, both official and unofficial, are aware that your son, Joseph Daniel Murphy, is the biological father of Ms. Emma Littleton."

While all of what she was saying was logical, Murphy felt pain as she mentioned his son's death and his granddaughter as "factors" of an analysis.

It seemed to him that Janeson let the pause hang for a moment before she continued.

"Unfortunately, your son killed Rebecca Littleton's brother, Anthony Littleton, and his girlfriend, Emma's biological mother, which led to her being taken in by Rebecca and her sister, Samantha Littleton. You can see how the situation is complicated at best."

Murphy felt a wave of anger, guilt, and shame all at the same time. He felt helpless that he could not save his son, and for being removed from his granddaughter's life. He felt shame that his son cared little about his own children and their well-being. Worst of all, he felt guilty for letting his loved ones and family be taken from him.

He was at a loss of words for some time, but finally spoke.

Rosemarie must think I'm a monster.

Murphy found it difficult to make eye contact with anyone in the room as he thought about the past.

"I found out years later what happened. I didn't even know she was alive for a few years," he said, more to himself than to Janeson. His voice weakened and trailed off as Janeson answered the unasked question.

"Regrettably, since the loss of Samantha Littleton, Rebecca Littleton has no siblings. The man who composed that document killed her, and your son killed her brother. While she has reported having some resolution with her brother's death, the relatively recent death of her sister has seemingly reignited Ms. Littleton's sincere grief that she did not kill your son in retribution for her own brother's death."

So there it was. Murphy knew that Janeson's words were simply a report, evident in both her review of the situation and her concluding remarks, which were without malice or emotion. Janeson was responding, in detail, to Murphy's question. Somehow, it made Murphy feel much worse.

Murphy began to turn and walk away, but turned to see what his granddaughter was doing.

"I'm sorry my father killed Ms. Littleton's brother," Rosemarie offered. She was standing behind her grandfather and had put a hand on his shoulder.

Again, there was a change in Janeson's presentation that seemed to deviate from her calm, cool demeanor.

"I did note that Ms. Littleton expressed ambivalent feelings about you, Ms. Flores," Janeson said while making firm eye contact with Rosemarie.

"Ms. Littleton is of the very strong belief that Emma should have some contact with her half-sister. Both Rebecca and David Caulfield have made Emma aware of your existence. There was and still is discussion about setting up a meeting with you. Ms. Littleton believes that if Emma has a sibling out in the world, she should make the choice about contacting you or not. Not them."

Murphy's eyes welled up. He had always been heartbroken about his son's death, while disappointed that his son was reckless, that he did not value family, and didn't seem to care that he had children out in the world. Murphy found that to be unfair to Rosemarie. He had struggled for years to make it right, but pushing a reunion with his granddaughters would not only be met with resistance, but his competitors would know his secrets, his granddaughters, and exploit them. Maybe his attempting to help Emma might pave the way for Rosemarie to have a relationship with her only sibling. *Blood is thicker than water,* he thought.

He watched as Rosemarie broke from Janeson's gaze and fell behind him to follow Agent Gilmore.

Well, that was the most stressful meeting I have ever had. And I've had a life time of "difficult meetings."

Chapter 3

"In omnia paratus" – "Ready for anything"

Denise Cratty watched from a distance with Becky Littleton as her team escorted David and Emma to their car. Actually, it was a new SUV with extra protective metal for door and windshield reinforcement.

About time. Those sedans were death traps, she recalled. *It only took a couple of years to get an upgrade.*

Still, she was glad to have her charges and team in some real protection.

She watched as David and Emma were heading home from school. David had started teaching second-grade children English and Latin. Unofficially he also taught American music. Today was an extra treat because Emma had a day off from school allowing her to volunteer to help David teach.

Damn it! Where are my binoculars when I need them?

She adjusted her eyes and watched Emma in her navy-blue dress and matching jacket over a white blouse, animatedly talking to David.

My God. She does love to talk. She always has something to say.

There was little secret that Cratty enjoyed being in charge of the team to protect Emma and her family. She felt unusually close to Emma and Becky, for very different reasons.

Emma was innocent, smart, and simply open to new experiences. A "free spirit" was close to what her nature was, and she was very trusting at the same time. It was routine for Emma to seek her out to play games and to have her tell her "adventure stories." Cratty tried to maintain distance so as not to get emotionally involved, but that was impossible.

She also felt as if she had a "unique" relationship with her boss, Becky Littleton. She was hard, quick, and constantly vigilant. She always seemed to be scanning and figuring out new strategies, whether they were a particular type of strike or an elevation with moderate wind for a shot.

I guess living underground, under threat of being discovered and trained by Burns, would do that to a person.

While she enjoyed watching the family interact, it was clear that Becky was the "alpha" male, while David simply enjoyed both Becky and Emma. Cratty respected and even admired Becky's dogged determination to survive, at any cost, and at the same time be a mother and a wife.

Jesus ... the new modern-day woman. Get dinner and make sure I clean my rifle for practice tomorrow. My kind of woman, Cratty thought as she watched her team expertly put the family in their new SUVs.

Today was different from the routine. Usually Emma was home schooled and David and Becky would do food shopping for the week and see some of the local neighbors. However, Becky and Emma had an argument that morning and Becky wanted a bit of "alone time," so David offered to take her to school to volunteer while the "girls go shopping."

Cratty had a hard time not bursting out laughing when she heard David say, "Yeah. Why don't you and Denise go out and do a little shopping? Get some shoes, check out the new fashions, see if you can get a good deal on some gunpowder for the hollow points. Oh! Play your cards right, I bet you could score a deal on a spring-loaded biped stand with matching infra-red scope. And don't forget the flash guard; a fire arm isn't complete without a flash guard."

Cratty marveled at David's deadpan presentation as she waited for Becky's classic response; she hit him in the arm, got her purse, and walked out of the room. What made it worse for Becky, and difficult for Cratty to contain her laughter, was the fact that Becky had mentioned to her earlier her desire to find a larger capacity magazine for her modified AR-15.

Cratty was still smiling about that interaction of that morning as she now watched the convoy of SUVs drive away.

"Ready to go?" Becky asked.

"Almost," she responded somewhat distractedly. Cratty did not like it when she split the team. Worse than that, and much to Cratty's chagrin, David was a creature of habit. While she did have the latitude to alter routes, the location of the school and the size of the town precluded many options. There were few changes in the routes to take to get from the school to home, or out of the home to market. At two places there were four natural choke points. The only thing Cratty could do, in addition to petitioning the town to make two more roads, was to vary the times so as to be less predictable.

Typically, Ramsey and she would transport David and Becky to school and then shop for supplies in the middle car while Horowitz, Fitzgerald, and Belben drove the lead vehicle. The trailing car taking up the rear typically was under the purview of either local law enforcement or Spanish field agents.

Today, however, this change meant the need to improvise. Horowitz and Fitzgerald also wanted to be the primary bodyguards of the family rather than riding in the lead car. Ramsey, being the most senior agent next to Cratty, was designated to command the unit and arrange the transport and route any way she wanted. To accommodate everyone's needs, Cratty planned to go with Becky leaving Ramsey in charge of David and Emma. From a distance, she watched to see how Ramsey was going to deploy the troops.

As anticipated, Ramsey placed Horowitz and Fitzgerald together in with David and Emma, while she and Belben, the youngest agent, drove in the lead vehicle. Cratty had questioned Ramsey earlier about why she wanted to take point in the lead SUV, rather than riding with the family. She asked the question in full knowledge of the answer: Ramsey preferred the danger and risk of being at point. Cratty respected Ramsey's tough exterior, but knew she would put her life ahead of her team and the family.

"Okay. I'm ready," Cratty said as she turned toward the car. She managed a faint smile as she watched Becky put a small but powerful set of binoculars in her bag.

Always prepared. Always watching. You sure learned a lot from Burns all those years, she thought as she started the car and headed in the opposite direction. Looking out the window, Cratty thought about what life might be like if and when she would no longer be needed to protect Becky, David, and Emma.

I guess I'll go home...wherever that is now. Thinking back, her time in New York was brief while her time in Massachusetts, while nice was fraught with emotional baggage. Pushing the thought of "what next" out of her head, she made the decision to just leave her meager personal belongings in storage and worry about that when the time came.

Why do you always think so much?

~

Dillon lost track of time as she continued to look at the memorandum about her former employees that had started a fire storm of events two years ago. If it hadn't been for the fact that she fell in love with her best friend and now lover, she would be with Cratty, Ramsey, Fitzy, and everyone.

Murphy and his granddaughter had just left and now her thoughts were running rampant.

I should have stayed with them. Who the hell leaked this out? Dumb question! We know who did.

"Christine!" Janeson said with urgency.

"Yes, Boss," she responded, somewhat startled by Janeson's level of emotion. Janeson was the only person other than her family to call her by her first name. She liked it. Coming from her, it was all right. While Janeson's lack of social skills was legendary, working with her these past several months had been instructional and informative. While Cratty had her strengths, Dillon found it easier to communicate with and learn from Janeson. She could tell that Janeson wanted her input as to how the *Rising Phoenix* memorandum, still classified, was now public.

"Sorry. This has to be from Daniels. He also must have help from my old shop," Dillon said as she held the document.

"Agreed," Janeson said now, standing with one of her many color-coded tablets, which Johnson and Gilmore also carried.

She could see this tablet was programmed for all information in Torrox, including present time and weather.

Janeson turned to face Johnson directly first.

"Give Gilmore ten minutes, and then go get him. I want both of you in the Control Room. I need you two to accelerate your research on the present location of all past employees who might have had the security level to ascertain this memorandum. I also need you both to personally see if you can locate and acquire satellite and audiovisual communication over Torrox, Spain, at Cratty's position. I need this done immediately; all operations are secondary, with the sole exceptions of watching Murphy and his enemies watching him."

Janeson turned next to Dillon: "Dillon, get in direct contact with Cratty. Her team is over their head and need to get Emma, David, and Becky to a safe house. They are to trust no one."

Is this fear? Is she really that worried? Is it so bad that even Janeson can see it?

"Boss, you seem pretty nervous. What's wrong ... other than the obvious?" Johnson said. They all exited the conference room; it had to be clear to anyone watching that things were in motion and speed was of essence. Dillon knew her anxiety was tied to being in Boston when her team was in Spain.

I should be there.

"I don't like the timing of this: The memorandum and Emma's half-sister showing up. I'd rather be safe than sorry. I am going to talk to Helms. Get going, people," Janeson added as she walked at her usual rapid pace and made a sharp right to her office.

Dillon was easily in step with Johnson as they both went to get Gilmore and to take up their assigned tasks.

"Just like old times," Johnson muttered, more to himself than to Dillon.

"I'm guessing they were not necessarily 'good times,'" Dillon commented.

"Merrimack Valley Crisis on May 2nd, Burns's national security breach and eventual flood of data on the Ides of March, the entire planet's opinion of the US hits an all-time low, our allies check out, your old agency implodes ... you're right. Not really the good old days," he confirmed.

"Jesus, Johnson, thanks for the rally speech. What are you like when things go bad?" Dillon sarcastically asked.

Dillon was taken aback by Johnson's sincere look of concern.

"I hope never to find out. If anything more happens to Burns's family, I think I'll cut my losses and go home. It'll be safer."

Dillon said nothing; *What can you say, when the man is right?* She was really worried and she couldn't move fast enough to call Cratty.

Damn it! I should be there.

Chapter 4

"Deceessit sine prole" – "Died without issue"

Ana Ramsey was still giddy to finally have some real protection as she smelled the "new-car smell," and felt the clean rug mats and supple leather seats.

"Isn't it beautiful?" Belben said to her as Ramsey was tinkering in the back seat of the SUV.

"And it drives so smooth," she added.

"You got that right, baby! She's got enclosed, recessed, and hidden compartments for weapons, radios, and shit. Even access to meals, ready to eat in the back, along with survival gear. Just a piece of art," Ramsey was saying as she moved around in the back while Belben drove.

"How come Witzy and Fitzy don't seem too thrilled about our rides?"

Oh Cindy. You are so young, cute, and naïve.

Ramsey too her time answering and scrutinized the holding brackets for a semi-automatic rifle.

"They love it, Cindy. They're just being cool and laid-back about it."

Ramsey had watched Horowitz and Fitzgerald earlier that day as they walked around and then looked in and out of each vehicle as if they were inspecting a naval ship of the line.

The SUVs were reinforced with extra plating to withstand direct assaults from gunfire. While it could resist improvised explosive devices and other explosives, Ramsey was sure it could not take a direct hit.

Once they had dropped off David and Emma at school, Ramsey had left briefly and returned to the compound to retrieve a case holding one of her favorite automatic rifles with extra-large-capacity magazines and collapsible stock. Once she returned, she had to walk her perimeter to make sure there were no security issues. Once David and Emma were back in the middle SUV, she returned to the lead SUV and carefully pulled the weapon out of the case and placed it in a gun rack in the SUV to see if it fit.

"Look at that. You were made for each other," she said with much adoration.

She could see that Belben saw her wide, radiant Puerto Rican smile that confirmed a successful fit.

"I don't think I've ever seen you happier," Belben commented.

Though the ride was short, Ramsey took the opportunity to explore more of the SUV's secrets. While still in the back, she made sure to see that Horowitz and Fitzgerald were a safe distance behind them before she thought about getting back into the front seat with Belben. She also noted that the trailing car followed suit at a respectable distance, though she would have wanted them just a little closer to the VIP vehicle. Shifting focus, and having passed worst choke point, Ramsey just wanted to take a few more minutes checking out more of the back seat interior.

This is a fine ride.

~

Fitzgerald had to admit that the new SUVs were smooth and easy to maneuver, but were probably hell on gas with all the reinforced plating.

Rather pay more money for gas than get shot.

She kept her eyes on the lead car, and in her rearview mirror on the trailing car, just to make sure her spacing was good. At the same time, she was thinking about where she was in the route and how many turns and choke points there were up ahead.

With home no more than ten minutes away, it was a simple trip through the center of the town, parallel to the coast. There was really only one bad choke point, but when they passed that vulnerable point, she focused her attention back on spacing. The problem she now encountered was listening to her passengers discuss the events that had occurred earlier that day. As David and Emma were talking about "the fight" Emma had with Becky, and how there was a better way to get Becky to listen to her rather than getting her angry, Fitzgerald saw a strange situation unfold. They were beyond the "bad" choke point, where an ambush would have been perfect to spring, when Fitzgerald peered through her rearview mirror and noticed the trailing car slowing down. Fitzgerald motioned to Horowitz to check it out and confirm it was true.

She had known Horowitz for years, dating back to their college days as roommates at Cornell University. After years of living together and now working and living together again, they were able to communicate volumes in mere micro-expressions and movements.

Shit. I was right.

Horowitz took out her cell phone to give the lead car a heads up when both she and Horowitz watched a sizable truck, maybe a garbage truck, crash right into the lead vehicle's driver's side. Both the lead car and truck vectored in the opposite direction, with the truck still upright but slowing to a stop as a result of the impact, as the lead SUV was hurled off of its wheels and flipped three times before landing on its roof.

Holy shit! Where the hell did that come from?

She hit the brakes and swore out loud.

Horowitz, who was the most taciturn of the group, broke form with her assessment of the potential crash:

"What the fuck!"

Emma, who had picked up on Fitzgerald and Horowitz looking behind them, turned upon hearing the impact of the SUV and truck, and she instinctively screamed. Emma's scream snapped her out of watching the carnage, and she let up on the brake and started to speed up again, but then a vehicle, a larger SUV, blocked her from going forward and three men exited with rifles.

"Hold on, everyone!" Fitzgerald yelled out. She braked violently and then approached the SUV in reverse.

"It's a set-up, Fitzy! The trail car is in on it! Ram them!" Horowitz advised as she extracted her gun.

Damn right, she thought as she built up speed to smash into the trailing car as it attempted to block their escape route. The fact that their own rear car slowed down and gave no warning meant they knew something was up and let them walk into a trap. Fitzgerald concluded that they were the enemy too, and the thing Fitzgerald hated most was someone who back-stabbed you.

Screw you, you traitors! She was very anger as her foot depressed the gas pedal.

The trailing car had spun to a halt, putting its full length across the majority of the road, blocking the exit with walls of building enclosing them in. However, the trailing car and its occupants were caught by surprise at how fast Fitzgerald had reacted and did not have enough time to exit their own car before it was hit.

The SUV smashed right into the passenger's side and made a satisfying crunch of metal on metal and glass. Although the late-model car might have been made well, it was not reinforced like the SUV, and was pushed back several feet on impact until it was stopped by a construction dumpster.

Fitzgerald's head felt as if she had a bad case of whiplash, but she recovered quickly and put the SUV in forward with the full intention of smashing into the larger SUV.

"Hang on!" she yelled as she felt her wheels grip the ground and pick up speed.

Horowitz had to know what was coming, and to her amazement had jumped in the back to pull Emma on the floor, with her on top. Fitzgerald took one more look to see where David was and then she saw that he was now lying on top of Horowitz.

Should be the other way around? Witzy should be on top of you and you on top of Emma.

As she turned her full attention on the narrowing gap between her and the larger SUV, she caught the telltale exhaust stream of a rocket-propelled grenade as it hurled directly at her.

"Shit! Stay down" she turned back to yell at her passengers. She pushed the accelerator to the floor and swerved the SUV to avoid a direct hit.

Suddenly, Fitzgerald could swear she felt her body lift in the air as sharp stabbing pain penetrated her entire left side, while the sound of the explosion was deafening. But it was the bright light and the sense of wet warmth that made her feel both surprised and at the same time, almost relaxed. She had an image of her sister, who died when she was twelve, and had always wondered what it would be like to see her.

She kind of looks like Witzy. Taller, and smiling. She reached out for her. Her sister remained in place as if she were alive and well.

Then, as the light faded and she saw her world go from brilliant white to gray and then slowly to black, everything remained silent and her body felt numb and light. But her sister's image remained solid, with outstretched arms as if she was waiting to embrace her.

It's as though I'm weightless ... Fitzgerald thought as she melted into her sister's embrace.

~

David had endured many things in his fifty-three years of life-- almost two separate, distinct lives in that time. But from the moment he sensed something wrong in Fitzgerald's voice to Horowitz's yelling out "What the fuck," and Emma's screams, he didn't need sight to tell him something was very wrong.

Damn it! This is it! I wish Emma wasn't here!

David fought the force of rapid acceleration, deceleration, and then back to acceleration. There were commands being yelled out and directions given, but he could focus on only one thing.

Emma?! Where are you?!

All his thoughts were desperate and he pushed himself out of his seat to feel for her. If it hadn't been for Horowitz's jumping in the back seat and pulling Emma to the floor by his feet, he was sure he would never have found her, with all the rapid movement in the SUV. As David took in his breath to fight the acceleration so that he could move again, he heard Fitzgerald yell "Hang on" in his direction, as if she were looking back.

"Damn it," he said to himself as he hurled his body on top of the human mound by his feet.

Feeling a larger pile than expected, he realized he was on top of both Horowitz and Emma.

Oh my God! I hope I don't crush her. He suddenly felt the SUV's velocity violently stop as sounds of steel crunching reverberated through the vehicle.

Winded and slightly dizzy, David felt himself accelerating forward again and then the SUV felt as if it arced to the right as if to avoid something. He instinctively tightened his body more to cover Horowitz's and Emma's as much as possible as he thought, *I hope we make it.*

A clap of thunder exploded right next to him as he felt thousands of sharp shards pierce his body. While initially there was great pain, David felt suddenly relaxed, more relaxed than he had felt in years. No longer able to feel Horowitz and Emma under him, he realized he felt nothing--no pain, no sensation, and no sound in his darkness.

David felt himself smiling as Dickens's words flashed before his inner mind's eye: "... it is a far, far better rest that I go ...."

Feeling suddenly exhausted, he was caught by the vivid memory of how beautiful Emma must have looked at her baptism and how happy Becky was when Cratty asked her to help her train her team. He held the real vision of how Alex looked the day he remembered everything and the time he went out to lunch with Samantha so many years ago. The smell of Becky's skin after she showered, and Jenny's warm smile filled his mind as she sipped her coffee and he listened to her sing when she left to work. It all came back.

It's just so nice. I just want to sleep ... it's so nice.

He felt his face relax and then his entire body as if he was falling into a deep sleep.

~

Eyes wide, fists tight, and teeth clenched, Glenn watched the carnage from three stories up. When the SUVs showed up, he knew that he had been left out of loop on some critical data. He knew that his skin was naturally pale, or at least very white. He was sure he was white as a ghost as his mind did somersaults as to what to do next.

"I thought you said they had sedans? Cars? Those SUVs are probably reinforced!"

"Smiley," the "monkey" holding the rocket launcher, had a smile on his face when he gave his answer in fairly good English. What made his "smile" look all the more grotesque was a set of scars that flared from his chin to the right cheek.

"No worries. We got it covered," he said with more confidence than Glenn expected.

No worries? What the hell? They're civilians! Capture – not kill! Damn you assholes!

Glenn looked down the street that ran perpendicular to the road where the VIP convoy was heading. He grabbed a set of binoculars and focused on a garbage truck that was barreling down to hit the lead SUV.

He was glad there was a small, waist-level wall in place to keep him from falling over the side.

Fuck! That's not an SUV, it's a garbage truck! That means these assholes knew the convoy had SUVs and made adjustments. That's why they wanted the rocket launcher! Glenn pieced everything together.

Once again I'm the stupid patsy!

He watched helplessly as the garbage truck hit the lead SUV and sent it hurtling, flipping over for what seemed to be forever. With glass and metal strewn everywhere, the lead SUV finally landed upside down.

My God. They have to be dead, Glenn thought bitterly.

His attention was pulled away by another crash.

"Shit! Now what?"

He turned to the other side of the building and saw that the VIP vehicle had rammed their own trailing car, pinning it against a huge dumpster, and was now speeding toward a very large SUV.

No way they're going to get through it.

Glenn heard the high-pitched shriek of a rocket being launched from a reusable shoulder-held launcher. It was not the first time he had heard it. Two years ago he saw Rebecca Littleton take a helicopter down. Point and shoot. *Damn it!!*

His eyes shifted to Smiley, who launched the rocket and followed the trajectory. As everything seemed to move in slow motion, from his perspective, if the driver had not sped up and swerved, the rocket would have hit the vehicle dead on. Reinforced or not, the SUV would have been destroyed and its occupants dead.

He peered at the impact site and saw that the explosion had caught the entire length of the passenger's and driver's sides, even though it hit closer to the sidewalk and building.

If these condominiums weren't empty, there would be a lot of dead bodies.

Glenn watched the SUV flip on the passenger's side and skid several more feet, carried by momentum.

"Hey! I almost got it! What do you think?" Smiley said enthusiastically to Glenn.

Glenn took only a second to answer, and it was with a smile.

Remembering an old phrase he had once heard from the Chairman of the Foreign Intelligence Agency about covert operations and leaders, he decided to implement a new strategy: *Acting!*

"Good job! Do you want another rocket?" Glenn asked with a broad, encouraging smile.

He could easily see that Smiley seemed to be happy at his positive response.

You must be very proud, you God-damnned idiot! Pay peanuts and you get monkeys!

"Yes," Smiley said as he handed Glenn the rocket launcher to reload from atop the small wall on the roof.

While he filled the launcher, he watched and waited for Smiley to turn and look at the damage he caused.

You just can't help yourself but to look and gloat, can you, Smiley?

Predictably, as Smiley leaned over, he came up from behind and pushed him off the roof, as one might push garbage off a ledge. While

Glenn ignored the falling man's screams, he was positive the other members of his team would be bunched up around the large SUV as he finished reloading the rocket launcher. As he rechecked to see if it was ready to fire, he mounted the small wall along the roof and brought the rocket launcher to his shoulder. He saw that the three men from the SUV, and the driver of the garbage truck were clustered together, and they were closer to the building than to the SUV.

You see. If you had any military training, you'd know never to bunch up. An explosive or grenade could kill all of you at the same time. Sloppy, just sloppy.

"It's been nice working together - Ha sido un placer trabajar juntos," Glenn said as he squeezed the trigger, launching the rocket toward the middle of the group. A moment later, once the sound and dust settled, he peered over the ledge and saw that "his team" were dead and mostly in pieces.

He looked back at the VIP SUV as it lay on its side, motionless, with shards of glass and metal concaved on its entire left hand side. Taking in a deep breath and feeling free of the "monkeys," he felt no guilt as a wave of calm came over him and silence fell all around him. The smell of gasoline, oil, tires, and discharged explosives filled his lungs as he drew in another breath. Right now he had to make only one decision.

Do I stay and help, or walk away?

~

Ramsey was in the back of the new SUV, farthest away from Belben, attempting to unlock yet another secret compartment in the floor when she was thinking about just giving up and getting back in front.

How many more secret compartments does this thing have?

Belben was looking in her rearview mirror and got her attention.

"Hey, boss. Fitzy looks as though she is slowing down for some reason."

Ramsey was about to get up from the floor when she saw a large shadow suddenly appear in Belben's window, and something massive pushing in through the reinforced driver's door. Suddenly Ramsey felt as if she was spinning and bouncing inside a huge can as it bounced and crunched along the ground. The time she spent colliding was nothing like she had experienced before; it was long, jarring and it just went on forever. Finally, as the somersaults stopped, she found herself face down on the ceiling of the now slowly spinning SUV. She tried to move but grayness filled her vision and she felt as if she might be slipping away until she found her voice and uttered "No ... no. Don't pass out."

While still awake but not moving, she had no idea how long she had been lying there but she could feel what felt like sharp glass in her chest and cheeks as the spinning came to a stop.

"Jesus, Mary and Joseph ..." she uttered as she slowly moved her limbs to see if anything was broken.

With all the SUV's windows smashed out, Ramsey looked out and saw the ground and nothing else. She heard what she thought was another explosion, but her hearing seemed hollow and tinny.

Suddenly, she remembered that she was not alone--and then something hit Belben's door.

Putting the pain aside, Ramsey rolled on her side and looked for her. She looked toward where the steering column and driver's seat were, and saw Belben hanging upside down, crushed into the dashboard and steering wheel. Her body was so contorted and misshapen that she had to look away and catch her breath for fear she might throw up or do worse.

"Fuck no ... Cindy ..." was all she could say. After a minute she felt for a pulse, but she was sure from the severe, odd angles Belben's neck and torso were in that she probably died on impact from whatever hit them. Finding no pulse, Ramsey lay back down again feeling dizzy and nauseous. Tears burst from her eyes.

"Damn it, Cindy! Why you?"

She was the youngest! No! Not fucking fair!

Ramsey found herself drifting for a moment, and was not sure if she passed out, or how much time had elapsed.

It's too quiet.

Suddenly, she remembered she was there to protect Emma and David. She had to help her team. As Ramsey fought to move, she remembered that her rifle might still be clamped in. For what it was worth, she noted that the SUV's concealed rifle compartment with clamps held the rifle perfectly in place. With effort, she pulled and unclasped the rifle, and as she crawled out of the wreckage she grabbed three loaded magazines off the ground.

She was still sniffling and only peripherally aware of her own pain.

Cindy ... she kept thinking.

Ramsey crawled faster, as her hearing was returning, but there seemed to be silence.

Maybe I'm deaf? No, it's temporary. Must have been a crash.

She was now on her feet, wobbly and attempting to run, but the best she could do was to walk quickly and not fall down. She jammed two clips in her pocket and struggled with slapping a clip in her weapon, priming to a bullet in the chamber and move quickly at the same time without tripping over her own feet. With a magazine in the assault rifle, safety off and set for full automatic, Ramsey peeked around the corner of the building where she was sure the other SUV was located. As she now fully rounded the corner she saw the extent of the damage.

"Sweet Mother of God."

With bodies everywhere and a slightly damaged, large SUV blocking the road, it was easy to make out a major crater beside a construction dumpster, with body parts radiating out from the blast's epicenter. Down the street, she could see that the trailing car looked completely t-boned and crushed in another construction dumpster, and her team's SUV was on its side, with the entire driver's side concave and shredded.

She ran as best she could to the shattered windshield to see if anyone was in the vehicle. As she dropped to her hands and knees, she could see that Fitzgerald was still strapped in her seat, with large shards of rocks, glass, and shrapnel protruding out of the left side of her head and torso.

Ramsey felt for a pulse but knew she would find none.

"God damn it!" she yelled out. *Is everyone dead?*

Ramsey was looking for other bodies in the back, and swore she saw movement.

"Witzy! Witzy! Horowitz?"

Nothing.

Oh, my God. All dead? How was she going to tell their parents? How could she look Becky in the face?

"Ramsey?" she heard.

She yelled back as she pushed herself into the small crevices to gain access to the back seats.

Horowitz pushed the front seat down and emerged with her gun first. Looking dazed, with blood flowing in from her nose and mouth, Witzy seemed to take a moment to recognize Ramsey.

"Ana?" she asked.

"Right here," Ramsey said.

"Do you have Emma and Dr. Caulfield?" Ramsey asked as she continued to push debris out of the way with her own bloody hands. Appearing to orient herself, Witzy put her gun down and looked behind her.

"Emma? Give me your hand and be careful of the glass, honey," Horowitz said.

"I'm coming, Witzy. Can you help Papa? He needs our help," Emma asked in a remarkably calm voice, Ramsey thought.

"Absolutely, honey. But you first. Come on," Horowitz said in a low, tired voice.

No! Shit no!

Ramsey had a sick feeling hit her as her breathing slowed down and cold chills ran down her back. She didn't think she could feel anything worse could happen until she heard Witzy call for Emma to come out first. Standard protocol would have the adult VIP exit first in a hot zone, and the child last. The fact that Horowitz was getting Emma out meant that either David could not be moved…or worse.

Ramsey gently pulled Emma out, making sure not to drag her through glass and metal. Once she was sure that Emma was not seriously hurt, she assisted Horowitz out.

Horowitz had a gaping hole in her left bicep and was bleeding badly. Ramsey pulled her torn, filthy jacket off and ripped the lining and sleeve off to put pressure on the wound to stop the blood flow.

Ramsey looked around for a workable vehicle.

The SUV blocking the road was dented, but clearly drivable.

"Okay, Emma. Help me get Witzy into our new ride," Ramsey directed.

Emma dutifully went to Horowitz's side to assist, but then she slowed down to ask, "Are we going to come back for Papa, next, Ana?"

She found herself avoiding her eyes, and did not answer the question. "Witzy's bleeding, honey. We've got to get her to lie down."

Ramsey opened the back of the SUV and gently put Horowitz in, and Emma beside her. Closing the door of the SUV, Ramsey went back to see if Horowitz was wrong.

This can't be happening. He's gotta be alive.

It took more effort than expected to get toward the back of the SUV, but she managed to get through.

She saw that David's back had more debris and shrapnel than Fitzgerald had in her side. Turning him around, Ramsey's eyes welled up as she looked at his peaceful face. No pulse, no life. Belben was so young; Fitzy was all attitude. To see them all dead was unreal. But Dr. Caulfield looked as he did when he was alive: serene. Ramsey didn't want to leave him.

"I'm so sorry, Dr. Caulfield," she said as she made the sign of the cross. More tears threatened to burst from her eyes, but she pushed them back.

"I gotta get Witzy and Emma out of here."

She shook herself out of her grief and crawled out of the wreckage.

My God. Belben. Fitzgerald. Dr. Caulfield. All gone in minutes.

Ramsey saw movement coming from what appeared to be a walk-in dumpster. Her hands snapped up as she honed her automatic rifle onto a limping, dirty man whose arm also appeared to be broken, if she could surmise from its odd angle.

"Please! Don't shoot!" he cried out. He moved slowly out of the dumpster.

"Who the fuck are you? Who did this? Tell me now or I'll shoot you," Ramsey demanded.

She saw that Horowitz had pushed Emma to the floor and had her own gun drawn and door closed. She made a gesture with her hand as if she was turning a key, and Horowitz seemed to have said something to Emma and then maneuvered into the driver's seat.

The man fell down and turned on his back with his working hand up. There was something about his face ... *are those scars or something else?*

"Please! The American! He pushed me! He killed my friends! Please ...."

Ramsey heard the SUV start up as she closed the gap between him and herself.

"Who is the American? What is his name? Give me a name! Tell me or I'll shoot you right where you are!" Ramsey was standing over him and pointed the rifle at his torso. She became aware of sirens getting louder.

"Please! He pushed me and took the rocket and killed my friends," he kept repeating.

"A name! Give me his name!"

The man seemed to be struggling with trying to remember, but then finally seemed to come across it.

"Glenn ... Mr. Jethro Glenn ... I think," he said as he seemed to start to cry.

Ramsey's heart stopped.

That name! That sack of shit was here? No!

"Jeffrey Glenn? What does he look like? Quickly--or die!"

"He's tall ... blond hair ... pale-colored man. Much lighter than you or me. Very white."

The first responder sirens were closing in on the crime scene and Ramsey felt she had all the useful intelligence she needed for now.

"If you are lying, I'll be back to kill you and your family," she hissed out as she stepped on the man's broken foot until she heard more crunches and his scream.

I'm going to find you, Glenn, and I'm going to cut you deep! Sack of shit!

She used all her strength not to shoot the screaming, crying man.

Ramsey bolted to the SUV's back door, where presumably Emma was on the floor, and jumped in. She suddenly felt the SUV lurch forward and speed away.

"You okay to drive?" Ramsey asked as she put her rifle's safety on and checked on Emma.

"Yeah," was Horowitz's short, weak answer.

She was about to question her as she watched Horowitz's nose starting to bleed again, but felt a little hand pulling at her.

It was easy to see that Emma was aware that the SUV was moving, but as she looked around she saw that her father was not with them.

"Ana? Where's Papa?"

Chapter 5

"Improvidus, apto, quid victum" – *"Improvise, adapt, and overcome"*

Becky found herself truly baffled by what to make for dinner. While she was very annoyed with Emma's attitude and spoiled behavior, she decided to focus on making a "special dinner" for David rather than her. He was, as always, a Godsend. Ever since Emma hit puberty, she had been acting as if she were in charge of the family, and often got in power struggles with Becky.

Just like you, Sam, she thought as memories of Samantha's teenage years came to mind. *I wish David was there when you arrived. Mom and Dad could have learned a lot about how to handle you. We all could have.*

Returning to the present, Becky was amazed, as David had a way of dealing with her that she just couldn't mimic. Emma never fought with him, and he was able to just talk to her in such a way that made her think.

Kind of what he does with me. Taking in a deep breath, she continued her thinking as she stopped to readjust her shoulder holster under her short jacket.

You know, I know Emma has no blood relation to Tony or Sam, but I swear she channels them both. Becky went back to her search for the ingredients for fried ravioli. She was not hopefully she would get all of her supplies from the meager choices on the shelves.

It was very warm outside and the air conditioner in the small store was off. The store door was wide open, giving her a full view of Cratty pacing. Then she heard Cratty's phone ring. She could see her smiling as she started to answer her phone.

"Now that's just weird," she heard Cratty say to herself.

"Dillon? I was just thinking of you and then ...."

Becky smiled as she remembered that Christine Dillon had gone back to the States to be closer to her boyfriend.

That's nice. She found only two ingredients but still pressed on. *I wonder if Denise has anyone special, other than Emma and me, of course.*

Feeling suddenly hot, Becky regretted having her semi-automatic weapon, as she needed a jacket for concealment. Looking around, she lost track of Cratty.

Hmm. I wonder what's up? Maybe a break on the case. Maybe Burns has found Daniels. Feeling frustrated with the lack of supplies and wanting to know what was happening, she decided to pay for her meager ingredients and find out. Paying the bill, she carefully picked up her small bags and walked to the open door to see Cratty squatting down on the porch with her back against the door, and a hand on the wall as if she needed support.

What the hell? Are you all right? Becky thought as she took a step to help Cratty up.

As she closed in and her worry for Cratty's health jumped to mind, Becky heard Cratty speak with such urgency that she knew something was wrong.

"She's fine? Thank God! Why is she crying? Where's Dr. Caulfield?" she heard Cratty ask.

Emma? Emma's fine? David? What's happened to David? Becky felt her blood run cold and she froze in place.

"Horowitz? Did you confirm that he's gone?" she heard Cratty demanded from whoever was on the line.

I thought she was talking to Christine ... Emma's fine but David ... is gone? Gone?! David?! No, no, no,

Becky's mind kept repeating as she felt frozen in place with the sole exception of hot tears streaming from her eyes, and her heart and stomach sinking to the ground. She lost track of time as her whole being, weighed down by the memories of Tony and Samantha, filled her in eye as she feared for David, the last adult left for her to love. *No! It can't be true. I know where David is! I can find him!*

Becky felt her eyes dry in the heat of the day as salt from her tears settled on her cheeks. She suddenly became aware that Cratty was now standing and was clearly angry yet resigned about something or someone.

"That son of a bitch!" she heard Cratty say with great vehemence. Becky felt her heart race as hope seemed to emerge.

Maybe it's not Emma or David. Maybe something else. Maybe something with Burns or Dillon.

"Get to the safe house. Keep Emma safe. Contact Helms. Find us a way out of this shit," she heard her order.

Her hopes were dashed as rapidly as they were raised.

No. She said nothing about keeping David safe ... David ... no. Her mind kept saying over and over again. Seeing herself standing on the porch, she watched Cratty as she turned to face her. She had never seen Denise Cratty look distraught, frightened, and infuriated all at the same time. The last thing that she remembered seeing in Cratty's face was recognition: recognition that Becky knew David was gone.

"Becky ..." was all she heard her say as she took a step toward her.

No ... I can get to David. I can save him! I can run there if I have to! I can make it! I can save him! He's all I have left!. Becky's mind was racing as she backed away.

Feeling a scream choke in her own throat, she turned to run.

I can find David! I can save him! Her thoughts raced as she began to run.

~

Cratty was debating whether she should suggest that she and Becky actually try the shooting range that was two miles away before they continued their shopping, or just let her relax and take her time.

Emma's been getting on your nerves. I don't think I'll rush you.

She knew that the small shop Becky was in wouldn't have the supplies she needed for a special dinner she wanted to make for David. *But if Becky wants to try this place; that is fine with me.*

Cratty's eyes narrowed as she did an immediate risk assessment of her location and noted that the place had more men hanging around than shopping.

No kids, few women, and the guys looking for trouble ... I'm glad we are both armed. I think Becky's armed. Why else would she wear a jacket on a day like this?

As she looked at the area again, she found herself thinking of David and Becky as a couple, and tried to figure out how their relationship worked. Clearly they were close and always seemed to be on the same page in regard to raising Emma, but she had a hard time envisioning David and Becky ever being intimate. This was often the kind of discussion that occurred among "her girls," especially when Dillon was around.

I wonder how she's doing? I hope things are working out for her and her boyfriend.

Cratty's attention was broken by her ringing phone. The caller ID had the listing as "Dillon."

"Now that's just weird," Cratty said to herself.

"Dillon? I was just thinking of you and then ...."

Cratty was surprised by the fact that Dillon not only cut her off, but her tone was deadly serious.

"Boss. There's a problem. You remember that operation a couple of years back? *Phoenix?*"

Cratty's stomach sank. *I'll never forget that memorandum,* she thought.

"What's happening, Dillon?"

"Emma's grandfather just handed me a copy of it ten minutes ago. Move the family to the safe house. Await instructions for a return home strategy ...."

Grandfather? Shit, Boston organized crime. Murphy. Emma's biological father and a half-sister. Shit!

Cratty's phone beeped, indicating another call.

"Hold on, Dillon," Cratty said. She was now jumping out of her own skin, but when she saw the caller ID was Ramsey, she was partially relieved, as it was close to the time she would check in. *They should be home,* she thought.

"Ramsey. We are going to have to move David and Emma ... Ramsey?"

Cratty listened and could hear screaming.

Her stomach dropped even more as tension pressed on her chest, and her heart was racing. It took every bit of will power to try to hear what was actually being said.

She listened closely, and clearly heard Ramsey trying to console Emma: "No, honey ... I checked. He wasn't faking, honey ..."

"No! No! He's alive! We have to go back ... no ...." Emma kept saying.

Cratty leaned against the store's wall with her back against the door. If the wall hadn't been there, she would have fallen over.

"Ramsey! What the fuck is going on?" she yelled. *God damn it! I knew I shouldn't have left them! God damn it! Someone answer!*

"Boss ... it's Witzy ..." Cratty knew it was her, but she'd never heard Horowitz sound so tired ... so exhausted.

"Witzy. Where are you?"

She could tell that something was deadly wrong with Horowitz, since her tone was low and voice was heavy, as if she was struggling to breathe.

It was also hard to hear her, as Emma was now in a full blown crying fit.

"Boss, we're heading to the safe house. We were ambushed ... Fitzy and Belben are gone, Denise."

As Cratty heard Horowitz's voice telling her that half her team were gone, she felt her knees buckle. She continued leaning against the wall, but she slowly squatted down with one hand on the ground in front of her for more support. She thought being close to the ground might keep her from falling over.

"Witzy, no ... Emma?"

Horowitz anticipated her next questions:

"Emma is shaken but absolutely fine."

"She's fine? Thank God! Why is she crying? Where's Dr. Caulfield?"

Horowitz's delay in responding was telling, and Cratty felt truly ill. When she spoke next to Cratty, it was so low that she could barely hear her.

"Denise. He didn't make it. We were hit with a rocket and it killed Fitzy and Dr. Caulfield at the same time."

Cratty found her mouth getting dry and she was trying to get her head around how everything had gone to shit in a matter of twenty minutes.

"Horowitz? Did you confirm that he's gone?" She started to slowly stand up with her hand on the wall for support as she felt herself getting angry. Anger at herself for not being there, anger at her team for getting ambushed, and that someone she swore to protect was dead. Cratty found herself just getting angry at the whole world.

"Yes, Boss. Ana went back in the wreckage to check. The Spanish guards were in on it too ...."

"Where are they?" Cratty asked as she looked around the parking lot at her car and felt for her gun.

"Fitzy rammed them. I think they are either dead or unconscious. Boss, we're heading to the safe house. See you there in thirty," Horowitz said.

"Yes."

"Boss? Ramsey talked to a witness before we left. He identified Jeffrey Glenn as being there," Horowitz said.

It took a full thirty seconds for the name and situation to register. When they did, Cratty was filled with rage.

"That son of a bitch!" was all she could think to say.

Her free hand balled up into a fist as she imagined beating Glenn to death with her bare hands.

Cratty focused on the exit plan and listed out next steps: "Get to the safe house. Keep Emma safe. Contact Helms. Find us a way out of this shit."

"Done, Boss."

Cratty heard Horowitz close the line while she stood still, motionless for a moment, trying to figure out the fastest route to the new location. As she slowly turned around, reorienting herself to face the store's entrance, she saw Becky standing still, holding a small bag, looking directly at her.

She locked onto Becky's eyes, which were rimmed with tears, with tracks already running down her cheeks. She could easily see that Becky had heard everything.

Oh my God. She knows her husband is dead.

"Becky ..." was all she said. No lie, no excuse, no reason came to her as she watched Becky emotionally collapse while standing still in front of her.

Cratty watched as Becky slowly back away from her and threw the bag on the ground. As she took a step closer, Becky cried out and started to run to the back of the parking lot toward the road.

"Becky! No! Wait!" Cratty said as she ran after her.

She knew she would have to sprint faster and catch her before she gained too much distance. She knew that Becky was a runner and she would run all the way to the compound without thinking about the danger.

Maybe through will or adrenalin Cratty shortened the gap as quickly as her smaller legs could carry her, and tackled her to the ground by grabbing her legs. As she tried to grab hold of her and try to talk to her, Becky started to fight back.

"Let me go! I have to help David! I have to save him! Fucking let me go," she kept yelling, while striking out.

Cratty made sure to keep her head close to Becky to keep from really being hit hard as she moved up her body to try to control her arms. She pressed into her body and moved behind Becky as she continued to flail out.

People, mostly men, stopped what they were doing and watched, clearly wondering what was going on. Cratty was finally getting control of Becky, but was also becoming aware of a large group of onlookers crowding in. She knew she had to get control of the situation fast.

"Becky! David's gone! Emma needs you! If we don't get out of here, they will come for her again! Becky! Emma! Emma needs you. She needs you now!"

Becky's struggling decreased significantly at the mention of Emma's name and her being in danger. Her yells changed to moans.

"David ... Sam ... no ... Tony ... no more. Please, no more ...."

Cratty looked up and noticed more people were coming and the crowd was getting large. She began to feel that this group was closing in too fast, and noticed that they were all men now. The talking among themselves increased in volume, and the laughter was far from pleasant. Cratty did not like it at all.

She spoke low but firmly into Becky's ear:

"Becky. We need to get out of here and get to Emma. You need to follow me. Are you armed?"

It took a moment, but Becky responded through her tears and sobs. "Yes."

Thank God.

"Becky. You need to follow my lead and stay with me. We need to do this together to get to Emma as soon as possible. Right?"

Cratty could see that Becky was now focused on the men looking down at her. She watched with approval as Becky turned back to look at her, and timed her own hand movement toward her shoulder as Cratty moved her hand to her shoulder holster under her jacket.

Cratty pulled out her semi-automatic weapon and yelled out, "Todo el mundo! Fuera de aqui!" To punctuate her point, she fired two shots in the air.

The crowd of men was startled by the order and shots, and stepped back. However, it was both women jumping up from the ground pointing guns at the crowd that Cratty was sure sent them running.

"Mover! Fuera de aqui!" Becky added with additional shots above the receding crowd's heads. Cratty noticed that while her own warning shots were well above the crowd's heads, Becky's were substantially lower, and that was when the crowd took off like a stampede.

"Becky! Follow me!"

Cratty chased the crowd as a way of cover as she searched out a car. She had no intention of taking her own car; in light of the ambush, she couldn't take a risk. It might be bugged or set to explode.

As she ran, she was looking for a car already moving, until she saw two young men getting into a very small but fast-looking car.

She jumped in front of the car before the driver could start the car, and pointed her gun directly at him.

"Salir del coche o te mato! Ahora!" she ordered.

Though the men slowly exited their car, they were obviously moving too slow for Becky's taste: "Ahora mismo!" she added with two shots at the driver's feet. Seeing that the armed women pointing guns at them meant business, the men ran in the opposite direction without looking back.

Cratty jumped in the driver's seat as Becky took the passenger's seat. Cratty handed Becky her gun with an assigned task:

"I need to focus on driving and getting there fast. You handle this."

Becky nodded affirmatively.

As she gunned the engine and pulled away, her phone rang again.

"Has it been ringing all this time?

She realized that she had never gotten back to Dillon. Cratty didn't even look at the caller ID when she answered.

"Dillon! Belben, Fitzgerald, and Dr. Caulfield are down. Becky and I are en route to the safe house; Ramsey, Horowitz, and Emma are heading there too. Will contact you in twenty minutes. Jeff Glenn is involved in all this. Dillon? Find us a way out of this hole! Got it?"

Cratty had a sharp pang of guilt, saying out loud the names of her friends, and her charge who died.

"Glenn?! ... That rat bastard!" she heard Dillon hiss out.

"Dillon! Focus! I gotta get Becky and Emma out of here! Embassy, airplane, or ship. Anything. Got it?"

"On it, Boss!"

Cratty accelerated and took the road's turns aggressively to get to her destination fast. She spied a look at Becky, who continued to watch for any threats through her tears. Becky's intake of air and sighs were audible.

Poor thing. She really has had a lot of bad breaks, Cratty thought. *I gotta get her to Emma fast.*

As the road passed rapidly, Cratty kept thinking about her team.

Belben, Fitzgerald ... dead, and Horowitz is injured ... all in twenty minutes.

~

"That fucking rat bastard, slack-jawed, blond pig!" Dillon blurted out as she slammed the phone down forcefully. She had already been on her feet after she lost contact with Cratty the first time, and the ensuing no answer for the longest eight minutes on record.

Dillon had made the call in the middle of the FBI's control room, which was filled with analysts, and operations specialists Johnson and Gilmore. While she had been waiting for Cratty to pick up, Gilmore was attempting satellite linkage over Torrox, Spain, via CIA, as four other analysts were listening in on first responder scanners with eavesdropping provided by the CIA and Spanish Secret Service. Johnson was updating Janeson as she kept her tablet open with Director Helms on the line.

When Dillon turned around and focused, she noticed she was the center of attention. It was Janeson, as always, who was unfazed by the emotional outburst and requested an update.

"Christine? I have the director on the line. Quickly! What's going on?"

Dillon took a moment to breathe and to put her thoughts into bullet points. Finally composed, she did her best analytical report she'd made in years, in light of the loss of her friends.

"Boss, Belben and Fitzgerald are dead. Dr. Caulfield is also dead. I have no details on how ...."

"Jesus H. Christ!" Gilmore said.

Recovering from Gilmore's remarks, Dillon continued.

"Cratty and Becky Littleton are en route to the safe house and will be there in twenty minutes. Horowitz and Ramsey have Emma and they are also en route. Those three are alive, but nothing more than that. Cratty is requesting a way out of Spain, ASAP."

Dillon felt water in her eyes, but she would be dammed if she was going to cry.

"Witness at the scene named the presence of Jeffrey Glenn."
That rat! I'll kill him myself!

As she was talking, Janeson had walked over to a control panel, and plugged her tablet into a dock which put Director Helms on a portion of the floor-to-ceiling monitors for all to see.

Dillon was still thinking of killing Glenn when she was brought back by Janeson's round of orders.

"Crepes? Do you have an update on the first responders in Torrox?"

"Yes, Boss," a young man in his late twenties responded.

"There's a report of a major car accident that's involved a car, a garbage truck, and two SUVs near a condominium development. There's also chatter of some kind of explosion where there are a number of body parts. Varying reports seem to point out that the drivers of the SUVs are dead, as well as possibly a passenger in one of the SUVs."

Cindy ... Fitzy ... Dr. Caulfield ... no ....

She just couldn't believe it.

"Gilmore, anything on satellite?" Janeson asked.

"No, Boss. If there were crashes or explosions, we missed it. I do have ETAs on the teams getting to their safe house, and they should be online in fifteen minutes. I'll have a dedicated monitor and phone link ready."

"Thank you. Johnson, get hold of our contact at the CIA in Torrox. Give them what we've got and have them cover all ports. Dillon, contact your people at the Spanish Secret Service and the police department and find out what they know, and get them a picture of Jeffrey Glenn as a person of interest. And to be clear--I want him alive. I get no answers or intelligence if he is dead," Janeson said, with her attention focused on Dillon.

"Yes, Boss. Can I make sure he's hurt?"

Dumbass! That mouth of yours! If Cratty was here, she would have me doing a thousand push-ups and cleaning the head with a toothbrush. Can't I just keep my mouth shut for once!

Dillon waited for Janeson to explode. And then she remembered she had mouthed off to Janeson.

Janeson looked at Dillon as if she were considering it.

"No. I don't want him hurt, either. The attempt to hurt him might escalate, and that could lead to his demise. No. Just get him to the authorities in one piece, thank you."

Dillon felt bad for mouthing off to Janeson and felt she needed to apologize as soon as possible. Dillon liked Janeson a lot, but forgot that she did not pick up on sarcasm.

"Yes, Boss. And I apologize for my sarcasm," she said.

Janeson looked confused for a moment, but then decided to let it go. Dillon watched Janeson turn to address Director Helms on the big screen.

"Director, I recommend that we bring Mr. Burns in to have him assist us find these attackers."

"And to keep him from going offline and killing everyone," Helms added.

Dillon's heart sank. *Shit! Dr. Caulfield was his close friend. Shit!*

"That too. Also, I am sending two cars to watch Murphy's home. Director? Could you ask Mrs. Welch if she could make contact with the American Embassy near Torrox? I am sure that between you and Mrs. Welch, you will have an effect on the Marine contingent stationed there. They are more likely to help than if I ask."

Dillon watched Helms smile.

"You got some serious skills there, Janeson. I'm at the airport and will talk to Welch. We'll call from the road. Get a chopper ready to transport me and Andersen to that landing strip in Easton. Brief Davis, but keep her in the field. I got a feeling this is a three-pronged strategy and I am sure Daniels has something else in play up there. Maybe they'll show themselves if they think Burns is gone. Dillon?"

Dillon had heard everything, but was still focused on her friends' death.

She looked up and saw Helms's face was stern yet soft.

"I'm very sorry, Christine."

Dillon felt her jawline set hard and her eyes begin to swell.

"Thank you," she croaked out. She then turned and sat at her monitor, looking away from the group as she called the police department's number she remembered from her days in Spain. Dillon sniffled and felt hot tears fall on her cheeks.

Helms and Janeson were still talking, but Dillon was not listening. She had her assignments and needed to focus on them or be consumed with sadness, anger, and guilt.

I should have been there. That rat bastard, she thought as she stabbed at the phone pad.

~

With a sudden burst of heat from an emerging hot flash, Diane Welch was struggling with her overhead bag in the compartment that was over her close friend's head.

It's a curse, I tell you. What kind of God curses a person with no sleep, aching muscles, and hot flashes?

While she was spending more time flying from Boston to DC, it was nice to travel with Steve Andersen, as it offered her a chance to catch up on personal things rather than work. She had spent months leading the background investigation of former Chairman Eric Daniels, and his role of the now-defunct Foreign Intelligence Agency. Since his disappearance, her role and duties had intensified as she was now involved in the search for Daniels in addition to her ongoing investigation. While she and her colleagues had anticipated Daniels's exodus, it was still difficult to coordinate both search efforts and investigation at the same time. Andersen was now on leave from the North Reading Police Department, and on loan to her and the FBI. This greatly helped as her own team, Thomas "Nine" Williams and Dan "Ice" Maddox, were themselves in the field looking for Daniels under the command of Jillian T. Davis.

"Looking" is more of an overstatement. "Watching to see if Daniels goes for the bait," is probably more accurate.

It was evident to her that Andersen could see she needed assistance with her bag, and moved in to help. When she was younger she would have pushed the help aside and done it herself. But because it was Steve, and because she was tired, she accepted without resistance.

She smiled as he pulled down her luggage with less effort and gave it to her. The only other man she would have acquiesced quickly to would have been her husband, Joe.

I miss you, Joe, she thought as she pulled her other belongings together to deplane. If he had been alive, she could expect to smell food cooking in the Crock-Pot, and sounds of him and their dog howling a song together at home. When Joe died three years ago, so did the sounds, smells, and feel of her home. Two months after he died, their poodle, Collin, died as well.

Collin couldn't live without you, Joe. There are times I can't, either.

If Andersen had not pulled her into the "whole Burns affair," she would have moved and probably would have withered away.

Thank God for work. What would I do if didn't have this? I'd give it all away for you to be here, though.

Still, coming home now was less comforting.

"So? Are you going to tell me what the 'T' stands for in Davis' middle name?" Andersen hounded her.

"No. No, I'm not, Steve. You will only make fun of her. You know, she's a lot more like Darlene than Terry. She's sensitive. She really wants to be liked. Even cared for. She's definitely more like Darlene," she said as she and Andersen walked toward the gate area.

For a moment, Welch thought that Andersen was actually being considerate and respectful of the request. Maybe he believed that he should be nicer to Davis, rather than constantly busting her all the time.

She looked over to see if it were possible to have a change of heart.

Andersen turned and asked, "So you're really not going to tell me? It's got to be something weird like 'Tatum' or 'Toto' or 'Tickle,' or something like it."

She shook her head and recalled when she had first met Steve and his younger sister, Darlene. While he was protective and actually very considerate, he would crack on her once in a while--not too different from how he would tease Davis.

Andersen was still listing off names when Welch noticed that John Helms was waiting for them right at the arrivals gate, with his FBI windbreaker on, and one other in his hand.

Now this can't be good. Waiting at the airport to pick us up when we never scheduled it? Something bad must have happened.

When she saw that Andersen had noticed Helms, he confirmed her fears as well: "Ah shit. This can't be good."

As Welch and Andersen approached him, Welch was the first to ask.

"How bad is it?"

Helms took Welch's carry-on, handed Andersen the spare windbreaker, and led the way to a waiting vehicle.

"Murphy came in with the 'Phoenix' memorandum that he obtained from another crime family. Burns's family was hit an hour ago. Fitzgerald and Belben are dead."

"Shit!" was Andersen's response as his pace picked up speed.

"The others?" Welch asked.

"The girl, Emma, is fine. Ramsey and Horowitz should be at the safe house. Cratty was with Rebecca, and should also be at the safe house. Dr. Caulfield is dead."

Damn it! This is going to set Burns off. Is that the plan, Daniels? Kill Burns's family and have him come after you?

Welch noticed that Andersen was no longer in step with her and as she turned around to see where he was, she saw that her friend had seemed to slow to a stop.

She could see that his eyes had narrowed and that hearing about Dr. Caulfield's death was more of a blow than she had anticipated. While she had thought about how Burns was going to react, she had not anticipated that Steve might have a personal response as well.

Welch turned and saw that Helms stopped his rapid walking as well, and had turned back to talk to him.

"Steve?"

Welch could see that he was trying to look for the words to describe why he felt the way he did. She knew that Andersen had spent hours with Dr. Caulfield years ago on May 2nd. Then when Samantha Littleton was killed, it was Dr. Caulfield whom he spoke to, and then finally returned to North Reading so they could move to Spain. Andersen spent days with him and the family at that time. While he made no bones about the fact that he did not excuse or condone Caulfield's involvement in the death of sixteen federal agents, he did understand how it had happened. He confided in her that he was very ambivalent about Caulfield because he had always wondered whether, if he was in his shoes, would he have done what Caulfield did to save Emma, Rebecca, and his friends Samantha and Burns? He was convinced he would have wanted to, but was not sure he would have had the strength to do it, the will and drive to prepare for years to execute a plan that was, at best, impossible.

Hearing that this man was dead had to be unsettling to him for many reasons, Welch thought. Exactly how, she was not sure.

"Steve? You Okay?" Helms asked.

Welch watched Andersen as he finally responded.

"I'm sorry ... I didn't expect that. How did it happen?"

He began to walk again and picked up the pace.

"Rocket-propelled grenade hit the rear passenger's and driver's sides. The rapid report is that Fitzgerald and Dr. Caulfield probably died at the same time," Helms reported.

Welch could see that Andersen had regrouped and was now moving ahead.

"I've got a car to take you back to the control center, Diane. Steve and I are going to fly to Easton Air Strip in New Hampshire to pick up Burns," Helms said.

"What's the plan?" Welch asked as she stepped into the waiting SUV and Helms packed her and Andersen's luggage in the back.

"Go to the Control Room and talk to the Marines at the embassy in Torrox, Spain. See if you can get them or the CIA to transport Cratty and her team to either the embassy, or military transport out of there. Janeson has already briefed Davis and her crew. They will get Burns to the airstrip. We will tell him there, and probably take him back to the control room as well."

"Is he part of the team, or protective custody?"

There is no way he's going to stay in protective custody.

"He's going to be part of the team that finds Glenn...."

"Glenn? Jeffrey Glenn of Webber's group? How the hell is he involved?"

Memories of Glenn flooded her head. He'd had a chance to keep Webber from sending in those federal agents to their death, but didn't hold ground. Only after Burns had trapped his men, compromised

Alpha Operations Center, and watched Webber march to his death, did he finally do something. And then only after Cratty stepped in.

"Reports are that he was on site when Cratty's team was attacked. He has to be somewhere in Spain. Also, there's Murphy and his granddaughter whom we need to consider. You know Daniels. He doesn't do just one linear attack--he does multiprong, like Burns," Helms said.

Glenn? That bastard. After what Cratty did to save your ass, and this is how you pay her back?

Welch shifted her focus back to the plan.

"All right, Helms. I'm all over it. I also need to talk to the Secretary of State about a summit meeting with foreign intelligence agencies in our search for Daniels. If all goes to plan, I'll have to convince the Secret Service director, Bob Tombs, to be the emissary."

Welch could see Helms was smiling at the thought.

"You mean 'Mr. Risk-Taker Tombsy'?" The sarcasm was not lost on her.

"Yes. The one and the same."

"Sounds good to me. See you back at the ranch," Helms said as he continued to shake his head in disbelief.

"Good luck!" she said to both Helms and Andersen.

He still looks shaken.

Welch looked back at Andersen as the SUV pulled away.

Jesus. How did it get this bad so fast? She knew how. *As long as Daniels is out there, it will always be this way.*

Chapter 6

"Aut viam inveniam aut faciam" – *"I shall either find a way or make one"*

Jillian T. Davis was sitting in the booth toward the side of the restaurant where she could see both the entrance and the back door. Her "usual seat" had a commanding view of the parking lot, as well as of the kitchen, wait area, and bar. In front of her were her props of cameras, maps, binoculars, and all the gear for a photo journalist looking at various birds in the White Mountains. In many ways, she fit in, with relaxed khakis and light Saharan shirt that was very comfortable and roomy for her "concealable items" – semi-automatic weapon, and spring-assisted knife. And then there was her mother's white gold necklace with a crucifix that shone prominently on her neck. While she had given Burns her other necklace, she was making a serious effort not to touch or play with it, as she often noticed that Burns touched his constantly. Even as she peered up from her text, she could see him absently looking out his own window, fiddling with his cross as he watched both his dog and truck.

What the hell is his dog's name again? Moxie? Rosy? She tried to remember. She did notice that the dog was clearly high-maintenance; cute but prickly. The "cute" and "prickly" matched its owner, but he was far from high-maintenance. She'd had plenty of opportunity to watch him for several months, as he made himself bait for Daniels.

While she was the point person in the field, Thomas "Nine" Williams and his quiet friend "Ice" were watching her and Burns. Nine would periodically break cover and be in the field at the same time, but parallel to her and Burns. Ice was always more than five hundred yards away, with a 30-caliber sniper rifle, watching everything. With the sole exception of updates, Ice didn't talk much in Davis' ear. Nine was the more chatty of the two.

At that moment, her ear piece was silent as she moved her gaze off of Burns to see that Nine was putting gas in his car across the street. She welcomed the silence as she was looking at her texts.

The restaurant, *Meg's Eggs*, was more than a breakfast place for the local color. It boasted having two New York chefs and an impressive array of desserts, with an extensive list of liquor. While there were many families, mostly tourists, that visited the establishment, it was the hang-out stop for the town. With the hotel up the road and the general store it shared the parking lot with, it was the hub of most of the adult activities at night. Though Davis was a tall, athletic woman who could typically adapt to any environment, she found the booths of the establishment just on the small side, making it uncomfortable to actually enjoy sitting, let alone eating.

Right now, though, it was closing in on late breakfast, and she was hunched over looking at her smart phone again, rereading the bad news in Spain via Dillon in Boston.

Shit. Fitzgerald and Belben. Unbelievable. Caulfield too. This is bad. Real bad.

She was shocked when she first read the report. Two of her colleagues in Cratty's team were down, and Burns had just lost the last person he knew who had helped him six years ago.

Caulfield wasn't just a friend. Mentor? Father figure? Something. If it wasn't for him and Samantha Littleton, Burns might have been dead and long forgotten. This is going to be bad. My God, poor Denise. She's got to be pissed and upset. She built that team. Half of them gone in a minute.

Davis was shaken out of deep thoughts by Ice talking in her ear.

"Davis? 'Brown Eyes' is back," Ice announced from wherever he was concealed. She looked up and saw an all-too-familiar small SUV pulling up to the restaurant.

Beyond her, she watched Nine pull his car up to the air gauge and pop his hood for ostensibly further service as he chimed in,

"Oh yes. She broke up her routine a little just so that she wasn't obvious. And would you check out what she's wearing? The jeans are too perfectly worn to be real, and the tight tee just screams of 'I wear this thing to bed.' Come see for yourself," Nine filled in.

As Davis listened to the running commentary she watched a very pretty, petite young woman exiting her mini-SUV. The woman had been scouting the place out for several weeks now and had focused on coming in during breakfast of late. Originally, she and the team thought she was just a local woman hitting on Burns, but she was a newcomer as well, and all the men were interested in her. She worked at the bank where Burns cashed his checks from painting, and she seemed always to open her window and serve him. She was always on duty when he came in and she had shifted her time to now dine in the morning where he typically ate.

"A bit too coincidental and convenient, if you ask me," Davis said.

Nine was right; the woman looked too well-put-together to still convey that "just fell out of bed" look.

Sorry, honey ... Burns likes his women a bit older and way more experienced.

"Maybe she's just interested in dating," Ice commented.

Kind of chatty today, aren't you, Ice?

"No way. She's wearing heels. She's working it too hard. It's too planned out. She trying to be sexy and it is coming across too well-done, well-rehearsed. She just doesn't exude ... sensuality," Nine said.

"Big word for you, Nine, and well-used. I'll let the boss know how you've become more articulate and sensitive," Ice added.

God, they're chatty today. After months of working closely together, Davis and her team were pretty tight as a unit. She liked them. It reminded her of the "old days," when she had been part of an agency she once believed in.

Wasn't too long ago.

Davis watched the woman closely as she entered the establishment. She looked to her left, as if she was looking for an empty place to sit; there were plenty of seats. She then seemed to decide it was too empty, and moved toward where Burns was sitting.

As she moved around the bar that divided the restaurant in half, Davis made sure she looked busy with her camera as she carefully scrutinized her. The only data that came up on this woman, Susan Lee, were her birth certificate, license, education and some jobs. No records, no prior places of employment, nothing.

The very thing that was supposed to make her "normal" was to have a history; since there was none that meant she was not, and as such a probable threat.

Davis watched as the woman seemed to slow her pace, and then turned to the bar as if to order after she located Burns. As Davis looked at her menu, she could see that Burns was still not paying attention to the woman and was looking out the window. The woman ordered and then she looked at Burns and seemed "surprised" and walked over to him.

"Oh, this is going to be good. She's gone over to talk to him. And ... wait for it ...."

Davis watched Burns stand up to acknowledge her and then seemed to offer her a seat.

Always a gentleman.

"Yes. She's asked if she can sit down. Okay, it's a set-up, boys. So here's the deal--Dillon just told me the state troopers are on their way to bring Burns to Boston. FYI--Cratty's team was hit; two of them are down and the VIP Caulfield is dead. When they take him, let him go. I want all eyes on her. Copy?"

It was silent for a moment. Davis knew that it was a lot of data, hard data at that, to hear all at the same time.

"Copy," Ice responded. His voice was lower and more somber than usual.

"Copy. I'm sorry, Davis," was Nine's response.

Davis was too pissed to let it interfere with her job. *I'm not going to let their deaths be in vain. I bet this woman will lead us to Daniels.*

"Let's do it. Once he's gone, converge at a distance on her. I'll leave before the troopers do and be in the car. Ice, you take over when I back off. Nine picks up after you. No tracking or GPS on her car. I don't want her to catch on. Copy?"

"Copy," Ice and Nine said at the same time.

"We're green. Let me know when the troopers arrive."

"Done," Nine said.

Davis started fiddling with her own necklace again and stopped. She started to pack some of her props.

~

From the restaurant window, Burns watched Roxie sitting diligently in his driver's seat as he finished his coffee and sandwich. He found himself periodically eating an egg-bacon sandwich with mustard and ketchup on it. As memories of Sam emerged and when he felt most lonely and depressed, he would eat that particular sandwich, which was her favorite. He had been thinking of her more and was beginning to reconsider the entire plan until the "bank teller," Suzy Nee as her name plate said, came in. He knew he was not the best in picking up on dating rituals and the subtleties of flirting, but he had learned a lot from Samantha about what to look for when a woman is "trying too hard." And this one had all the hallmarks.

Burns casually looked in Davis' direction and saw that she noticed her too. As the woman approached him, he saw Davis talking to herself. She did it well, and if you weren't looking for it, her lips moving might have gone unnoticed. At the rate they were moving, it looked like she had a lot to say.

This Suzy is the link to Daniels.

Burns made sure he had returned to looking outside when Suzy came up to him.

"Mr. Tennyson?" she said.

He turned to look her in the eyes as he stood up to acknowledge her.

"I'm not bothering you, am I? I just ordered and I don't like eating at the bar. Would you mind if I joined you?"

Not bad. Not too flirty--and yet how could I turn you down?

"Well, my wife might have a problem with that, but she's pretty open-minded," he said in total seriousness as he stood up.

The woman's face contorted in surprise, and then it turned a slight auburn color.

"What? Oh ... I'm sorry ...."

A bit too surprised. She noticed there was no other place mat. Yeah ... she observed everything.

"I'm sorry. I was joking," Burns said. He pointed to the free seat and waited for her to sit down before taking his own seat.

The woman's composure rapidly returned and her regrouping was faster than average.

"You had me worried there for a moment. I thought I might be a home wrecker."

"Home wrecker? Are we having breakfast, or something more?" Burns threw out as he softly smiled. He thought of Samantha as he said it. It was a genuine, warm smile but it was all for Samantha. He found it difficult to be in the company of women and be smiling without feeling sad and missing her. So he thought of her when he heard something like this, and his response was often misinterpreted as relating to the person at the moment.

"Well ... for now it's only breakfast. Have you tried their House Special...?" she asked as she turned to see if her order was coming.

You see. That was too much. Too over the top for a flirt, Burns was thinking when he noticed that Davis had pulled all of her belongings together and rapidly exited the restaurant.

She stole a look out the window and noticed that Davis's shadow was nowhere to be found. As he surveyed the area he noticed a state trooper car pulling into the parking lot.

Something's up.

"So what did you order?" the woman asked.

Burns came back to the conversation.

"I found I like their egg and bagel sandwich with bacon, mustard, and ketchup," he said without thinking.

He turned and saw that Suzy was making a face.

"Mustard and ketchup? That is ... interesting," she said, trying not to make a face.

Burns smiled again.

You have no idea--it's not about you.

"Well ... it's an acquired taste. Once you get beyond the initial assault on your senses, it grows on you."

Burns saw two large state troopers enter the establishment and talk to the manager.

"I guess I have to at least give it a try. You can't refuse to eat because you're afraid of choking," she said with a smile.

Burns's eyes shifted back to her and narrowed. He noticed his heart quickened and he came up short on air intake. He closed his eyes for a second and then he composed his next sentence.

"I'm sorry. I didn't hear that. Something about choking?"

She smiled and repeated as she looked deep into his eyes.

"You can't stop eating if there's a chance of choking. I think it's am Arabic saying," she said.

He smiled, which ran completely contrary to his strong urge to reach across the table and force her to tell him where Daniels was--no hate, no desire to kill or to even real harm her, but a deep- seated anger to force her to tell him everything.

Looking away from his guest, Burns watched the state troopers approach his table. He motioned to her to let her know that they were going to have company. As she turned, his smile evaporated as he looked at the back of her head.

It's a Chinese proverb. You should read more.

She turned back to Burns.

"Do you know what this is about?" she asked.

"No ... hey, Suzy? Do you do a lot of reading?" Burns asked.

I'm sure that sounded out of context.

At first she looked confused, but then answered.

"No. I find I don't have much of an attention span for reading," she said as she turned to see the troopers upon them.

"Mr. Tennyson?" the larger of the two troopers asked.

"Yes," Burns said.

"Mr. Tennyson, we have a report that the truck you purchased might have been stolen. We need you to come with us to identify the person who sold it to you so that we can press charges," he said.

Burns was still thinking of the woman in front of him when he responded.

"Does that mean I can't drive my truck?"

The trooper remained calm as he spoke.

"For now, we will drive you and we will need to impound the truck. Do you have any belongings in the truck you need to take with you?"

"Just my dog. She has to come with me."

The troopers looked at each other, clearly weighing whether the presence of the dog would be a problem.

Well. Something big must have happened for the troopers to come pick me up, not knowing if I can take my dog.

"All right. As long as she is leashed," the trooper said.

As Burns exited the booth and left money for his meal on the table, he took a moment to find the right words to depart.

"I guess I have to take a rain check on having breakfast with you," he said.

"Sounds like a date," she responded, her eyes blinking a bit. Too well-timed.

Again, too much. You should be asking more questions about why the troopers are here. That's what a civilian would have done. You'd look forward to seeing a guy again who was just picked up by troopers? Really?

Burns smiled as he walked out with the troopers. He was still thinking of the woman as he noticed that Davis was in her car. He knew she would follow the woman.

"Is this going to be a long trip, or local?" he asked the trooper.

"Long. We're heading to the landing field in Easton. A chopper is on its way to pick you up."

Burns frowned.

Yeah. It can't be good.

He pulled out Roxie's leash and took her out of the truck where she preceded to growl at the troopers.

"You are such a baby", he said as he pulled her into his arms.

Burns was happy to sit in the back of the cruiser; the more distance his dog had from people, the better.

"I wonder how you're going to do with flying?" he asked her. Her eyes looked into his eyes. Roxie began to shake as the car pulled away with them in the back.

"You don't like change, do you, girl?"

He held her close and felt her breathing heavy and squirm.

Burns held her as his mind drifted to what must have gone wrong to warrant a chopper coming in.

Daniels.

~

Lt. Steve Andersen was feeling very conflicted. For years he had pursued ghosts, and he found himself ruminating during the entire ride to the Massachusetts State Troopers air field and the majority of the helicopter ride to New Hampshire to pick Burns up. To anyone who didn't know him, he knew he had to look as if he were brooding.

Maybe I am. Maybe I'm entitled. These damn ghosts just keep coming.

The ghosts started on the anniversary of Oman Sharif Sudani, May 2nd, when he had been incorporated in a master plan to divert all resources so that a federal agency could be attacked and secrets stolen to bargain for innocent people's lives. Alexander Burns and David Caulfield entered his life with explosions and bomb threats, and melted away in a shroud of mystery hours later.

Then, in an attempt to reel the ghosts back in and keep national secrets from flooding the world, one of their sister agencies interfered with the plan and ends up killing one of the "innocent" civilians, Samantha Littleton. And in response to this betrayal, secrets were released, Burns killed six federal agents, Littleton's sister killed four, and Dr. Caulfield pushed the button that killed sixteen agents with a house bomb.

Twenty-seven deaths in under twenty-four hours. One civilian. Twenty-six federal officers. Christ. I should hate them. I should hate Caulfield in particular. I shouldn't even care he's dead.

Eyes narrowed and brow furrowed, Andersen kept wondering why he did care, why it affected him. To add insult to injury, to stop the flood of data, they negotiated money and amnesty. They negotiated with terrorists per presidential mandate to end a world crisis. As a set of old ghosts exited, enter the biggest ghost of all, Eric Daniels. Creator of the now-gutted Foreign Intelligence Agency, Daniels still had more money than God and the same level of entitlement to exact revenge, as if he were still running the agency in good standing.

It just never ends.

Andersen started to shake his head, which drew the attention of Helms, who up to now had let him reflect in piece.

"Steve? What the hell is wrong with you? We got to be on the same page when we pick Burns up. It could all go south real quick, depending on his reaction," Helms warned.

Andersen almost said nothing, and then thought better of it.

Maybe Helms has figured this out. He was the one who assembled us to find Burns and his crew. He was the one who kept looking for Daniels.

Andersen took a moment to form his thought before he articulated his question.

"I'm trying to figure out why I am upset that Dr. Caulfield was killed."

Helms looked at him as if he was either crazy or very dumb.

"Is that it?" Helms asked over the din of helicopter rotors and engine.

What do you mean, "Is that it?"

"What's with you Marines, anyway? You have a simple answer for a complex question," he started. Andersen often found himself annoyed at how Helms and Welch could seem to be at peace with their world when it was filled with ambiguities and complexities.

"The guy killed sixteen agents in less than three minutes from when they entered the house!"

"I know. Steve. If Caulfield's wife hadn't been killed, and he hadn't been put on the short list for 'termination' by one of our agencies that's supposed to protect citizens, I would probably agree with you. If Rebecca Littleton hadn't watched her sister being gunned down by that same agency, I would also say you were right."

But? Go ahead? Tell me why I shouldn't be ambivalent?

"But, we started the whole thing. We put them in a no-win situation and expected them to just go away. Instead, they fought back. They organized and fought back. The first time around they focused on getting some leverage, didn't hurt any civilians, and wanted to disappear. But we didn't let them. Maybe we should have. I guess if the same thing happened to us, would we want to do what Burns did? Caulfield? The Littleton sisters? They just wanted to be left alone and raise a little girl in peace. I've had a hard time damning them for something I think I might do if it happened to me." Helms took a breath and added a little more.

"I don't approve of the killings. None of them. I believe in a higher power that will judge us all. Caulfield will be judged. You and me. But if we hadn't put Caulfield and the Littletons in that position in the first place, and then pushed them, I don't think they ever would have harmed anybody. David Caulfield would be practicing and healing people, and then he would go home to his wife. Samantha Littleton would be alive, and visiting her sister and niece. They were civilians in a war that we started and kept them in. They were desperate."

Andersen found himself staring at Helms for a long moment, and then he smiled.

"Pretty reflective for a Jar-Head," he said.

Helms smiled, shook his head and asked, "So are you better?"

"Yeah. I guess there's a little bit of Burns in all of us. But it's eerie that you gave the same reasons to excuse their actions that Caulfield gave me years ago in interrogation room 8." It was strange that both men came up with the same rationale. Caulfield reiterated the classic "they started it," and invoked the Bible. It was then that he recounted needing to figure out if Caulfield was either crazy or innocent. As it turned out at that time, it was neither. At that time, he was just smart and able to keep him distracted from what was really going on.

That made Caulfield dangerous.

"Well, Caulfield and I are older than you. We're gifted with not just good looks, but wisdom," Helms said with sincerity, and then smiled again.

Andersen smiled as he felt some relief.

"Thanks, Socrates," Andersen said, and sat back in his seat to figure out how he was going to tell Burns that his friend had been killed.

Fifteen minutes had passed when he got the word that they were preparing to land. As they descended, Andersen saw that a New Hampshire state trooper's car was parked. He felt the same kind of anxiety he did when he told a spouse of an officer or a civilian that a loved one was dead. He was still having a hard time imagining how he was going to tell Burns that his friend was dead because we couldn't protect them, as they got the all clear to exit the chopper.

As they ran across the field, Andersen saw Burns exit the trooper's car holding a small white dog. He had heard from Davis that he had the creature, but it seemed to be a mismatch--a small, nervous- looking dog being held by America's most dangerous former spy.

As he and Helms stood together for a moment in front of Burns, and as the troopers took up watching for anything suspicious, Burns was the first to ask the question.

"What's wrong?" Burns asked.

Here we go.

"Emma and Rebecca are fine and are heading to the safe house. Dr. Caulfield and two other agents did not survive an ambush we think was set by Eric Daniels," Andersen said. It flowed out of his mouth. He wished he had planned it that way, but it was all spontaneous. He had assumed that Burns would want to know who was safe and who didn't make it.

If it were me, that's the way I would want it.

Burns's eyes seemed to become very still, and then he looked down at his dog and patted its head very gently as he stepped away and turned his back on them while looking at the trees on the other side of the road. It was a very long minute as Andersen made eye contact with Helms.

He waited and wondered if Burns would set the entire planet on fire again for this loss. Andersen had always thought that Burns kept some copies of the secret data he stole in the case of another betrayal.

Would it be this time? First Samantha Littleton and now David Caulfield?

Burns slowly turned around and looked at Helms.

"Emma and Rebecca are safe?"

"Yes," Helms said. "They're en-route to a safe house and Janeson is working on extractions with Welch."

"Is there a plan to get Emma and Becky back?" he asked.

Without hesitation, Helms filled him in on the details.

"Welch has already spoken to the Marine contingent and CIA contacts to get them out on a military flight by this evening. She is also talking to her contact in the West Wing to shut Daniels' flow of money down from abroad. Cratty and Ramsey identified Jeffrey Glenn, who was there on the scene. We have put Emma's half-sister under surveillance, and her grandfather is already on heightened alert. He was the one that brought us the evidence that Daniels was probably behind the strike."

As Helms talked, Burns's hand went to his necklace for a moment, and then to pat his dog, who seemed very anxious as it looked around.

"What evidence?" Burns asked.

"Reports of another mob family being in contact with a former government agent, probably Glenn, and a plan to get at Murphy by holding Emma hostage. Additionally, a copy of the 'Phoenix' memorandum emerged, and it's not declassified for public knowledge," Helms said.

Burns seemed to take all the data in with little emotion.

What's going on with you, Burns?

Another tense moment passed as Burns spoke next.

"All right. I'm coming with you. Whether you like it or not, I'm part of the team," he said.

Without skipping beat, Helms responded.

"That's the only reason we're here. We know Daniels is going to do at least three things at the same time. We want you to help us stop him. Fitzgerald and Belben gave up their lives to save Dr. Caulfield and Emma. Cratty, Ramsey, and Horowitz will do everything they can to save your family. We need to know where he's going to hit next."

Burns shrugged his shoulders, and at first Andersen thought that he was not going to have a clue, but the answer surprised him.

"They're going to hit me and Murphy next. They already made contact with me. I'm sure Davis and her team already sent you data. Since I'm here, the next logical targets are Murphy and his granddaughter. We need to focus on them for now. Let's go," Burns said as he walked to the waiting helicopter.

As Helms and Andersen walked behind Burns, he was still having a hard time seeing Burns as a 'national threat' as he marched to the chopper to help his family, holding a frightened lap dog.

Fact is stranger than fiction.

~

He's dead. Becky's without her husband and Emma's without her father, Burns continued to think as he held Roxie in the helicopter. As the scars on his scalp, arms, and hands burned, itchy and painful, he vacantly looked over the swiftly passing landscape, wondering where his hate for Daniels had gone.

It was so easy before, he thought. *I could just focus on the feelings and then act. But what will hate do? Bring him back? Like it brought Sam back?*

Feeling his dog shiver and seemingly clutch him with her paws, he couldn't believe that he was now deprived of his only friend, in addition to losing Samantha.

Kill everyone responsible? Flood the world with more classified data? It didn't bring Sam back. It bought a future for Becky, Emma, and David. But now David's gone. Both of them.

Feeling eyes upon him as his scars burned, Burns decided to keep looking out the window and patting his dog. While not reflective by nature, he owed his ability to figure feelings and thoughts out to both Samantha and David. Looking deep inside of himself, remembering all the prayers, he genuinely wondered if maybe it was a less of a divine plan to take his friends away, but rather a punishment by God, for all the early years of carelessness with other souls under the excuse of "collateral damage."

Maybe. But it's not about me right now. It's about Emma and Becky? Burns refocused on where he was and continued to slowly pat Roxie, who now buried her head in his jacket. While still holding her close, Burns covered her head and ears with his free hand. After a moment, her body seemed to become less tense as she now snuggled further into his chest.

"It's okay, girl. You'll be all right."

No. No hate. Focus on finding Daniels and destroy his network. Make sure Becky and Emma are safe, and finish the job with Daniels. It's not about them. He's pissed at me.

"Time to end this," he said to himself as he held Roxie tight.

Chapter 7

"Animus facit nobilem" – The spirit makes noble

The first call with an old Marine sergeant at the American Embassy in Spain would have been nothing short of a delight if it hadn't been for the fact that the safety of American citizens was at stake. While violating protocol, he made a promise to make sure he got the citizens home.

"We got it covered. We'll go to them. I promise. One Marine to another. Oorah?" he said.

"Oorah!" was the only appropriate response Welch could think to give. For a Marine, that was the one that mattered.

The conversation with her other non-uniformed colleague, on the other hand, was as difficult as she anticipated. Fortunately, she was able to use Helms's office at the regional office to make the call, since she knew the ensuing conversation was going to be fraught with questions and doubt.

Well, the President did ask me to use all resources to investigate and bring Daniels and his crew to justice. If we can re-establish some communication, and build some bridges with other countries, that would be a bonus.

"Are you out of your mind?" Robert Tombs demanded to know.

Welch had to agree that involving both the Chinese and Russian secret service communities warranted that question.

"Come on, Bob. You know my research on this matter is thorough, reliable, and valid. Crazy? Yes. But then look at who I'm dealing with?"

There was a long pause, as it was evident that Tombs was thinking about the proposal. The box of data and information with a summary report was more than thorough.

The more silence, the better here.

The problem with phone calls was that much of the non-verbal communication was eliminated, leaving only verbal communication as the sole means to understand what the person might be really thinking.

"I don't know, Diane. It's crazy, but it might help us get on the map of re-establishing some friends on the planet. I wouldn't mind getting a piece of Daniels at the same time," he said.

"It's a pretty 'big' piece of Daniels, when you look at the total value of assets he squirreled away from insider trading, research development, innovations, and patents alone. While we think we have confirmed likely foreign accounts and industries, we have no idea of the exact figure. We do know that it's in the multi-millions, and that quarter earnings combined is about fifty thousand American dollars. That's a lot of spending money," she said.

It is truly amazing that he was able to accumulate such wealth right under our noses in foreign countries. The irony was not lost on her that a private, national security agency focused on American security from abroad, simultaneously investing in those same 'enemy' countries, made a lot of money doing it. *Only in America.*

Helms had been looking for the assets of the Foreign Intelligence Office for more than a year, until he handed it over to the IRS. Not one to leave something undone, Helms continued to have a couple of people continue their investigation to see if they could find something. John Martin, former accountant, now logistics specialist, was the guy who found the pattern. Welch smiled when she heard it was him--the same guy who several months ago "acted" his way into a fire fight and then rescued Helms, Andersen, and Davis from a no-win situation.

Before Martin's interest in acting and field work, he had been the Bureau's accountant. After months of research, digging, and collaborating with the IRS and CIA, he found how Daniels left a sea of corporate shells and invested his money. While she didn't pretend to know entirely what he was talking about, she did know that Daniels invested his money solely into emerging economies in such services as computer innovation, software, social networks, communication, private security, and profit/private human services. The top places he invested were Afghanistan, Iraq, North Korea, Iran, China, Russia, Cuba, and Brazil.

When Martin had vetted the data, documentation, and evidence with the IRS and CIA, they were shocked at both the audacity and simplicity.

The money was hiding in plain sight. A hallmark of men like Daniels and Burns.

While the CIA wanted to freeze accounts from the US end, the money was inaccessible in those foreign countries. In order to access those, Welch would need to ask their countries' governments to do it. In order for them to do it, they needed to be approached by a respected government agency not connected with Homeland Security, Department of Defense, or any agency that had even a peripheral connection to Daniels' Foreign Intelligence Agency.

And that's where Robert Tombs, Secret Service Director, came in. Since it was the President of the United States who had publicly indentified Daniels and his agency as rogue, and demanded it shut down and investigated, he became the symbol of one part of government that was not tainted by corruption. Welch had to admit that she never thought she would live to see the day when the President's office would be seen as "America's last semblance of justice and order."

The guy doesn't even have to campaign for another term. A coronation should be just fine.

In regard to Tombs, he was many things, but he was not a risk-taker, and did not like covert operations. This was well-known in the intelligence community, both state and foreign. She had met Tombs a number of times; she also knew a number of people who knew his work but not him personally. Still, he was known as a straight shooter and pretty honest guy.

Now that's something you just don't expect in DC. Maybe that's why he's not well-liked. Too honest, and not political.

So if someone was going to take the lead on asking the Chinese and Russian secret service to take action on the US's behalf, to shut down the money flow to Daniels, it might be better received from someone like him rather than if National Security Agency were to ask. Now, the hard part of the entire plan was convincing Tombs to actually extend the olive branch to see if it would work.

Welch was suddenly pulled back to the conversation by Tombs's litany of questions.

"Why the hell would they trust us? Didn't Daniels have a plan to infect China with a drug-resistant flu through poultry? Didn't Russia and China pull all their embassies and expel our diplomats? Didn't we kill North Korea's leader?"

"Bob, I'm not asking you to ask North Korea. I'm asking you to ask the two largest countries in the world, before they slip back to the old ways and we're all building missiles for a new arms race again."

Hyperbole? Could it happen? Maybe. If North Korea or Iran gets them, the missles will be launched.

More silence, except for the sound of Tombs rubbing his chin.

Has to be five o'clock shadow. It's got to be itchy when it's so stubbly you can hear it over the phone. I don't know how men can simply forget to shave.

"You know what? Screw it, Diane. I'll do it," he said.

She was surprised by the sudden turn-about. *A guy like him doesn't do "sudden" changes of heart or "surprises."* She had to know why.

Careful not to undo her work, Welch asked as softly as she could muster,

"That's great, Bob. But just so I can tell my friends here at the Bureau, what changed your mind?"

I hope I didn't just blow my only chance by having him think about it and then explain it to me.

Welch could tell by Tombs's voice that this was not a sudden decision. Rather, it was a well thought out one that he must have made long before her call. Maybe she was just the reason or the opportunity to do something.

"For more than two decades, I made every effort to establish working relationships with my counterparts in those countries, while maintaining the Constitution of the United States. So when Daniels and his agency make a habit of violating that Constitution and then documenting it, it really pisses me off. We're America. We're not supposed to do that shit. Do you know what it's like to duck calls from counterparts as they try to figure out what other shit we did and if I knew about it?"

Is that a rhetorical question, or real? When he continued, she knew it was the former.

"So I'm going to give Vladimir and Liang a call and see if we can plug the money up. If that flushes Daniels out and we get him, that's fine with me. In fact, I'll even give Seo-yeon a call. She's still a somebody in the North Korean Directorate. I bet they'll send their fleet to help find him."

Welch smiled. The idea of getting the secret service agencies talking ran contrary to conventional thoughts. *Is it possible that Tombs, of all people, could re-establish diplomatic relationships? Could finding Daniels be the binding force? "The enemy of my enemy" thing could work?*

"Well, Bob--what can I say except 'thank you,'?" was all she could think to say.

"Don't thank me yet. They could all hang up on me, or not take my call. If I was Liang, and my country was the target of genocide, I might have some ill feelings about talking to me."

Excellent point. This may be a fool's errand, but it's the only thing we've got to hurt Daniels.

"True. But I'm sure they will at least take your call." Welch could swear she heard more enthusiasm in his voice. *Jesus. He's just like Helms. He wants to make it right.*

"Don't worry about it, Diane. I'll field this one. Just find that bastard. Oh--and by the way, I'm keeping the Israelis out of this. Chatter is the Mossad and key Israelis Special Forces commanders are really pissed at Daniels, and are coordinating their own team to find and kill him. And for whatever reason, the French are helping them."

Welch took a moment to digest that data before asking her next question. *What are the French doing with the Mossad?*

"What the hell did Daniels do to them to warrant a death sentence?"

"If it wasn't for the fact that I'm a federal officer, I would probably say 'happy hunting.' Unfortunately, you now that the Israelis don't respect national boundaries. If Daniels is still in the US, they will come here to kill him. I have a problem with that, especially with the Israeli agent called "Ruth." She's a real piece of work – gets the job done regardless of international treaties, federal and local laws and pesky national boundaries."

"Are you kidding me? There's a female version of *James Bond* who is a Mossad with just the name 'Ruth'? Kind of cryptic and mysterious?"

"I don't make this crap up, Diane. I just try to keep America safe. And I don't like other foreign intelligence agencies, no matter how well intentioned, walk in and out of my country doing whatever they want, when and how. I got issues with that," Toombs said.

Old school. Learn a new thing about someone every day, I guess.

"Anyway, Diane," he continued with renewed enthusiasm, "I'll make my end work while you go find him. Good luck and have a nice day."

"Thanks. Good luck to you too," she replied.

As she hung up the phone and sat back in Helms's large leather chair, she took a moment to sigh and rest. After approximately thirty seconds, she was paged to the control room.

"Mrs. Welch? Dillon here."

"Yes."

"Burns is ten minutes out, ma'am. We are going green on the Murphy situation. Thought you would want to know."

You're damn right I want to know.

"On my way," she said.

As she pulled herself out of the comfortable chair, she felt her bones creak. Still, she was more worried about what Burns's mental state would be. Would he be all vengeful and in a "kill everyone" mood, or the quintessential professional who would compartmentalize his feelings, and focus on the mission even though his friend had been killed?

"I wonder how it's going to be," she said to herself as she entered the corridor to the control room.

~

John Helms was glad to be back in his regional office, where he could be at the center of things rather than running errands. In the past, he would have deployed junior staff to get Burns, but as he approached retirement he found himself grooming the younger staff for control and command duties in addition to field experience.

You got to just do it. But there were times he appreciated being "back at the ranch."

The helicopter flight back to Massachusetts and the ride to the office were silent for the most part, as Burns looked out the window, patting his dog.

As he led Burns and Andersen through the mazes of offices, he made note of the level of activity that appeared too high.

More must have happened.

Upon entering the conference room he was glad to see Welch, Dillon, and Janeson already in place with a series of laptops, tablets, and folders in front of them. Cups of half-drunk coffee and water suggested that there had been a number of people in the room prior to their arrival.

"All right, people. I think everyone knows everybody, so let's get to it. Updates--and what will Daniels do next," Helms announced as he sat. He turned to see where Steve was sitting and noted he was flanking Burns's left side as he covered the right.

Funny, we're all keeping our jackets on. Guess we don't plan on staying here very long.

Janeson was the first to start the briefing. She was known for her memory and her exquisite level of detail.

"I will summarize as rapidly as possible. Mr. John Murphy came in with his granddaughter, Rosemarie Flores, to give us a warning that his other granddaughter, Emma Littleton, might be in danger. He produced the 'Phoneix' memorandum, which outlined the necessity to bring in Mr. Burns and his family to justice."

Helms sighed, and heard a similar sigh of relief from Andersen. He had been hoping that Janeson would refer to the Littletons and Caulfield as Burns's "family crew," and not his "family." Somehow, revisiting the memorandum just seemed too painful, in light of Burns's loss and questionable mental state.

Helms spied a look at Burns, who continued patting his dog while periodically looking up.

"As we were in the process of warning Cratty and her team, they were ambushed, leaving three of our people dead."

Yes. Someone briefed her on how to brief Burns: keep it simple but don't refer to people as things. Thank God.

"Also at the scene were approximately seven other victims. It appears that Fitzgerald rammed the two guards who betrayed them, and some kind of explosion killed four or five others. Ramsey was able to obtain intelligence that Jeffrey Glenn had apparently killed the attacking men. Reasons for this turnabout remains unclear. Reasons for him being there to begin with are unclear."

Helms noticed that Burns slowed his patting down when he heard Glenn's name, and then started up again.

Janeson continued without skipping a beat.

"Presently Emma is safe with Ramsey and Horowitz. Horowitz's degree of injury is unclear. Rebecca is with Denise Cratty and should arrive shortly."

"Where is Glenn now?" Burns asked quietly.

Janeson took a moment to consider the question before she answered. Obviously her briefing on how to present did not entail what she should do if Burns asked her a question.

"Well, Mr. Burns ... I am speculating that he was part of the original plan to ambush our people. He must have thought or changed his mind, and decided to kill the attackers. As a result, he can't go back to Daniels, nor can he come in to us. We discovered that Mr. Glenn had a gambling problem that was suddenly resolved last month. He wired money to his sister and niece. I am guessing he plans to get to them and then to get out."

"Where are they?" he asked.

"Germany, just outside of Berlin. They are presently under surveillance by German police."

Helms watched Burns as closely as he could without seeming rude. He was impressed with his ability to listen to the briefing without demonstrating emotions. But it was unsettling when you considered his loss. Then he was really surprised.

"Ms. Janeson. Is that your name?" Burns asked.

Helms saw that Welch's eyes locked onto Andersen.

I know. This is weird.

"Ah ... yes. Rachael Janeson, sir," she responded. Although she seemed not thrown by this change of questioning, Helms could tell by the delay that Janeson was completely thrown.

"Okay. You can call me 'Burns' or 'Alex' but the 'Mr.' part has to go. Also, you don't have to refer to Dr. Caulfield and your people as 'our team.' They had names. You can use them. Who are the people that died?"

Stay with it Rachael. You're doing good.

Janeson seemed delayed in answering the question. If it were any other person, one might have thought she had forgotten their names. But she didn't forget things like that.

"Kelly Fitzgerald, thirty years old. Survived by her mother and father. They lost their other daughter eighteen years ago. They now have no surviving children. Cindy Belben, twenty-seven years old. Father and mother deceased. Survived by two brothers and one sister. Dr. David Caulfield, fifty-four years old. Survived by Rebecca and Emma Littleton, and close personal friend Alexander J. Burns."

Burns had stopped patting the dog as Janeson listed the personal data. Helms was attempting to make eye contact with Dillon when he noticed Janeson's eyes becoming an even deeper blue, and still.

What the hell? Now? You feel and experience emotions now, he thought. Again, to the casual person they would have thought she was only pausing but for Janeson, this was an emotional breakdown on par with tears.

Dillon also noticed and couldn't help but respond.

"Janeson? Are you all right?"

With still, deep blue eyes fixed on Burns, Janeson sat back in her chair and folded her hands on her lap.

"Yes. It's just that we didn't get to them in time. Maybe we could have done something if we'd just moved fast enough. It's .... It's just too much loss. Three deaths on May 2nd. Twenty-six federal agents killed starting on the Ides of March. Dr. Caulfield, Ms. Belben, and Ms. Fitzgerald. Seven other dead bodies. All of them somehow connected to Eric I. Daniels. We have to end this. We have to end it soon."

Janeson stopped abruptly.

Though she spoke with no emotion in her voice and it stayed level throughout, Helms knew that this speech reflected more than a random list of obvious events. It was her "emotional moment." After a moment reflection, it made sense.

Janeson, Dillon, Johnson, Gilmore ... they're all young and they take all of this personally. For Welch, Andersen, and me, it's just another tough bastard we have to find and finish, now.

Helms found himself still looking at Janeson when she spoke again.

"I am sorry ... Alex. I am frustrated because I want to catch Daniels and end this. And I can't find him. I cannot pick up his trail. I can't even locate his place of birth and birth date. I am unable to even find what the 'I.' stands for ...."

"Icarus," Burns said matter-of-factly as he patted the dog while holding eye contact with Janeson.

There's some connection between you two, Helms thought as he watched the interplay. His attention was interrupted by Andersen's remark.

"'Icarus' as in Greek mythology," Andersen said.

Jesus. Janeson has an emotional breakdown and you're all of a sudden literate in Greek mythology. What the hell?

"Yes. That gives you some insight as to who we're dealing with here," Burns responded.

"There are two pieces of additional data," Dillon offered.

All heads turned to her as she looked at her tablet and turned it over for everyone to see the picture of a pretty young woman with a stern face talking on the phone while walking to her car.

"Telophoto picture via Davis. It took us a while, but she was on the same list as Jeffrey Glenn, who went MIA after Daniels disappeared. Her name is Alica Wise, twenty-five years old. She was groomed for deep cover, something called, ah, 'intimate contact.'"

Helms turned to face Dillon so that he could ask what "intimate contact" meant, but Welch beat him to it.

"What? Does 'intimate contact' mean what I think it means?"

"I'm not one hundred percent sure, but I think it has to do with becoming very close to your target. My security level when I was at the agency didn't give me authority to see the details. This is the first time I'm seeing this classification of operatives," Dillon clarified.

Helms's attention was drawn by Burns's deep intake of air.

"'Intimate contact' means just what it says. The operative has carte blanche authority to create any kind of relationship they need to get close to and stay with their target for weeks, months, or years. That includes becoming a lover, the 'other woman,' a girlfriend or boyfriend or spouse if necessary. Once the mission is completed, the operative has the choice to either stay or be reassigned. Sometimes it's divorce. Sometimes it's faking a fatal accident. There have been a few occasions where the operative stayed with the person even after the mission was over. Not often ...." Burns's voice trailed off as he must have noticed the slackened jaws that almost everyone had. *Except maybe the dog and Janeson*, Helms thought.

"Are you shitting me?" Andersen asked. Helms could thoroughly understand why he was dumbfounded.

For the first time since they had been together, Burns seemed almost to appear "guilty" of something he had done.

"I'm not condoning the program. I'm just telling you what it was. Trust me, there are other agents and programs in place that make this one look tame by comparison," he added.

Helms was surprised by Janeson's timing in changing the subject away from the discussion back to key data.

"One point of interest with regard to Ms. Wise," she said as she pointed to a large computer screen behind her, "is her brother, Robert Wise." An image of a very tall, blond, muscular man in military fatigues appeared, along with other images of various military-type people and camps.

"Robert Wise is a corporal in the Republican Citizens' Army, or RCA, who are preparing to 'fill the void when the US government falls,' or so their literature says."

"What? Intimate contact and this? You are shitting me? A federal agent for an armed agency has ties to 'preppers'?" Andersen asked in astonishment. Again, Helms could understand the shock. All agents were carefully screened to eliminate candidates with ties to survivalists or any paramilitary group.

Burns answered the question almost distractedly as he patted his dog.

"Daniels picked those candidates specifically. Anyone who can pretend to be in love with someone for a mission for years at a time might have a history far from the conventional two-parent, intact family. That said, if Alica is continuing to be loyal to Daniels, I bet Daniels will know where Robert Wise and this RCA group is as a possible point to retreat. It may make sense to delve more into Alica Wise's past relationships to see if there might be other possible ties."

"That's okay for now. Maybe we can take that one offline. We don't need to know right now for this mission. Dillon, do you want me to fill in the money trail?" Welch said to change the subject.

Thank God. I don't want to hear any more shit about Daniels and his fucked-up agency.

It took time for everyone to refocus on Welch so as to deviate from Burns's report.

"Our resident logistics analyst and former accountant, found how and where Daniels has stashed his money. And Robert Tombs has agreed to pursue his contacts in Russia and China to shut the source of his money down."

"Well, that is some good news. Tombs didn't strike me as the type of 'lock and load' guy," Helms said.

The conference speaker phone suddenly beeped and Gilmore's voice came on the line with great urgency.

"Sorry for the interruption, Boss. We just got a call from Murphy's second-in-command, Fitzpatrick. Murphy's car never made it back to their house. Martin and Crepes just located the bodyguards in the garage--two are dead, one critical and might make it. It appears Murphy's phone is off, as is the girl's. But she still has the tracking device and we are picking it up loud and clear."

Damn it! People killed in my garage!

Feeling his jaw tightening and fists clenching, Helms did his best not to yell at the messenger.

"Get security to pull any video and secure that crime scene. I want every inch covered. No one comes in my house and kills anyone," he said angrily.

"All over it, Boss," Gilmore was quick to say.

"I already have a team in the garage and two teams in pursuit of the trace," he added.

Good. Something going right.

"Heading?" Helms said as he stood up along with everyone else.

As Burns stood he put the dog down, slapped a leash on, and walked over to Janeson.

Yeah? What are we going to do with that creature?

"Heading 93 south. They are fifteen minutes ahead of us. Two SUVs are ready to go. Johnson is loading it up with weapons. I'm rounding up others. How many of you are going?" Gilmore asked.

Helms looked around the room.

"Andersen, Dillon, Burns, and me," he answered.

"What the hell?" Welch said.

Here we go.

Helms knew that would come. He was more than aware she had more experience in the field than the team he pulled together.

"I can't have all of the senior team out with us if everything goes bad. Janeson is in command of the control room operations and you are the lead back here if it all goes bad. Getting the Littletons and Cratty's team back is the number one priority."

Helms could see that she was not happy and took a moment to make her decision.

"All right, this time. But next time, Steve stays back and I go. Fucking men ...." he heard her say as she walked out.

Helms smiled knowing that he would be pissed if she'd done it to him. As he turned to look for Burns, he caught the last part of what he was telling Janeson.

Thinking back on the bodies in his garage, his smile evaporated and his fists clenched again. He thought he was about to grind his teeth down to the gums until he overheard Burns talking to Janeson.

"... she'll pee on paper if you put some down. Do not pick her up. Do not get close to her or pet her. When she's motionless or snarls or growls, she means it. Keep her on her leash and she will follow you. She eats hypoallergenic food. Venison in particular."

As Burns started to walk away the dog started to howl. He stopped and returned to the creature.

I can't believe this. He terrorized the East Coast and destabilized the US government ... and now he's a pet owner...

"It's okay, Roxie. I'll be back," he said. Helms really didn't expect tenderness from Burns; he rubbed her face affectionately for a moment, and then fell behind Helms to walk out.

Helms had a hard time seeing Burns as a dog owner, especially a lapdog. His expression must have conveyed that thought as Burns stopped and said, "She was abandoned, and has issues." He then gestured for Helms to lead the way.

Shaking his head, Helms gave his departing order: "Janeson! Get to the control room. Locate possible destinations. Start with the mob. Get a status on Cratty and her people, and find out which son of a bitch killed people in my parking garage!"

"On it!"

All right! Here is the second prong.

Chapter 8

"Nil desperandum" – "Never Despair" Horace

It took Cratty a full minute to remember where the safe house was, as it was not a house per se, but rather two large ship cargo containers, significantly modified to keep a small group of people safe. The containers were outfitted with air filters, cots, food, air conditioning, weapons, clothes and a very sophisticated satellite communication system. Two containers similarly arranged and separated meant team and family were split so as to reduce concentration in one target. Cratty's thoughts were filled with anger, loss, and logistics as she slammed on the brakes in front of the second container, assuming that Ramsey would be in there with Emma while Horowitz would be in the lead one setting up communication, providing reconnaissance for Ramsey's position.

With weapons drawn, both Cratty and Becky were out of the car in seconds, as they sprinted to the doors as fast as possible.

"Ramsey! It's me. Wolf. Repeat--Wolf!" she yelled as she pounded on the metal doors.

As the door popped open, a brick fell in place to keep the door ajar so that Ramsey's gun could have a clear shot at whoever might be on the other side of the door.

"Nice," Cratty said as she pulled the doors open.

Becky had been silent, and ran by both Ramsey and her as she spotted Emma behind a small couch.

"Mommy! Oh Mommy," Emma cried out as she ran toward Becky. Cratty watched as the two embraced with Becky nearly enveloping her daughter. Emma's tears were flowing as she cried out, "Papa's gone! Mommy? Why? Why, Mommy ...."

Becky was barely audible and Cratty decided to focus on protecting what was left of her crew.

I just can't think about it.

"Boss ... I'm sorry ... I should have ...." Ramsey started to say before she cut her off.

No time for "could haves, should haves, would haves."

"No time for that now, Ramsey. I saw your deployment from the base and it was fine. You were outnumbered and outclassed with weaponry. It's a wonder anyone made it out. Where the hell is Horowitz? If she was doing recon, she either knew it was us or she's busy. What's the deal?"

Cratty could see her short speech had the desired effect as her seemed to physically push herself to focus on the survivors rather than the dead.

"Last check-in was fifteen minutes ago. She's in the lead container. She diverted much of the electricity here because we had none until ten minutes ago. She was going to set up a link to the Bureau to get an exit strategy. I'll go check."

"No," Cratty said. "I'll go check on her. Lock us out. New entry word--'Miranda.' Got it?"

"Miranda. Got it, Boss."

"Good. Get the weapons ready. Full automatic rifles and side arms, vests, and ordinance if necessary. Clear?"

"Full gear, Boss. Got it."

Cratty turned to exit but stole a look at Becky, still standing rocking Emma in place, who was still crying.

It's just too much. No way I could stay here and watch this.

Cratty ran the seventy feet between containers with her gun drawn and her senses on fire. As she approached she saw that the door to the container was ajar.

"Damn it ...." she said to herself. She quickened her pace, pushed the door open and dropped down to the ground to peer in with her gun pointing inward. Her stomach felt as heavy as lead, and at the same time she found her blood boiling with anger. As she rounded the very few shallow corners, she eventually saw Horowitz slumped over the communication desk with everything nearly set up for a communication link. Without taking her eyes off the surrounding environment, she felt for a pulse in Horowtiz's neck. There was none.

Shit! Damn it! Shit!

Cratty spent at least five additional minutes searching the small container to make sure there were no explosives, bad guys, or toxins floating around before she closed herself in with Horowitz's body.

Once locked in, she went directly to Horowitz's body to figure out the cause of death. She carefully pulled Horowitz to lie on her back on the floor. At first view there were no exit wounds or bleeding, nor had rigor set in. There was dry blood at the nose and mouth, and her arm was bandaged very well. She was puzzled until she noticed that Horowitz's normally dark complexion was pale, and had bluish lips while her neck seemed too dark. As Cratty unbuttoned Horowitz's blouse, the cause of death seemed evident, with large hematomas covering the majority of Horowitz's chest.

"Oh, Molly ..." she said to herself. "I'm so sorry."

The internal bleeding had to be massive. She probably suffocated to death in her own blood. Kelly, Cindy, and now Molly. Fuck! The majority of my team wiped out. With adrenalin ebbing from her body, Cratty felt suddenly empty and tired.

The only thing she wanted to do was sit down and weep.

No time! Not now! She refocused on a plan.

After buttoning up Horowitz's blouse, Cratty slowly got up from her side and set the final configuration in motion to make contact with the FBI's Boston Regional Office's control room.

The set of three monitors came to life as the middle one displayed the woman that Cratty knew as Janeson, with two familiar men nearby, Gilmore and Johnson, and in the background, Diane Welch in some heated discussion with someone on the phone.

My God. It's nice to see friendly faces.

"Ms. Cratty? Are you all right? What's the status of your team?" Janeson asked.

Cratty took a deep breath before answering.

"Kelly Fitzgerald, Cindy Belben, and Dr. David Caulfield were KIA on site while en route. Molly Horowitz appears to have died of severe internal bleeding while setting up communication. Three guards and one VIP are down; two are left, as are two VIPS."

As she continued with her report, she could see both Gilmore and Johnson pausing what they were doing as they heard the list of casualties.

"Again, Becky and Emma are fine, while Ramsey and I are the only ones left of the protection team. We will be refitted with weapons. What's our exit?"

Before Janeson could respond, Diane Welch spoke up as she came up from behind Janeson.

"The Marines stationed at the American Embassy are mobilizing and will be at your location in twenty minutes."

Cratty looked closer at Welch without trying to be rude but to see if she was really sweating as much as she appeared to be.

"Can you hold out, Ms. Cratty?" Janeson asked.

"Yes," she said, but she was distracted again by what seemed to be a leash attached to Janeson's hand.

Does she have a dog or something? Cratty forced herself to pay all attention to Janeson.

"Yes, we can. Once the VIPs are secured, and if there is a period of time before exit, I want to take Ramsey and go find Glenn. He has to still be local," she said.

Janeson took a moment to respond as Welch started to shake her head, meaning no.

"No, Ms. Cratty. Your first responsibility is to your VIPs ..." Janeson started.

"And I'm guessing that a fully armed platoon of Marines with heavy weapons and probably air support will be able to make sure they are safe once they are in their custody. We need to get to Glenn before his trail goes cold. Glenn will lead us to Daniels."

Cratty could see that Janeson was processing the data before she responded.

Come on ...

"All right. Find him. You will have eight hours to do it before you exit the country. Helms, Burns, Andersen, and Dillon are pursuing an abduction of the Murphys even as we speak--so the sooner you move on this, the better," Janeson said.

Cratty was about to terminate the link when Janeson broke in with one final requirement. *Not an order but close to one.*

"And Ms. Cratty? Don't kill him. The authorities think he's planning on exiting through Tangiers," Janeson added.

"Thank you. I am shutting down here and will be in contact via the satellite phone. New code name--'Miranda,'" she said.

Without skipping a beat, Janeson confirmed.

"'Miranda.' Confirmed. Contact us once you transferred the VIPs and once you enter Tangiers. We will get you any intelligence from the local agencies as soon as we get it. Good luck. Janeson out."

Cratty closed the line out. She found herslf wondering what had shocked her more--the fact that Daniels had already moved on Murphy and Emma's half-sister, or the fact that Burns had joined the team to assist after the loss of his friend.

Unbelievable.

After she shut the communication system down, she went back over to Horowitz to remove her side arm and any identification from her body. It was then that she noticed that clutched in Horowitz's hand was a picture of her, Fitzgerald, and the entire team.

Cratty looked at it and knew the occasion captured was Dillon's going-away party back in the States. It was a rare picture of them all together, in varying degrees of inebriation. It was hard to look at the picture knowing that of the five in that group, only two, Dillon and Ramsey, were still alive.

Jesus ... I'm sorry I got you guys involved in all this.

She felt tears welling up as fury build in her stomach.

"Fucking Glenn!" she said to herself as she finally stood up to leave. With the container secured and locked, she walked quickly to the other container with her handgun, and her eyes everywhere.

She knocked on the door quieter than she had the first time and uttered the pass code.

Ramsey did the same thing she had done before to make sure she had a clear line of sight to shoot if she had to.

"It's me, Ramsey," Cratty said as she walked into the container and closed the door behind her.

Ramsey looked puzzled as Cratty locked the door.

"Boss? You keeping Witzy in the front? I'll take over for her. She's had it rough today, and she seemed kind of woozy and out of it after we got here ...."

Trying to keep out of earshot, Cratty positioned herself between Ramsey and the VIPs so as to shield them from Ramsey's expected response to the bad news.

"Ana. Molly's gone. It looks like severe internal bleeding," she said quietly, waiting for Ramsey's response, which was first to blanch and then to jump from shock to anger.

"No, Boss! She made it," Ramsey said. Her shoulder's tensed and she started to walk toward the container's exit to leave.

Cratty stopped in her path with hands on Ramsey's shoulder and made solid eye contact. She knew that having at least one survivor from your team after such an attack was profoundly better than being the only survivor with all dead in your command. *No survivors? Just you...*

Ramsey stood still for a moment as the anger faded back to shock, and glistening moisture formed around her eyes.

"Ana. I'm sorry, but Molly's gone," she said a bit more softly. She had known Ramsey as long as she had known everyone on the team. She liked her because it was clear that she was tough, and it would take a lot to rattle her.

This has to be a lot, Cratty thought. *It's just too much ....*

It was. Ramsey's shoulders rounded and she backed away from Cratty.

She then turned to walk to the table where she had pulled together the weapons, ammunition, maps, money, and other essentials to go out in the field. She stood quietly for a moment. Cratty could see that Ramsey was going to focus on what was next. It was her voice and sniffling nose that made it clear to Cratty that she was hurting, but determined to move on.

Poor thing. She's the only survivor--along with Emma.

"Okay. Okay. Ah, Boss? I've got all our gear ready to go. Do we have an exit strategy?" Ramsey asked through her clenched jaw.

Cratty shifted her gaze and located Becky, now sitting on the couch holding Emma, who was still crying with her head in her mother's lap. She felt her blood boil and her resolve thicken to steel.

Turning her gaze away from Becky and Emma to focus on the array of weapons, Cratty organized her thoughts as she handed Ramsey the picture she had found in Horowitz's hand.

"Yes. The Marines will be here in fifteen minutes. We'll hand them over to them, and you and I will track down Glenn and kick the living shit out of him until we find Daniels."

Ramsey accepted the picture with hesitation at first, but knowing what it was, she carefully put it in her front pocket as she cleared her throat to respond.

"Sounds like a great plan to me, Boss."

Yes. Find him. I might kill him. Or Ramsey might kill him. But we gotta find out what Daniels is doing before all that.

~

Waking from sleep, Murphy found his head feeling heavy and his breathing labored. As consciousness returned, he realized he could lift his head, which helped with his breathing. As his eyesight cleared, he could first smell what he thought was the ocean, and then he was able to see the form of his granddaughter sitting in a chair next to him. Seeing that she was bound, he attempted to get up, only to find his strength sapped and his limbs bound as well. Blinking his eyes, he remembered heading to the car and getting ready to get in when he saw his driver slumped over the wheel and felt a sharp prick in his neck. Confused, he stood back up as his hand felt for what was sticking him, and then the world got very hazy as he felt himself falling to earth, light fading to darkness. Taking in even breaths now, he could see that someone had gotten the jump on him and his men, and now both he and Rosemarie were in a very bad place.

"Ah, shit. Rosey? How long have we been here?" he asked.

"I don't know, Grandpa. It's been awhile," she said in a brave voice.

Focusing now, Murphy asked a very important question, and depending on the answer it would be the difference between life and death.

"Did you see their faces? Were you blindfolded?"

Rosemarie looked down at her lap, knowing the meaning of the question. Murphy knew that her mother, though paranoid, was right in this case, and told her that if she was, ever kidnapped she shouldn't fight if they kept her from seeing their faces. "If they don't care and you see their faces," she had instructed, "fight for your life and don't go to the next crime scene, which will be your grave."

"Yes, Grandpa. They didn't even cover their faces, and I saw how we got here. Route 3 south. Near the beach--like near Plymouth. I'm scared," she said as she started to sniffle.

Murphy found himself angry at himself for having her caught up in his shit...and now she was going to die. *Not if I can help it*, he thought, as he continued pulling at his bonds. As he pulled and shook his chair, Rosemarie started asking him questions.

"Grandpa? Is it true about my dad? Did he kill my sister's mother and her boyfriend? Is it really true?"

Murphy sighed and truly thought about lying. At least she could have some peace and positive thoughts about her father. He shook his head.

Only dead men think that way.

Taking in a deep breath, Murphy decided the truth, for once, was the best thing.

"Honey, my son didn't appreciate family. He had children, and to him they were a burden and a pain in the ass. He saw everyone as strangers, even his own flesh and blood," he said. It was very difficult to say these things about his son, but Rosemarie was more important now. Pushing his own guilt and sadness aside, he continued for her sake.

"I should have spent more time with him, and been a better father, a better person for him to follow," he said as his voice trailed off, hearing his granddaughter's sniffling. She was seventeen years old and an "old" seventeen at that--but it still pained him to think that he had hurt her. He took another approach, which was to focus on distracting her with a real imperative, such as escaping. Still pulling at his bonds, he attempted to see if his cell phone might be in place. Rosemarie must have seen what he was trying to do as she answered his unasked question.

"They took my cell phone too," she pronounced.

"Oh," was his only response. *We really are screwed.* He felt a sudden rush of anger at putting himself and his little girl in such a bad place.

"Grandpa? The FBI cell phone is still on and stuck in my bra. It's been on all this time from the ride to this place," she said very quietly.

Murphy's heart jumped with excitement and relief as he smiled adoringly at his smart granddaughter. Smiling, he said, "Thank God one of us is thinking. I bet that Janeson woman has a whole group of FBI guys on their way," he said more as reassurance for Rosemarie and a prayer for himself.

For a minute he thought he could relax, but the basement door opened, letting bright, blinding sunlight fill the dark room as two people bent their heads to safely enter. As the door closed and Murphy tried to will his eyesight to return as soon as possible, he could tell by the high-pitched female voice that he was in the presence of one of his major rivals, Regina Panelli.

"And so," Regina announced, "I think it's about time that you and your family take a long vacation, and leave the business to us. Anyway, don't you want little Rosemarie and her half-sister, Emma, to get to know each other? Spain would be a nice place for a reunion, don't you think, Angie?" Regina, tall, thin but sturdy, and impeccably dressed, truly lived up to her name as "Queen."

Angelo's voice was markedly different from his tall sister's, in that his thin body and small stature had an unusually deep voice that must have made people do a double take to make sure it was actually him talking, and not some old cinematic dubbing technique. Similar to his sister, he could easily have modeled clothes if it were not for his short height.

"Yes ... nice time of year I hear," he said as he sat in the empty chair just opposite Murphy with the sole purpose of staring at him.

Shit. A little man with "little-man complex." Just when you think you have hope, the sea gulls shit all over you. Gotta keep them talking.

"Gina, Angie ... you don't call, you don't text or Skype. You don't stop by anymore. If you wanted to see me, why didn't you just ask? I love the North End ... haven't been there in years, and would have loved to get a cannoli," Murphy calmly said.

Angelo narrowed his eyes while he continued to size him up. He noticed that Regina was in a more chatty mood.

"You see, John. If you had only sat down and talked to us about being in business together rather than taking a high and mighty stance, and cleaning up the city, we could have met under better circumstances. But your newfound desire to keep the city clean of drugs and crime, while noble, should have just stayed in South Boston rather than claiming the entire city and suburbs. That really affects my bottom line and offends my principles of free enterprise. Really, John? Do you think coming into my turf was going to be okay? Did you think your actions would go unanswered?" Regina asked. She looked calm and poised as she leaned against her brother, who continued to stare at him. Murphy decided now would be a good time to broker a deal, before they reached a place of no return.

Being tied to a chair in a basement is as good a starting point as any.

"I can see how that might come across as offensive," he said bluntly.

As the silence lingered, Regina's eyes also narrowed in unison with her brother's, as if waiting for more to come.

"Anything else you'd like to say?" Regina asked.

"Yes," Murphy responded. "I would like to apologize for my arrogance and my lack of consideration for your rights to run your family business in your own back yard. I fundamentally agree with the principles of free enterprise and appreciate your concern and anger."

While Murphy did enjoy the surprise on both siblings' faces, he was positive that the longer he kept them talking, the better. His attempt at candor, although growing over the past few years, was still new to him.

Regina stood up straight for a moment and walked around Murphy as her brother cocked his head to the side with an apparent question.

"So that's it? You 'apologize'? You think you can shut my business down for two months and simply say 'sorry' and all is forgiven?" Angelo asked in a lower voice than Murphy thought was humanly possible. With eyes unflinchingly glaring at him, he caught sight of Regina walking slowly around him with her frosted fingernails gliding firmly over his shoulders. The smell of vanilla was subtle but strong enough to hold Murphy's attention.

Under different circumstances, this might be nice.

As suddenly as his thoughts were hopeful, his heart sped up out of anxiety as he watched the femme fatale casually walk to Rosemarie. Fighting his urge to tell her to get away from the child, he continued with his tactic of engaging the siblings to buy time.

"Yes. Look, Angelo. I'm an old man. All I want to do is get some dignity back to my name. But stepping on your toes was stupid, and I plan to make it right. If you want to kill me, that's fine. But my granddaughters? I know family is important to you."

Angelo's eyes seemed to soften for a moment, but then glazed over with anger.

"Gina! Something's very wrong here," he said, breaking his gaze for the first time to make eye contact with his sister, who was now motionless right beside Rosemarie with an intense look in her eyes. Murphy noticed that Regina was not paying attention to her brother, but continued staring intently at Rosemarie.

"He gave no reaction to this girl Emma in Spain. Something is very wrong for sure," Angelo continued.

Murphy looked over again and was surprised at the speed and dexterity Regina's hands demonstrated as they suddenly clasped Rosemarie's breasts and dug between them to pull something out.

He tried to stand up in response to Rosemarie's startled yelp.

"Hey Gina! What the hell?" he yelled out, still bound to his chair.

Stepping back, Reigna retracted a dark, old-style flip phone and carefully looked at it as if she was looking for something specific. Her face showed recognition that the phone had to be law enforcement as she continued to inspect it carefully.

"Crap! Angie, it's the Bureau and it's on. Son of a bitch! Which one of your morons missed this?" Regina said accusingly to her brother.

Angelo shook his head and looked briefly back at Murphy before responding. Regina opened the cell phone to turn the power off.

"Maybe a signal couldn't get through in the basement," she offered as she looked at her brother.

"Doesn't matter. I bet little Ms. Muffet over there had it on all the way here. We got five minutes or less. Time to move," he said as he stood up and took his sister by the arm to help her out the basement door. As light streamed back in, obscuring both their lean features in the bright light, Murphy heard Angelo's disembodied voice, making it more foreboding than expected.

"We're not done with this, old man," he said as he closed the door behind them, leaving Murphy and Rosemarie alone again. After a few long seconds of silence, Rosemarie asked her usually bright, intuitive questions.

"How much time do we have?"

Murphy sighed and calculated what he would do and how long it might take before he answered. He was not proud that he knew the answers, but it was his line of business.

"I'm guessing ten to fifteen minutes at the most. Walk to the car, yell at people for their idiocy. Maybe ...."

Murphy suddenly heard a relatively loud gun report, which drew Rosemarie's attention back to the basement door.

Murphy sighed again before he continued.

"...Maybe kill the lead person for making the mistake as an example for everyone else to see what happens when you screw up. A couple of minutes for Angie and Gina to drive away, while the others get rid of the body, and then they come in here, move us to another place." Murphy stopped at that point, as the thought of his granddaughter being hurt was too much for him to actually say out loud.

"And that's when the FBI come and save us," Rosemarie said.

Murphy turned and looked at his beautiful Rosemarie and smiled.

"Absolutely," he lied. "That's when the Bureau comes in with guns blazing."

Chapter 9

"Non mortem timemus, sed cogitationem mortis" – *"We do not fear death, but the thought of death" Seneca*

Helms had watched the black limousine drive in through the gated estate that possessed a commanding view of the ocean in Plymouth. While he watched the wrought-iron gate close, he saw Burns clearing the top of a ten-foot wall with little to no effort.

"I'm in," was all Burns said. Feeling that several minutes had passed, Helms looked at his watch to see that only five minutes had passed before he spoke again.

"How does he do that?" he asked to no one as he thought back on how Burns had scaled the wall. Forgetting he had a headset on, he got an answer.

"My guess is he has probably done this a million times," was Andersen's response. Helms smiled as he heard his voice and was glad that Andersen knew a lot of people on the south shore to mobilize a three-county police drag net without any sirens announcing their arrival.

How does he know so many people?

Suddenly, Janeson's voice came over the line. She was sounding older, more mature these days.

"Boss? Data indicates that after several steps removed, the land and home is 'a business' for Angelo Panelli. He and his sister, Regina, are key suspects in an array of charges such as racketeering, drugs, prostitution, money laundering, and three murders."

"Competitors of Murphy."

"More like victims, of late," she continued. "Murphy has made some significant changes in his life and business, which has made trying to do organized crime in Boston--and in the state, for that matter--very difficult. The Panellis have not been happy with his sudden changes to walking the straight and narrow, especially in their area."

Squinting his eyes in surprise, Helms wondered what was wrong with Janeson's use of "straight and narrow."

"'Straight and narrow'? Janeson, that's kind of an old-fashioned statement, even for your vast knowledge of idioms."

Helms peered back through his binoculars and counted the positions of his men. He did not like sending one man in, let alone Burns. Any other guy he would have benched due to personal involvement with the case. Why he didn't was unclear.

"Mrs. Welch recommended that I attempt to use more terms that might be more consistent with your timeline," Janeson said innocently.

Helms broke his gazing to fully appreciate the insult. He heard Andersen's laughter erupting from his microphone. Shaking his head, he opted for another approach.

"What's the status on Cratty's team and exit?"

"Marines have Emma and Ms. Littleton in protective custody and are en route to the embassy. They will leave the country in eight hours under very tight security. Cratty and Ramsey are following up a lead to find Glenn."

Helms was about to express his reservations about that strategy when he and everyone on his team heard a distant single gunshot. Helms put his hand up to get everyone's attention, and for them to remain silent.

"Burns to Helms. Stand down. Stand down. Do not come in. I've located the probable location of prisoners. One of the owners, a tall, attractive, well-dressed woman just killed one of her own men. The man she is with just threw a cell phone on the body, and now they are leaving. The others are collecting the body. I'm moving in on location. Wait for my next signal. Burns out."

"Confirmed" was all he said. He switched signals for all other parties. "Radio silence from now on. Prep to go in hot. Helms out."

A series of team acknowledgments went up. "Boss? We got satellite coverage. Looks like a car is leaving. Heat signals show three men carrying something in one direction away from the house as one signal is approaching."

There was an uncomfortable silence for a moment as Helms covertly watched the same limousine that had entered several minutes ago now leave at a faster pace than before.

"Boss. Burns must be inside the house. We lost his heat signal," Janeson reported.

"Confirmed. We hold position. Janeson, follow the car. See if Welch can round up some of her state troopers to pick them up--unless you have another idea, Andersen."

Silence, and then Andersen's voice kicked in.

"I gotta better plan. I'll coordinate with Welch, but I have to go. You got this covered?"

"No problem. Go. Helms out."

God, I hope this works.

He went back to looking through his binoculars hoping that all would go well.

~

Once Burns was over the wall in the well-manicured estate, he found himself tired from pent-up grief and loss. Kneeling while still behind the bushes, he scanned the immediate area, as his mind drifted to how empty he felt with his friend David's passing. All his scars continued to itch furiously. He had come to understand that the scars on his hands, arms, and scalp were always an indicator of painful emotions. And right now, David's death was on par with losing Samantha. Additionally, there were the other names and faces of the dead that haunted him. When he heard that David was dead he immediately prayed for him, Sam, and all the others.

First Sam and now David. Maybe it is punishment. Samantha had been the one to find Burns and get him the help he needed. David cured his fractured brain at the expense of losing his wife, his eyesight, and his happy life. It had been both David and Samantha's idea and push to take the fight to his former bosses to get back their lives.

He was shaking his head as he continued his careful footing and pacing along the bushes behind the house.

They weren't soldiers. They were civilians. It's just not fair-- they were my friends, companions, and compatriot. But instead of feeling anger or vengeance, he found himself wondering what David and Samantha would want him to do.

Easy. Save the civilians. Protect Emma and Becky. Find Daniels. Destroy his network. Destroy him. Burns found that when he had objectives, it helped him to redirect the pain.

I'm sorry, Sam; I couldn't help him. I'm sorry, David. I wish I could have been there ....

Taking in a deep breath, Burns immersed himself in the next step. *Locate the limo. They must be there to see their guests.*

Burns had a semi-automatic weapon holstered on his hip as he continued his search. In the past the gun would be drawn and ready. But if it wasn't for the insistence of Helms making him take a gun, he wouldn't have brought one at all. Over the last five years he had come to rely on his wits. Reliance on a gun made people dumb; it was an easy go-to step. Focusing on past experience, wits and intelligence, that was the key especially for covert operations and hostage situations. Also, ever since losing Sam, his heart for killing had dropped off. Maybe with one exception.

I may have to kill Daniels to stop this. I just want him to stop. And then there were the others. Debbie Foley, Anthony Maxwell, Kelly Fitzgerald, Cindy Belben, and scores of others.

Taking longer than expected, Burns finally stopped behind the house where he saw a parked limo, and four men talking as a basement door started to open. A very well-dressed couple was emerging with a short man in front and a very tall, regal woman being gently escorted out. The short man waved the lead man of the four to come closer to talk, and was clearly angry. With a great deal of pointing, the shorter man eventually turned to face the woman, with his hands on his hips. He then casually stepped to his right, giving the woman, who now had a gun in her hand, a clear shot at the larger man. The loud crack it created indicated a large caliber, as did the man's falling backwards on the well-sculptured rose bushes. Burns immediately got on the small headset to tell Helms to keep his team at bay, and described the situation as it unfolded. Then the woman casually handed the gun back to the short man and the man continued saying something to one of the other men as he dropped a cell phone on the body. The three men began to collect the body as the couple got back into the limousine and drove away.

While both parties were going in the opposite direction, Burns seized the opportunity to cover the distance from the hedges to the house basement. It was easy to deduce that the civilians were held hostage in the basement the couple had just left from when he first saw them. After pausing for only a moment to listen for any noise inside, he opened the basement door and closed it as quickly and quietly as he could. With the door closed firmly, he noticed the deadbolt and latch and made use of them. It took some seconds for his eyes to adjust to the relatively dark room when he saw an older man and a very young woman in a school uniform of sorts.

"Mr. Murphy, I presume," Burns said as he produced a knife and cut his bonds.

"Not that I don't appreciate the assistance--but who the hell are you?" Murphy asked.

Burns smiled for a moment as his first thought of Emma jumped in his head, the only thing that made him smile at all of late. Freeing Murphy's hands first, Burns took a moment to hand Murphy his own gun. In another lifetime, turning over his gun would have been unheard of, but that was another time. It was evident that Murphy didn't know what to think of this action.

"I used to be an agent. I'm here because Director Helms of the FBI wants to make sure that you are safe before they come in hot. I want you to cover me while I free you and Rosemarie. I'm also Emma Littleton's uncle, Alex Burns," he responded as he finished with Murphy's legs and now turned to free the young woman. "And you must be Rosemarie?"

As Burns cut her bonds, he took a moment to look at her face and found himself stopping briefly. This sudden change in behavior drew the obvious question.

"What's wrong?" the young woman asked. Even though he was in the middle of a mission and lives were at stake, he couldn't help but notice that Rosemarie's eyes and face seemed to be an older version of Emma's. Even her voice seemed similar.

"I'm sorry, Rosemarie. It's just you have a striking similarity to your sister, Emma," he said. He cleared his head and returned to his cutting.

"Is she okay? Did they capture her, too?" she asked.

Burns felt his hands and scalp itch intensely as he felt his heart fall heavy. Pushing his grief aside, he sighed deeply and answered as well as he could.

"She's all right. Right now the US Marines have her and her mother, and they are heading back here. We've gotta move, though." Burns looked at the other end of the basement and saw a set of stairs going to the rooms above. Putting his fingers to his lips and motioning them to wait, he climbed up the stairs quietly, and carefully opened the door. As he looked around he could see he was in the kitchen area, with a connecting corridor leading to the main front rooms. He looked around each room to make sure it was clear before waving the family upstairs. Once they were all together, he secured the basement door with the kitchen table, keeping it shut while he talked into his headset.

"Burns to Helms. Murphy and Rosemarie are with me at the front door of the main house. Come in fast and hot. Once you've got the lead SUV passenger door open, we'll move. Have a pursuit car."

"Copy. One unit for your ride and three units for cover. Local PD will secure the crime scene. Out," was Helms's response.

Burns turned to Murphy and Rosemarie to update them on next steps when he heard shooting at the basement door in the kitchen. Flipping a large, heavy ornate center table in the main hall, Burns placed Rosemarie behind it while positioning Murphy there as well to cover her and have a clear line of fire. Burns held his position to the front entranceway and waited for the vehicles to arrive. More shooting drew his attention to Murphy's position when he realized he should have asked a critical question.

"Ah, Mr. Murphy? You do know how to use a semi-automatic?"

Burns was surprised by the warm smile he got.

"You're joking, right? Do you have a spare clip? We might have company real soon," he said.

Burns dug into his pocket, but then saw a sea of vehicles approaching at high speed and decided there would be no need for a standoff. As the cars stopped suddenly, doors flung open, releasing scores of men and women with guns. Burns caught sight of the lead SUV with the back passenger's side door open while Dillon was covering their exit.

"No need. Time to move, Go! Go!" he said as he pulled Rosemarie to her feet, and then Murphy. Burns made sure he was the last person out, and the only target when the shots from down the hall rang out, and started hitting the door frame and glass around their exit. He felt two sharp burning pains in his left buttock, and though it slowed him down a moment, he kept moving. The sun was still bright as they ran at top speed to the front SUV and jumped in the back while covered by Dillon and a whole bunch of agents. Rosemarie was first, then Murphy, and then Burns, closing the door. With a driver behind the wheel and Dillon back in front with her gun still drawn, he felt the SUV lurch ahead as he turned to see Murphy hugging his granddaughter. Dillon still looked vigilant and called back on her headset to make sure their convoy of protection was right behind them. Burns reached down his left hindquarters and felt something warm and wet, as Dillon seemed to relax a bit and gave an update.

"Nice work, Burns. We got everyone back in one piece," she said with a smile as she holstered her gun.

"Almost," Burns corrected as he looked at his blood on his hand.

Burns watched Dillon's brown eyes open like saucers as she sat right back up.

"Shit! Burns! Where are you hit?"

Burns found himself laughing. It might have been the result of the range of powerful emotions he had been experiencing throughout the day. Still, having survived a near-death experience, he could only think of what Samantha and David might say if they knew he had been shot in the ass. He was sure Sam would have said something smart and looked at him as if he was a dumbass, while David would have been far more sincere and referenced a number of heroes who were injured in that same region. Burns noticed that Murphy was looking and immediately saw the area that had been hit. Although he was not laughing, he did see a small smile emerge. It was evident that Murphy had seen that kind of injury before.

I guess by that look, the wound is not fatal.

"Back in the day, we'd pay good money for shots like that to get back home from the war."

Dillon was not finding this at all amusing as she took command.

"Damn it people! It's not funny," she said. She turned her headset on to talk to others. "Burns is hit. I repeat, Burns is hit. A non-vital area. Will need an MD at home. Hospital is not an option. The area is not vital. Will apply first aid. Dillon out."

As Burns felt the SUV moving in and out of traffic at top speed, Burns made a suggestion he thought made sense as he watched Dillon about to leap over her seat to apply first aid.

"Dillon? It might make sense if you give Mr. Murphy the first aid kit and he can at least pack my ass for closer inspection later. It's bad enough I'm hit in the ass, but let's not get into a pile-up over it. Stay up there. Mr. Murphy, would you mind in giving me a hand?"

Burns saw Rosemarie take a quick look at the blood on his hand as her grandfather handed his gun to Dillon in exchange for the first aid.

As she made a face Burns had seen on an older version Emma in Rosemarie. He smiled yet again when he heard the predicted "Ewwwww" as Rosemarie suddenly turned away.

Taking his jacket off and rolling up his sleeves, Murphy did give Burns fair warning.

"You may have a lot of padding there, but this is going to hurt."

"Yes. I know but I'd really be embarrassed if it somehow hit an important organ and I didn't take it seriously," commented as he shifted positions to allow Murphy access.

Dillon's reaction indicated that some question must have been coming over her headset as her face contorted and her response was as immediate as it was angry.

"Do you really think I have time to do a thorough abdominal exploration of the wound right now, Janeson? We're travelling in excess of eighty miles per hour and I can't just jump back in the car and poke around his ass." Dillon closed her eyes as if she had made an embarrassing mistake, and turned red.

"Sorry, Burns," she said apologetically.

He would have laughed again, but the pain was growing exponentially as Murphy applied pressure.

Just great.

~

Daniels had been frustrated beyond belief as he kept hearing bits and pieces of various Internet reports and first responders' communiqués half a world away. Alica Wise had talked to him early on that she was within feet of getting Burns alone when he was suddenly whisked away by state troopers. This did not bode well, as that meant his plan to strike the family either in Boston via the Panellis or in Spain by Glenn's team or both might have been compromised. His call to Angelo Panelli went right into voice mail, and Glenn's phone simply kept ringing.

Pushing himself up from his folding chair, he stood as straight as he could to release the tension in his back and try to focus on something new. With the sun high in the sky and the sounds of trees rustling in the light wind, he felt suddenly small and lonely. Being out of direct contact with key players in a multi-pronged plan and needing to depend on others was not his preferred choice of executing a plan. Pulling fresh Canadian air into his lungs, he found himself thinking of an apt Milton quote:

"'Loneliness is the first thing which God's eye named not good,'" Daniels said to no one as he looked beyond the treetops to spy two birds flying. It was hard to tell, but it appeared two birds of prey were engaged in some kind of aerial battle.

"Now that's ironic," he commented as he reflected on the

symbolism. Daniels's attention was drawn immediately to one of his beeping phones. The red one was Glenn.

"Finally," he said. He lunged to open the line and spoke like millions of times before.

"Report," he said, out of habit. After decades of watching and responding to national crisis, his language had been reduced to key phrases such as this over time.

"Report? Here's a report. The entire plan was clustered with the monkeys you and the Panellis stuck me with," Glenn said unceremoniously.

Just breathe, Eric.

"Jeff. What happened? I've got reports of a multiple-car accident," Daniels said in a calm voice.

"Is that what you call a complete fuck-up?! Nice plan! Your monkeys would have killed all the hostages if they didn't have reinforced SUVs--which by the way, thank you for that heads up," Glenn said in a low, angry voice.

"Intelligence is not what it used to be. Jeff. I got all the intel I could on their resources," he said, more defensively than he really wanted to. Silence filled the empty space and Daniels wondered if he had lost the connection.

"Here's the deal," Glenn continued in hushed fashion. "Leave me out. Killing the hostages was not my plan. Maybe yours and the Panellis', but not mine. If you wanted a hit you should have told me, and I would have shoved the money up your ass. Don't call me--and don't find me, unless you want me looking for you like Burns!" The connection clicked off and Daniels was completely dumbfounded.

Well ... that is different for Glenn.

Daniels waited for a moment to speak to an empty line. She shook his head in anger amd spoke to himself: "The plan wasn't to kill them. Just hold them for a couple of hours. What the hell happened out there?"

Daniels moved back to his various laptops to glean any more data he could about how the plan deteriorated so bad that mild-mannered Jeffrey Glenn just melted away.

I don't need another Burns out there.

Chapter 10

"Nolo contendere" – "I do not wish to contend"

Glenn had been moving from one side of the street to another along a relatively quiet mall of coffee and food shops in Tangiers for a few hours. It was close to 9:00 p.m. and he noticed an uptick in the number of groups, mostly men, trying to choose their place to eat and relax. For him, food was less of interest than cover as he missed the ferry and was now stuck for ten hours until the morning ferry left.

His conversation with Daniels was brief, but not without emotion. For the first time in years, he felt liberated from both Daniels and his work. Looking from one concealed part of the mall, he decided to settle for a busy establishment that would better hide him.

Fucking Daniels. I'll get the Mossad on his ass if he doesn't leave me alone. There are a couple of people who would pay a big price for his head.

Glenn looked over the chosen eatery for a booth in the back that was close to an exit, but from which he could see the front entrance. His mind wandered as he made a mental checklist of what he had told his sister earlier about dropping everything and leaving for Australia. He smiled at the thought of seeing his niece and sister soon. While initially resistant, he could tell that she was happy about the sudden move, and with the cash he had sent her, leaving was viable.

Settling back in his booth, he busied himself with his smart phone to confirm departure times and to see what was happening in the area that could provide him more cover as the evening pressed on. After the waiter returned with his drink, he took notice of two men that had taken up residence at the bar.

When did you come in?

Just as he finished scanning the two men, he saw another set of men enter the restaurant.

Shit! Local law enforcement.

The haircut, how they scanned the area, travelling in pairs and all their behaviors spoke of police. Ordinarily, he would have thought they were looking for someone else, but the crowd he picked were low key, professional men with a few young families interspersed, making it easier for him to pick out anyone who didn't fit.

And these four guys don't fit.

Looking around the room, he confirmed that based on demographics and other patrons' responses, they were not the target. He pulled his meager possessions for an immediate exit.

Time to leave.

He casually and slowly got up to retreat out the back door. While keeping his eyes on the men in front, he turned his gaze to the exit, where he felt rushing air and then a sharp pain erupted under his nose and above mouth. The force of the hit was so hard that he was dazed. In addition to being dazed, the strike to his groin made him lose all the air and ability to stand. Falling backward, he felt himself being roughly pushed back into the booth he had attempted to leave. He only became partially aware of hands all over his body as he was trying to clutch his balls and face, both still in shock and pain. As tears from his eyes cleared, he felt his hands being clamped down with some kind of binding. As he moved to spread his hands, he caught sight of Denise Cratty putting every ounce of effort into a backhanded slap he felt as it cracked along the side of his face. His mouth and nose bleeding, testicles throbbing, and lungs still depleted of air, he was now dazed again and blinking to orient himself. With no energy to offer resistance, Glenn felt his hands bound together, and then they were bound to his feet leaving him hunched over, looking down at the table.

"Shit ..." he uttered. He attempted to look up until he felt another strike high on his jaw and just below his eye. This was a closed-fist strike.

Fuck ... I'm going to look and feel like shit tomorrow.

Still unable to visually focus, he knew Cratty was there, but he was still wondering who else was manhandling him. That was until he heard a female voice and realized that it had to be one of Cratty's team.

"Well, Ms. Cratty. Now that we found the piece of shit, why don't we just off him and feed his balls and dick to wild dogs?" Glenn couldn't tell what the accent was... it wasn't local, but didn't seem American either. Still trying to adjust to his pain and trying to clear his vision without use of his hands, he heard his former colleague's calm, low voice.

"Look at me, Glenn," she said.

As he tried to look up and clear his vision, the woman beside him clearly didn't think he was moving fast enough.

"Ms. Cratty said look at her," the voice hissed out, with a firm hand violently pulling his hair back to make him move faster.

"I'm trying," he croaked out.

Through blurry vision, he watched Cratty going through his personal belongings--cell, passport, wallet, cash--all in a very casual fashion. As his vision cleared he saw her piercing blue eyes on tanned skin, framed by longer blonde hair.

"Denise ... You look good. Did you do something with your hair?"

Another sharp slap to the face made his already loose teeth rattle in his head just as the first barrage of strikes was beginning to subside. Facing down at the table and lap, he saw that the amount of blood from his nose and mouth was impressive.

"We can dispense with the pleasantries and be happy there are INTERPOL agents present. Ramsey's idea of feeding your balls to wild dogs seems too kind. So ... Jeffrey. Word on the street is you assassinated Alex Burns's family and you are working with Eric Daniels directly. The original plan was to find you and bring you in alive. Still, though ..." Glenn followed Cratty's gaze to the other agents who were busy clearing out the patrons. "... I bet it would be easy to say that you attempted to escape and I had to shoot you. Not lethal."

Cratty pulled out a high-caliber revolver and placed it on the table.

"Yeah ... good idea, Boss. I'll testify to that. Snowflake tried to run," Glenn heard from his side, said too enthusiastically.

You seem a bit more willing than I'd like. He resisted looking at the source of the comment.

"Maybe a warning shot in the knee. Ramsey, did you use hollow point or Teflon?" she asked as she pointed the gun under the table.

"I'm not sure, Boss. Hollow point, I think. But it would be easier to just cut his throat and let him bleed out," Ramsey offered. The feel of cold steel was piercing on his throat; her left hand violently pulled his hair back, exposing his neck.

"Excellent point. Well, Glenn, it was nice knowing you. I'll make sure to tell your sister and niece in Germany that you died in the line of duty. But I think she's trying to leave, so it may take some time. You know, on second thought, let her settle into the new place, check out the school system for her daughter ..." Cratty said.

Glenn took in a deep breath and carefully chose his words as pressure on his neck began to increase.

"If you kill me, you won't be able to find Daniels." That was all he could think of to say. It was a very long moment before he felt the pressure from the knife at his throat subside and his hair released.

Readjusting his view, he saw that Cratty was sitting back in the booth again as the woman beside him replaced the knife with a gun of some kind pressed against his third and fourth rib.

"Hey Snow White? I wouldn't sneeze. I might think you are trying to escape," Ramsey said in an unusually cheery fashion.

Where the hell did she find this one?

"Thirty seconds to tell me something I don't know. Counting," Cratty said as she went through his cell phone.

Taking in a deep breath, Glenn put together his briefing of sorts.

"I was called to consult for a team that was supposed to hold Caulfield and Littleton hostage for a couple of hours while another team captured another person of interest--John Murphy."

Looking at Cratty, Glenn was surprised when he saw her yawn and roll her shoulders, and then return to looking through his items again.

"Old news. Twenty-five seconds," she said without even looking up from her renewed investigation of his wallet.

"My group left me out of the loop on their own plan, which was less of a snatch and grab, and more of a hit. So when I got the chance, I killed all of them with a rocket-propelled grenade," he continued.

Sighing, Cratty started to go through his smart phone and stifled yet another yawn.

"Tired, Denise?"

Breaking from form, Cratty leaned forward and slapped Glenn across the face.

As the sharp pain rippled through his face, he heard Ramsey offer her suggestion.

"Come on, Ms. Cratty. Let's just shoot this white pig and be done with him. The locals can dispose of his body."

Without much effort, Cratty resumed her efforts of scrolling through his phone, but was taking note of some particular numbers.

Well, she probably just found Daniels and Panelli's numbers.

"Nothing new. There was one person alive who told us about you. Since I told you something new, you are down to ten seconds," Cratty said as she now peered into his eyes.

Shit! Smiley, he thought. Glenn closed his eyes and narrowed down his next critical statements.

"Daniels's last line of defense is either in Colorado, outside of Denver, or Maine, outside of Fort Kent near the Canadian border, or further inland at Mount Katahdin. Wherever the group called the Republican Citizens Army is, he will be close by. A brother of one of our former agents is involved. The agent, Wise, is also on Burns's trail."

He stopped. He could have added more, but he figured his ten seconds were up.

Well. I'll know in a minute.

Looking up, he saw Cratty was still, peering through him as she remained silent. Quietly, she finally spoke.

"You killed my team," she said softly.

"No. That monkey, that smiling monkey pulled the trigger that hit the SUV. When I saw what was happening and he was reloading, I pushed him off the ledge, and used the weapon to kill his friends. My biggest regret is that I missed killing him," he hissed out vehemently.

If I get out of here, I'm going to find that bastard and put him down. His fists tightened in anger that Smiley had escaped.

Cratty exchanged a look with Ramsey that easily registered to Glenn as recognition.

"I don't know, Boss. If this blanco rat hadn't been there...Dr. Caulfield, Belben, they would all be alive," she said with her gun pressing more in his side, her mouth inches away from his ear.

Ah, shit! Caulfield dead ....

Still silent, Cratty suddenly pulled together all of his belongings and put them in her own pockets. She waved the other agents over as she stood up.

Jesus ... He sighed a breath of relief.

"Ramsey, we're leaving. Leave this piece of shit to INTERPOL. We'll get him after he's spent some quality time with them," Cratty said. Turning to Glenn, she added more.

"We'll be keeping a close eye on your family. Like I said, it looks as if she is trying to get out, but she sucks at covert operations, so for now we'll track her. Ramsey, let's go."

Shit!

Glenn's shoulders and arms began to relax as he felt the gun move out from his ribs. While still thinking about his sister and niece, he first heard a click and then saw a sudden, blurred motion move toward the side of his face. Feeling a sharp cut across his cheek, he was startled not so much by the pain as by the amount of warm blood indicating the depth of the knife wound.

"The next time I see you I'll cut your heart out, you pig," Ramsey said as she closed her knife. The sting was really forming as he next felt two strong hands forcefully pulling him out of the booth.

Damn it! Daniels! Shit!

Chapter II

"Fas est et ab hoste doceri" – *"It's proper to learn even from an enemy" Ovid*

"What's the situation?" Helms said as he strode into the control room still wearing his windbreaker, with Andersen carefully removing his own. He had spent hours at the crime scene after apprehending the three assailants that had gone after Burns and company. It was easy to find the dead body, but the joy came an hour later when Andersen returned bearing great news: the Braintree police department and state troopers had coordinated a roadblock and captured the Panellis as they were returning to the North End. Between Welch's state trooper connections and Andersen's police friends, they now had both brother and sister in custody, with forensic evidence of placing a murder weapon in their possession. Helms was still smiling at the thought of getting an affidavit from Burns, who had witnessed the murder.

"I have to say that I'm impressed with Angelo trying to take the rap for his sister. Real family loyalty, don't you think?" Andersen asked. He took the moment to stretch his back.

"Real considerate. Shame both a witness and powder burns on Regina are going to put her behind the murder."

Helms started looking for Janeson. Unable to find her or Welch, he found the next best thing.

"Gilmore! Johnson! Where the hell are Janeson and everyone?"

Gilmore responded first as he looked up from his monitor.

"Janeson is with Burns in the infirmary, and Dillon is debriefing Murphy and the girl."

Helms nodded at first, but then had a follow-up question.

"We have an infirmary? Since when?"

"Makeshift, sir. Three small conference rooms have been converted into sleeping quarters, eating area, storage, and first aid. Once the Burns case became active, Martin prepped everything for twenty-four hour rotation for three consecutive days. He called in two nurse practitioners and a medical doctor on standby," Johnson filled in, never looking up from his laptop and tablet.

Helms's eyes narrowed; he was surprised at the extent to which his team had grown from technological nerds to seasoned field agents.

Ever since Burns's arrival years ago, Merrimack Valley Crisis, Ides of March ... they had to grow, fast. If this keeps going, I might actually retire, spend some time with the Mrs.

"Martin has a lot of talents for an accountant, former actor now turned logistics expert. Is there anything he can't do?" Andersen commented.

Shaking his head positively, Helms had to agree that he was impressed with Martin.

If Janeson hadn't used Martin to bluff us out of that cluster back at City Hall Plaza, I never would have noticed him. The man does have some skills.

As Helms considered his next steps, Welch appeared with an unusually pleasant smile on her face.

"Well, you have to have some good news to have such a smile on your face," Andersen said.

Welch's grin was firm, and her eyes were sparkling.

I have to have Andersen and Welch over for a barbeque or something. I think the wife would love to finally meet these people.

"Out with it, Welch," he said.

Helms could see that it was either for drama or for savoring the moment that Welch took her time. In an uncharacteristic move, Welch took out a pair of reading glasses and a small notebook, giving the impression that she needed to get things right.

"Well, gentlemen, just to understand each other, I would have preferred being in the field rather than being stuck with politics. But once in a while, steadfast work and true diligence pay off."

"Oh my God, it's going to be a long speech," Andersen said as he rubbed his temples.

"You are not in front of the Senate, Welch. Remember, you're a Marine. What's the story?" Helms said, undeterred.

Welch cleared her throat before she began.

"Well, here's the short version. Director Tombs has not only convinced his colleagues in Russia, China, and North Korea--and I emphasize, North Korea--to freeze Daniels's assets, they have also committed any resources we might need to find Daniels so as to put him up for crimes against humanity." Removing her glasses to make her point, Welch continued. "I guess China is still pissed about Daniels's plan to use biological warfare, and they want a piece of him. Russia is on board, figuring they would be next, and North Korea just wants to be seen as a good guy for a change and is glad to be at the table."

Sighing, Helms was glad to get good news for a change.

"Well, at least we are all on the same page about finding Daniels," Andersen said.

"The good news here is that the President's Secret Service branch is now seen as the more legitimate, honest agency when compared to all the other intelligence services. For now, I am very happy with Director Tombs being lead. Especially in the light of the bonus we got," Welch slipped in.

Helms caught sight of Janeson and Dillon, and waved them over as he pressed Welch to continue.

Welch smiled as she saw the two come in, and continued with her report.

"The mixed news is that French and Israelis already have their own field agents looking for Daniels, and it's unclear if that is on US soil or not."

Helms was shaking his head at the idea of covert agents, especially Israelis, conducting operations on US soil.

"That's 'mixed'? I'm sure I'm not the only one who could do without the Israelis' methods of 'fixing the problem,'" Andersen added, confirming Helms's belief that he should be worried. Welch nodded her head in agreement, but Helms decided that the Israelis' involvement was beyond his control, so he changed the subject.

"And the bonus is…?"

Returning to her pad more out of the dramatic sense than necessity, she happily went with the changed subject.

"Glad you asked. It just so happens that ever since our president was elected, there has been a surge in hate groups, local militias, and preppers not seen since President Obama's terms. That said, with our new President, there have been some groups that have made the 'watch list' of the Secret Service. Colonel Timothy Carter, leader of the Republican Citizens Army, is on Tombs's top ten list. As soon as he heard about our interest and connection to Daniels, he gave us carte blanche use of their, resources including satellites they borrow from the Department of Defense--and that's satellites, plural, so we can find and watch the RCA's movement and locations. In other words, gentlemen, we hit pay dirt as far as support and resources."

As Helms took in the information, he was very pleased with the ramifications.

With outside intelligence services on our side, Daniels's assets and cash frozen, and support to watch the RCA groups, we might have a chance to carry the fight to Daniels directly. Daniels better hope we get to him before the Israelis do.

Janeson and Dillon heard the last part and seemed to have understood the ramifications.

"Great work, Diane," he said.

"Yes, great work. See, Diane, if you were out in the field you wouldn't have been able to make such headway, and save the world … again," Andersen added dryly.

Not picking up on the sarcasm and not allowing Welch to respond, Janeson jumped in with her own report.

"Boss? Dillon and I have some behavioral impressions and possible next steps for Daniels, if you're ready."

While still looking at Andersen, Welch answered for Helms.

"Yes, Janeson. Sounds good to me. I'm sure you both have more value to add. Steve? You had nothing to add, correct?" she said with a raised eyebrow.

Nice slam.

Smiling, Andersen didn't respond, leaving Janeson the opportunity to speak as Dillon smirked.

Janeson took out her tablet and brought up a full photo of Daniels, as well as pictures of his Spartan appointed apartment with wall-to-wall books and a map of Canada on the big screens.

"Boss, based on further data and insights provided by Mr. Burns, Daniels has consistently carried out multi-pronged missions to obtain his goals. The attacks in Spain and the kidnapping of Murphy and his granddaughter account for two. With the sighting of Alica Wise, I would assume that she is the third prong, directed at Mr. Burns. That said, I think that we need to carry out our own multilevel approach and think in terms of three dimensions rather than two."

Helms nodded his head affirmatively and then asked the natural follow-up question.

"So what do you propose we do?

Without a pause, Janeson continued as Dillon stood silently beside her.

"I recommend that we allow Mr. Burns to return to his normal life and allow Ms. Wise to strike. We capture her and keep her out of the loop the same way we keep the others out of the loop. That will keep Daniels confused. Then I would allow some data to 'leak out,' such as Burns going rogue and dropping off the grid, with a possible destination of Maine."

Janeson paused for a moment with her tablet and added more maps of central Maine and towns near Route 1 right on the Maine/Canadian border.

"Once Burns is out in the field, I suggest we allow Daniels to find him. Initially I had thought about putting three fire groups out in the field at a distance to watch him, but I think some kind of discreet homing device and satellite resources available will be better. The fire teams, as good as they are, could be spotted and compromise the mission. Still, they should be ready for immediate deployment. My hope is that with Alica Wise off the grid, her brother, Robert Wise, will also seek out Burns and use RCA resources to find Burns."

"Okay. Let's say that Daniels falls for the bait--we are going to need some pretty good surveillance on Burns that is both long- range and unobtrusive," Welch said.

"Actually, that may have been provided, courtesy of Mr. Burns's recent wounds. Much of the lead that remains in Mr. Burns's buttocks in particular will provide some cover for a transmitter to be placed in a cavity of a tooth. The tooth will be encased in lead, blocking the signal, and will be visible once Burns pops the crown. The metal in his buttocks will draw most of the attention, hopefully leaving the actual location of the transmitter free from inspection, less likely to be discovered," Janeson said without emotion.

Helms could see that Andersen couldn't help but ask the obvious question.

"So you plan to plant a bug in Burns's tooth and leave lead in his ass for cover?" he said.

After a stilted moment of silence as Janeson assessed if there was another meaning to the question, she answered it directly.

"Yes. And to make sure the signal is not inadvertently picked up by Daniels's detecting equipment, part of Burns's wound dressing will be lined with aluminum so as to confuse and diffuse any residual signal should it leak out. Once Burns removes the crown, the signal should be loud and clear via satellite."

"But that will mean that Burns will have to somehow remove the crown, which might be difficult should he be bound, and taking it off might be a problem, don't you think?" Welch countered.

"Under normal circumstances, yes. But Daniels will want to ask Burns questions and at least torment him before he kills him. I'm sure that Daniels, being narcissistic, will allow Burns to eat, go the bathroom, replace his dressing, and maybe even sleep once he's convinced there is no tracking device on Burns. That's why Burns must be clean of any surveillance and devices except maybe his cell phone, which I'm sure they will not take. After that, we get a location and we move in," Janeson concluded.

Hmmm. It could work. Have to admit, a GPS in someone's tooth might get through if the lining really works. Crazy to think of.

"And Burns is okay with this?" Andersen asked.

Pausing, as if searching for either the right expression or phrase, Janeson took her time in answering.

"He expressed that he will do anything that results in either Daniels's death or incarceration. If he does this, he will disappear into the background and find Daniels or the RCA. More likely the RCA will be easier to find."

"That means human surveillance is off the table," Welch said.

"Yes. However the three fire groups, spotter and sniper teams need to be trained and mobile for immediate deployment," Janeson reiterated. Then after a pause, Janeson added a critical detail.

"Further, we'll need a field commander familiar with battlefield and urban tactics."

Helms turned to Welch, whose face moved from serious to surprise and then gleamed with her broad smile.

"I've never seen you happier, Diane. It's as if the dream job just landed in your lap. Again," Andersen said as deadpan as he could, while cracking a smile himself.

"Well," Welch started as she cleared her throat and attempted to contain her emotions. "Do I get to pick the teams, or have you already done that?"

It's like she's containing her joy after winning the lottery.

Dillon jumped in to list the teams. Stepping forward, she went to a laptop, and a series of names went on the big monitor.

"Alpha team is Davis and Nine, Bravo team is me and Ice, and Charlie team is Cratty and Ramsey."

"Wait a minute. Won't Cratty and Ramsey be on the team covering the Littletons?" Andersen asked.

All eyes looked to Dillon, who in turn looked to Helms.

Well ... I guess now is a good time to make that announcement.

"Teams," Helms started with hands on his hips as he addressed all in the control room.

"I've talked to the US marshals and they plan to put Rebecca and Emma in witness protection. I am recommending that Rosemarie Flores go as well."

Helms could see the surprise on everyone's face, with the exceptions of Dillon, whom he had spoken to earlier about it, and Janeson, who he assumed thought the plan was logical.

"People. We are in the investigation and law enforcement business, not protecting VIPs. I want to focus all of our efforts and strengths on finding Daniels and these half-crazed good old boys who are preparing for 'end of days.' To do that, we need to have the marshals do what they do best, which is to hide people. We need to focus on what we do best, which is to find the bad guys."

Helms waited for a response, which was mostly silence except for some quiet throat clearing. Gilmore, who had been quiet throughout the briefing, did pose a good question.

"Boss? What does Burns think of the plan?"

Great question ... I didn't ask him.

To Helms and everyone's surprise, Janeson answered the question for him.

"Mr. Burns wholeheartedly agrees. He's asked not to be informed of their location ...." Janeson seemed to stop again, but then continued as if she had found the right words again.

"He said once the mission is complete, and if he survives, he wants to be able to see if he can find them without assistance."

There were some smiles and smirks, nervous and real.

"Well, he is consistent. I bet he could find them," Andersen said as he leaned into one of the few poles spaced in the control room.

"Speaking of finding people," Dillon continued, "Cratty has sent the SIM information from Glenn's phone. We've narrowed down the contacts and found three numbers that could be Daniels's. At some point when we're green to go, someone is going to have to rattle Daniels's cage."

As Helms turned to Welch, everyone's attention shifted to her as well.

My God. You are in the spotlight today.

"Really? You do know the man hates me," she said. She was genuinely surprised.

"Exactly," Dillon said with a smile, and then produced a behavioral assessment.

"Daniels is intelligent, audacious, and creative. He believes he is right and the world is wrong. He hates Burns, but he especially does not like being shown up by anybody. As you were the one who led the investigation into his agency, and he became MIA when you were getting close, your contacting him will distract him and possibly unnerve him to act less logically and more in keeping with his narcissism."

As Welch looked thoughtfully at the assessment on the monitor, Andersen broke the silence first.

"You do have a way with driving men crazy. Second nature, almost. Wouldn't you agree?"

"I agree and wish I could do it, but it makes perfect sense that it be you. He will hate being contacted by you directly."

Shaking her head and concealing a smile, Welch turned and asked, "So when do I make the call?"

Helms looked at his watch, and then at a series of clocks with varying time zones.

"First we need to get Burns back in the world to pull Alica Wise in from the field and out of circulation. Then we need to get Cratty and Ramsey back for debriefing and redeployment. At the same time, we need to hand over the Littletons to the US marshals. I'm guessing ... eight hours from now. Oorah?"

"Oorah!" Welch immediately responded.

"Fucking Marines," Andersen said, a bit louder than he meant to.

Chapter 12

"Nulla vit melior quam bona" – *"There's no life better than a good life"*

As Burns laid on his stomach in a conference room filled with cots, Roxie snuggled into his side. He looked at a blank piece of paper. He had spent an hour just thinking of what to write to Becky, since he expected to be gone by the time she and Emma arrived. His memories flooded back to Samantha's death and how he had helped her to make Webber pay.

It didn't help ... it didn't bring you back.

Burns had been startled by his ongoing reflections on how once he had taken pleasure in "evening the score." Of late, even after he would think about Webber's death, there was more pity than anger, more disappointment in himself than feeling justified by his death. He was nearly positive that Becky had felt the same way, based on what David had told him.

She had David for a support back then. With him gone, she only has Emma. She's just a little girl.

Ever since hearing about his friend's death, the scars on his scalp and hands had itched intensely. Looking to his side to see Roxie sleeping, he returned to his task of trying to write something.

"I'm not the kind of guy who writes letters," he said to himself.

"Maybe you should tell Ms. Littleton and Emma what they might expect or prepare for," a familiar voice said.

Burns's eyes snapped up, as his hand instinctively went to an imaginary gun on his hip.

My God! Am I so distracted that I didn't even notice she was there?

"And how long have you been there?" Burns asked after catching his breath and keeping his blood pressure at bay.

"I just arrived," Janeson said. She pulled up a chair to sit across from him.

"I just wanted to tell you that Director Helms spoke to the US marshals about a relocation for Ms. Littleton and Emma. He also approved the plan of using you as bait for both Alica Wise and the bigger fish, Eric Daniels. Further, all of Daniels's foreign assets have been frozen and his cash has dried up." In his short time with Janeson he took no offense to her limited display of emotion. In fact, there was something about her clarity, honesty and real presentation that was comforting.

Burns looked at her for a moment and smiled. He looked down at the paper again so as to gather his thoughts.

"I'm sorry, Mr. Burns, but why are you smiling? Was it the content or the manner in which I expressed myself?" As anticipated she asked without emotion, but clearly curious.

David, I really wish you were here to help me with this one.

He looked up to re-engage her. She waited patiently.

"Neither. The content is great news and the delivery was succinct and to the point, the way I like it. I smiled because I think I see some similarities between you and me. They may be imagined or contrived, but I think they are striking."

He watched Janeson closely for a moment as she took in all the information and clearly thought about it before responding. He was truly impressed with her composure, with legs crossed and hands on her lap.

"Interesting thought. Your background and prior presentation would indicate that you had the great capacity to compartmentalize your feelings and to more fully employ your logic centers. While yours was achieved via training and years of experience, my abilities were wired into my brain in addition to training and experience. My unique neurology has both strengths and barriers, ranging from missing many social cues, and needing assistance with pragmatic speech while still maintaining a high IQ ....”

Burns watched as Janeson suddenly stopped and stared at him. For the first time in a long time Burns felt the corners of his mouth tighten in an upward position without his consciously knowing it.

“Mr. Burns? Your smile seems to have broadened?”

Shaking his head again, Burns curbed his smile and did his best to articulate both what he was thinking and feeling. His years of talking to David were now the only cherished insights and moments he had of him.

She doesn't remind me of myself....

“I'm not laughing at you as much as comparing you with Samantha Littleton. She was very intelligent, but had a great deal of emotions locked away. In the last months of her life I had the gift of getting to know her. Love her. You remind me a bit of her, save for her rough edges. Still, you and she have many similarities--difficult to be social with people, missing positives and social cues, intelligent, curious, and constantly watching and trying to figure things out.”

He was then granted another surprise when he saw Janeson's pale complexion slowly turn a rosy, flush red. He watched as her eyes narrowed and she placed a hand against her face as if to check for a fever.

“Am I blushing?” she asked, more out of curiosity rather than embarrassment. Burns knew the difference and didn't even ask if she was embarrassed. He smiled again at the thought of her experiencing a surprising, unexpected biological response. Before she had a chance to comment further, he changed the subject to more pressing issues.

“When do I leave?”

Janeson took a moment to respond as she was now feeling her hot, red face with both hands.

“0600 hours. Helicopter to New Hampshire and then dropped off at your car to return to the restaurant across the street from Dr. Cohen's office.”

“Good,” Burns said, as he had an idea of what to write. As he was about to start, he saw that Janeson was getting up to leave.

"Janeson? Do you have a first name?"

"Yes. Rachael. Why do you ask?" she responded as she sat back down.

"I have a favor. I won't be able to take Roxie with me and may be in the field for some time. I can't leave her with Becky or Emma, as they have enough to deal with, and Roxie doesn't like change or people. Are you married or with a roommate?"

Janeson looked puzzled for a moment as her flushed face was slowly subsiding. Burns re-evaluated his last question and clarified.

"It would be easier for Roxie if it were just one alpha in the house and less of an imposition if you lived alone."

Now why am I feeling ... guilty?

He thought he saw a small smile on her mouth as she now understood the question.

Maybe she does get embarrassed.

"Yes, I live alone. After my brief experience with Roxie I would like to take care of her while you're in the field. It actually will work out well, and you will be able to get daily reports on how she is doing."

Burns knitted his eyebrows as he figured out what Janeson was saying.

"So I guess I will be talking to you and others while I'm in the field looking for Daniels? It has to be via cell. No transmitter other than the one in my tooth," Burns said.

He moved his tongue to his rear molar to see if the anesthesia had subsided, as he felt a slow ache forming.

He watched Janeson's body language closely to see if she provided any clues. He was impressed with the fact that she had none he could decipher.

Not even micro-expressions. I can't tell if it is a byproduct of her neurology, training, or both.

"Absolutely. Director Helms and I keep our word. As does Mrs. Welch, who will be prepped and the leader of the insertion team once we have your location. All the members of the teams you know, except for one, a former medic of hers, Bobby Calandra."

"Davis, Cratty, Dillon, and the two snipers from Welch's team?"

"Yes, and Ramsey. She is the only survivor from Cratty's team at the ambush. Ms. Cratty tells me 'it's personal,'" Janeson said.

"I understand," Burns said as he felt anger surge in his stomach and his scars itched even more.

Yeah. It's personal.

"Thank you," he said to Janeson, and with a nod of her head she stood up, returned the chair to where exactly she first found it, and left with a computer tablet in hand that she pulled out from her pocket. Looking back, he saw that Roxie was awake and might have watched the entire conversation, and he wouldn't have known it.

"So I take it you have some questions and concerns about boarding with Rachael?" he asked as she gazed back into his eyes.

With difficulty, he reached back to pet her and she licked his hand.

"I'm going to miss you too, missy," he said.

Looking back at his paper, he took her advice and began to write a short note. He was going to focus on something Becky could do about the future, instead of wallowing in the sorrows of the past.

Chapter 13

"Fiat" – "Let it be"

Becky was staring at the first aid kit above Ramsey's head in a cavernous military plane heading back to the States. With Emma sleeping on her lap, she felt the airplane's vibration through her entire body as she absently stroked Emma' hair. Her time at the safe house, transport via Marines to the embassy, and her boarding the plane hours ago had been so surreal that it was as if it were happening to someone else. She found herself empty and removed from the world, with Emma as the only tether keeping her on the planet. Even when Denise told her about being turned over to the US marshals for relocation, she found herself nodding in agreement without even asking any questions.

How am I going to live, Sam? When you died, David kept me from going crazy. With both of you gone, how will I live? Why would I want to live? Why bother? Really?

She broke her gaze at the first aid kit to see that Emma was still asleep, bundled up in a large flight jacket to keep her warm.

I couldn't have raised you without him. How can I go on without him?

Even as she tried to conjure up the anger and rage she had experienced when Samantha was killed, she found she was hollowed out, empty, and depleted of anything but sadness and loss.

"Becky?"

She jumped at her name and nearly startled Emma, who was in a fitful sleep.

"I'm sorry to startle you. How is she sleeping?" Cratty asked.

Cratty was on one knee, wearing an ill-fitting flight jacket as well.

"She's okay, considering," Becky responded. As Cratty was starting to get up, she dug in deep to say something more than one sentence.

She tried. She really tried. Ramsey and Horwitz saved Emma.

"Denise. Thank you for protecting us. I know it was hard." She couldn't think of anything more to say.

Cratty looked down as if to avoid eye contact, but then looked right back at Becky.

"Becky ... I'm sorry I wasn't there. I'm sorry I couldn't save Dr. Caulfield ..." she started, but then stopped.

She still calls him Dr. Caulfield.

"If you had been there, you might have been killed. If I had been there, we might all have died. What happened, happened," Becky said. She found herself wondering if that was really her own voice. It seemed different, far away and foreign. She looked back and saw that Cratty had acknowledged the statement and walked back to sit with Ramsey, who appeared to be awake, but busy looking over her weapon.

She turned back to Emma and felt more tears welling in her eyes.

Damn it, David. How will I live without you? Sam, make him come back. Help me ...

~

Cratty slumped into the bench beside Ramsey as she readjusted her jacket and felt for her weapon.

"You okay, Boss?" Ramsey asked.

"No. Not at all," she said quietly so as not to be heard by Becky. "I wish I could go back and rip Glenn's eyeballs out and shove a red-hot poker into his brain."

Turning, she saw Ramsey smile for the first time since the ambush.

"Sounds good to me. But we have to cut off the head of the snake if we're going to win. You say that Christine came up with this plan with the Bureau to flush out Daniels? Burns plans to use himself as bait? Won't that pig Daniels know it's a trap?" Ramsey asked.

"Yes. But Dillon and her friend there, Janeson, say that he won't be able to resist, because he's an asshole," Cratty said. She turned a bit more to see that Ramsey was looking at the picture of her team.

Once my team. All gone but me, Ramsey, and Dillon. Dillon and I weren't even there when the shit went down.

Without moving her eyes, still focused on the picture, Ramsey sighed with her response.

"Don't worry, Boss. Looks like the plan they came up with gives us all a chance to kill Daniels and any assholes who are helping him."

"Yes. That is a good thing. He has to pay."

Still, her heart was not filled with rage as much as she wanted, since she was still thinking of her team.

Belben. Fitzy and Witzy. It won't bring them back.

Ramsey put the picture away and motioned to Becky and Emma.

"How they doing?" she asked.

"Not so good. I have no idea how she's going to get along without Dr. Caulfield. He was the glue for those two. He made it easier for them to get along. I hate turning them over to the marshals."

"Yeah. But Boss. If we do this right, we'll get Daniels and free them of all this shit." Cratty saw Ramsey shaking her head in disbelief as she continued. "I just can't believe that all this shit happened to them just because her sister helped Burns out years ago. It's crazy. They're just civilians, the people we're suppose to protect from shit like this."

It's unbelievable. A rogue agent comes back from the dead. A nurse gets him help, and then their lives are turned upside down. And then, just when they think happiness might be coming their way, they're killed. Unbelievable.

"I know. I know."

"Yeah," Ramsey replied.

Both women sat quietly as the airplane seemed to become a bit more bumpy.

Great. Just great.

~

John Murphy found the cots at the Bureau just too uncomfortable to sit on, let alone sleep on. He decided to sit in a chair beside Rosemarie as she slept soundly in her cot. Looking around, he saw at least fourteen people sleeping in the early hours. They were the same people he had seen earlier that morning.

Looks like the earlier shifts are staying over.

Murphy found himself worrying about what to do with Rosemarie. He always did but as she got older, his concern escalated.

Both the directors recommended that she go into witness protection program with Littleton and Emma until Daniels was captured. Initially Murphy was clear that he could protect her, until Director Helms pointed out that it was by the grace of God, Rosemarie's quick thinking, and a rogue agent that both of them were alive.

"You might not be so lucky next time," Helms warned.

Protecting her really didn't work out so well. He watched her sleep like a baby.

Now with the Panellis in custody, he was positive there would be a power void and a whole lot of "wannabes" would be clawing for the throne.

Yeah ... there's going to be a war. It will be safer if you're not around, Pumpkin.

Murphy kept thinking about what his meeting with Rebecca Littleton and Emma was going to be like. He was ambivalent, himself, but he had to admit that if he were in her shoes, he would probably want nothing to do with the whole situation.

Still. She took in Emma as a baby and could have dropped her off at a fire station. Could she really turn her sister away? Maybe. Her husband has just been killed. Her sister was killed not so long ago. My son killed her brother ....

He stopped thinking about her situation, as it always returned to his son, a constant reminder that he was gone. He started to think of something else. He focused on returning to business once he was sure Rosemarie was safe. Looking at her, he could see that she was still wearing her school uniform under her blanket. Fitzpatrick, his second in command, had brought a change of clothes for both of them. By the time the Bureau finished screening him and the clothes, she was sound asleep.

I guess when people are killed on FBI property, they get a little cautious.

It was nice to see one of his own men, though. But Murphy also knew why Fitzpatrick delivered the clothes himself; he needed to get the plan of what he wanted to do next. After the initial exchanges, Fitzpatrick asked, "so what do you want to do about this?"

Such a simple question, which will have ramifications in organized crime for years to come.

In one little sentence, he knew the Rubicon would be crossed, terminal velocity reached.

"It's time to put our house in order," Murphy simply said.

As expected, Fitzpatrick blinked a couple of times as if to give him time to rethink.

"Are you sure? Being tied up and threatened can make a man pretty reactive," Fitzpatrick said, looking for confirmation.

"You know me. I'm not reactive. I'm planful. Crossing the Rubicon has been in the works for a while. It's time to move ahead. Are you in?"

"Like Flynn," Fitzpatrick countered with a smile and a shake of the hand, and was off. It was easy to see that he was happy his old boss was back.

Murphy now reflected on that past conversation a couple of hours ago as he watched Rosemarie sleep. With the die cast, the wheels of war were started against the Panellis, and everyone in the Commonwealth of Massachusetts outside of his network.

Maybe you'll use your knowledge about Julius Caesar and crossing the Rubicon for good rather than war, Pumpkin.

Still, he couldn't escape his anxiety about meeting Rebecca Littleton and the granddaughter he had never met. Then looking down at Rosemarie, he shook his head as he realized he had a bigger issue.

How the hell am I going to tell your mother you're going in the witness protection program?

Going to war against the other crime families didn't seem so ominous after that thought.

~

Davis was uncomfortable lying in the back seat of the car, but she knew she needed to sleep. Nine was watching Alica Wise's apartment, specifically her car, since taking over from Ice earlier that evening. After spending "quality time" with both men, she had reached her saturation point of discussing wind velocity effects on long shots in excess of 3000 yards, and was looking forward to some good sleep. She was also frustrated about being out of the loop in Boston as Helms, Andersen, and everyone were in the thick of things as she watched and waited. The constant reports she received from Dillon and Gilmore were thorough and gave her a lot to think about.

A key piece, using Burns as bait, didn't sit well with her. She had firsthand experience of seeing what happened when Burns used himself as a lure, back at her home when eight agents thought they had the drop on him. Two well-placed proximity charges on parked cars leveled the field, leaving six dead and two critically injured. Adding to her troubled thoughts was how Cratty and her surviving team members were doing. A long time ago, she had a hard time believing that she would have anything in common with Cratty. While clearly they were physically different, they were surprisingly similar in disposition, attitude, and diligence. In fact she was genuinely surprised by how "dark" Cratty had become and how she gravitated to the dangerous task of protecting Burns's team. With more than half her team KIA, and Dr. Caulfield killed, she had no idea what to expect next time they met. Based on Dillon's last briefing, they would be spending a lot of time together training as an insertion team to wherever Burns was finally taken to. Adding Dillon, Ice, and Nine to the team, it was hard to imagine how all of them were going to work as a team.

Well, we do have something in common. We all want to kill Daniels.

She knew that Helms's official plan was to capture and charge Daniels, but with Welch in charge of the ground team and former

Foreign Intelligence agents making up the majority, she was pretty sure Daniels would not make it to his own trial.

He authorized friendly fire on Welch's team in Afghanistan, set up the ambush on Cratty's team, and betrayed the trust of the country. Jesus ... he just ruined my career. It's bad news when I'm the nice one.

Davis turned to face the back seat of the car to cut down on the light, and found the long coat covering her surprisingly warm and comfortable.

And what the hell did he do to piss off the French and Israelis?

Davis was used to sleeping on short notice, but was having more trouble these days with her thoughts racing on to next steps and strategies. Still, she was exhausted, and willed herself to relax and try to sleep. Davis first focused on her breathing, as it felt steady and deep. Her body felt light, and she began to drift. Her face felt relaxed and her arms and legs felt like stone. It was so dark, sinking, and warm that she actually thought she was in heaven…and she was so relaxed. Slowly, she felt a light breeze on her face and wondered why Nine had opened a window. Not wanting to move, she snuggled deep into the seat and still felt as if she was drifting. She experienced more wind and floating.

Why am I breathing so fast?

Her arms felt lighter than usual, and easier to move. Suddenly she found herself soaring high in the air. It was hard to see at first, but her eyes adjusted rapidly. She was well above the mountaintops that bordered a great ocean with pink and white sand for a shore.

Where are the others? Where are my charges?

Lost and alone at first, she continued to hear the air in her ears and felt wind lifting her higher. As gulps of air filled her chest, she found the ravens she had been searching for such a long time. There were twenty or so flying and circling above a smaller number of doves that were skimming the water and beaches as the ravens diligently flew above.

Finally! There you are. Where have you been?

Feeling the sun's rays, smelling the salt air and hearing the surf crash on the rocks and beaches, she sensed she was being watched. Turning, she was the first to see an eagle diving from above toward the doves, which were still skimming the water unaware of the danger. Screeching, she warned the others, who took after the eagle, only to find more eagles coming from all directions, above and below. Breathless, preparing to bare her claws and fight to the death as she and her ravens were outnumbered, the doves changed from soft white small dots against the ocean to larger, shinny falcons that multiplied by the second. Energized with the knowledge that she was not alone, she pulled her body even tighter to pick up speed as she dived. She was leading them. She was the tip of the spear. Her heart was racing and she was breathing faster, deeper, and harder. As allies matched the enemy in numbers and ferocity, she struck the first eagle she had seen, crashing into it with claws pushing through its feathers as her mouth clamped down on its neck. The eagle's screech was silenced as it tumbled away lifeless from her claws.

Turning to find her next enemy, surrounded by eagles, falcons, and ravens in the sky, she spotted a falcon chasing a much larger, stronger eagle as it lazily climbed closer to the noon sun. Turning, she saw that the falcon was alone, and raced to help. The falcon stopped short and flapped its wings to stay still as it watched the eagle fly toward the sun. Slowing her own pace, she circled the falcon in full understanding of why the falcon stopped to watch: the eagle's wings were *melting ... melting? Why are they melting?*

Davis felt herself bolt up when she felt a firm push on her back.

"What the hell!" she blurted out as she slipped from the back seat to the car floor, gulping in air and smelling popcorn.

Popcorn? Where the hell did the popcorn come from?

After a moment of reorienting herself, she remembered she was on a stakeout with Nine in front of Alica Wise's house.

"Where the hell were you?" Nine asked.

Not answering, Davis found she was still trying to catch her breath when she asked her own question. Moving to get up, her hand slipped on an empty chip bag. Upon closer inspection, she discovered it was an empty popcorn bag instead.

"How long was I asleep?"

"Are you kidding me?" he said. Nine's eyes remained transfixed on both the apartment and the car. "You've been asleep for six hours. You might want to get your snoring checked out, by the way."

She looked at him and wondered if he had been talking to Andersen or Welch about the last time her snoring became a subject for public discussion.

"I do *not* snore," she said emphatically.

Sitting back in the front seat, Nine was apparently not the kind of guy to simply say okay.

"And you would know this how? I'm the guy awake listening to your sleep for hours. What the hell were you dreaming about?"

Davis rubbed her eyes and sat in the back seat in an effort to stretch. While she felt as if she had been asleep for only a few minutes, she did feel rested and almost re-energized.

"Birds. Ravens, falcons, eagles. Birds. Last time I had a dream like that, Burns was sitting in my house about ten minutes before he took out about eight agents."

She was organizing her clothes when she felt Nine's eyes fall on her, staring intently.

"What?"

She did another quick check to make sure her blouse was buttoned and nothing was showing.

"Davis? Are you like Native American or something?" he asked slowly.

Jesus ... another crazy question brought to you by Nine ... famous sniper and Doubting Thomas.

"What? What are you talking about now, Nine? Why does shit like this interest you?" she responded as she fixed her hair.

Nine took a moment to reflect on her question before answering.

"Well, I'm a curious person," he answered. Settling back in his seat, he explained further.

Davis closed her eyes; she immediately regretted asking him any question, as she knew a dramatic monologue would follow.

"I knew this guy back in the day. He was part Native American and black. Ojibwe, I think. He did recon for us and whenever he had dreams of animals and shit, birds, bears, wolves, something big would always happen. He called them 'visions.' I thought it was complete bullshit until I kept seeing this pattern of his dreaming and then a big mission would come up. Sometimes it went really well. Sometimes it went to shit. It was never a dull mission and the dream always related to the outcome of the mission," he concluded as he drifted back to watch Wise's apartment and car.

She felt very uncomfortable, as she had dreams like this on a regular basis, though not necessarily as intense as the one she'd had when Burns was at her home and now. Typically they were of foxes and wildcats. But the last two times, they were vivid and all about birds.

And a lot of shit went down.

"What happened to the guy?" Davis asked, as a means of buying time so that she could think.

"You mean Ice? You can ask him. He's alive, and that's good. The last vision he had was the night before we found the terrorists' camp in the Swat valley, Pakistan. We lost three quarters of our team. Parks, Grimm ..." Nine said as he trailed off. Shaking off the past, Davis watched him return to the present.

"Anyway, Ice had this vision. It was about the sun, bears, ravens, and wolves. It was hot and when the cloud of dust and fire cleared, there were only a few wolves left surrounded by dead bears, fire, and ash, with two dark birds flying away. The real weird part was that after the battle, it all came true, especially the two birds we all saw flying away. That was just creepy." "Yeah ... the two black birds flying away were real. We all saw them after we pushed the bad guys back and waited for transport," he repeated. His response conveyed that he still couldn't believe it years later.

Davis remained silent, feeling unnerved at Nine's description of many of the animals and birds in her dreams. Heritage and culture were never important to her. Raised as a devout Catholic, an only child with no extended family to speak of, she knew her mom was Irish and French. Her dad, however, was more of a mystery, in that he never knew his biological parents and never spoke of family. He was a broad, strong man and rarely spoke. But when he did, he was kind, and everything was heartfelt. She loved him as much as her mom did. When he died when she was nineteen, she felt lost, and her mom was broken. It took years for her mom to find religion, and that seemed to help. By then, too much time and distance had occurred between them.

"Are you okay, Davis?"

She found herself getting angry as she was pulled back to reality by his question.

"Fine. I'm fine. And stop freaking me out with these dream interpretations. I got enough to think about," she said.

Crawling over to the front passenger seat, she caught him smiling.

"What is your problem, Nine?" she said, more annoyed than before.

Chuckling to himself, he continued his surveillance of the apartment as he spoke.

"Davis had a vision. I can't wait to tell Ice. Maybe he did, too."

~

What time is it?

Wise got up from her warm bed to get a glass of cold water. Looking briefly at the ledge just outside her bedroom window, she wondered if she had any milk left as well. Her apartment was functional, but she kept the heat down at night so that she could sleep better. She had to admit that the real reason her sleeping was much better had been her last conversation with her boss.

The conversation with Chairman Daniels was brief but to the point.

"Let me be clear, Alica. I don't want you to kill Burns. Capture and bring him to me. You have your team, and Burns should be off balance. The Bureau will be busy with Caulfield and Littleton, and the Panellis will have Murphy at bay. I'm sure he'll return to get his gear to go off grid to find me. I want you to make sure he gets to me sooner than later."

"And if he resists?" she had asked, hoping for a clear answer.

"Use whatever force necessary," he reiterated.

No, no, no, no ....

"That's not what I'm asking. Burns is a trained operative. The last couple of agents that tried to take him in were either killed or injured.

With respect, I'm not taking that chance," she had said firmly.

After an unusually long pause, Wise heard the chairman do something she had never heard of in her history of knowing him.

"All right. If necessary, you are authorized to kill. But only as a last resort," he said.

Thinking back as she drank her water, she still found herself smiling. Standing in the middle of her small kitchen as the refrigerator light bathed her small frame, she looked forward to picking up Burns's trail again, as she pulled out a near empty bottle of milk. Closing the refrigerator door, she poured the milk into two soup bowls, and then proceeded to throw the bottle away. Carrying the two bowls back to her room, she continued to think that after years of bullshit, someone was going to put an end to Burns.

Finally, someone is going to put you down for your treason.

Her brother had warned her that something like this, Burns's treason, would bring the country to the edge.

"Well, Rob, you were right. Looks as though when I finish Burns I'll be signing up with Colonel Carter after all," she said out loud.

After years of service rewarded with unemployment and blacklisting from other intelligence agencies, Wise figured it was time to take an easier path.

Walking through her nearly empty apartment, she smiled at its starkness. Unlike many people, Wise liked open spaces and found that furniture, drapes, rugs, and other normal items one would find in a home were too confining for her.

Clutter, clutter, and more clutter. How do people live that way? Pictures on the wall, knickknacks on tables, books, vases, things, and stuff!

Recalling past missions when she would have to live with someone, it wasn't the sex, spying, and dual life that had bothered her, nor the feigning of emotions such as love and caring, but rather the furniture and living with people that drove her crazy. Especially if it were a fully furnished home or apartment.

God, I hate confining spaces.

Stopping by her bedroom's window, she put the bowls down to

open it just enough to put both bowls out on the large window ledge. Closing the window quickly, she quietly walked back to her warm bed.

She fell into and sank into her pillow and mattress. Wise thought about what she was going to wear in the morning. She thought of all her clothes and all the things she enjoyed and that helped her sleep. Still, the best was thinking about her recently purchased clothes. For this mission, she hated her need to blend in.

Denim, camouflage, earth colors, boots and orange hunting gloves and vests...ugh! God I hate this place. She cringed at what she might have to wear just to blend. She tightened the covers over her as if to block out the thoughts. Pushing those images out of her head, she focused on her favorite attire that enhanced her own petite, athletic body.

Mini skirts, sweaters, lace and satin, stilettos, boots, jewelery, oh I miss those. She decided to count her clothes in storage as a way to sleep. After a few minutes, she started to get sleepy.

All I have to do is kill Burns and everyone will be happy and get back to their lives...except Burns, she thought as she felt herself on the precipice of sleep.

Looking out the window, she smiled as she saw two familiar cats drink the milk she had put out. Turning on her side she quietly said, "Good night."

Chapter 14

"Hinc illae lacrimae" – "Hence these tears" Terence

The ride to the Bureau's office in Boston was quiet and uneventful. Surrounded by US marshals in large SUVs, Cratty, Ramsey, Becky, and Emma rode in silence, traveling at high speed to arrive at their destination before the morning work rush hour started.

Once in the garage, Becky noticed a high degree of security and wondered if it was for her. Then she remembered hearing that Murphy and Emma's sister had been kidnapped right from the garage. It was still surreal to her that such a thing could happen in such a secure area.

But then, I walked into a police department and unleashed a computer worm that nuked everything with a computer chip on the East Coast. Anything is possible when you're determined.

Holding Emma's hand, she walked with Cratty, Ramsey, and the marshals to the elevator when she noticed that Cratty and Ramsey stopped short of going in.

She was confused and Emma was standing silently, unaware that Ramsey and Cratty were not getting in the elevator.

"Denise? Aren't you and Ana coming up?"

She watched Cratty look away at first, but then look directly at her. She felt pain in her heart as she saw tears glistening in Cratty's eyes and a low tone in her voice.

"No, Becky. The marshals will take you and Emma from here. Ana and I need to debrief and get ready for redeployment. We ... need to get going," she said, her voice cracking toward the end.

Becky looked at Ramsey for confirmation, who spoke volumes as she shifted on her feet, looking at the ground, and remaining silent. Sighing, Becky stepped toward Cratty and in an unusual expression of emotion, she pulled Cratty into a tight hug.

"You be careful, Denise. You and Ana are family. We need both of you to come back."

Becky felt Cratty's body remain still at first, and then she hugged her back. She looked at Ramsey, who was looking very uncomfortable, her eyes brimming with tears.

"I mean it, you two. No heroics. Just complete the mission and come back," she said as she released Cratty. "Especially you, Ana. That attitude will get you in some serious shit."

Revenge doesn't bring anyone back. I know.

Sniffling, Ramsey gave the thumbs up, as it seemed it was too much emotion for her to verbally respond.

Emma ran out to hug Cratty and then jumped into Ramsey's arms. As she bent over to hug Emma, Emma reached up and kissed Ramsey, and ran back to Becky.

The door closed and Becky felt suddenly small between three US marshals. But it was the elevator music's rendition of Barry Manilow's *I Write the Songs* that really made her feel out of place at first, until she realized where she heard it last.

David ... you loved that song ... that horrible song, she thought.

~

Cratty was still looking at the closed elevator doors when Ramsey roused her out of her trance.

"You okay, Boss?" Ramsey said through sniffles of her own.

Cratty felt suddenly lonely and empty.

She's right. They are my family. I have no others to speak of. Ramsey's part of my team. But Emma and Becky were more. Dr. Caulfield was kind and nice. I really have no one. Is this how other bodyguards feel when they're discharged?

"I'm fine," she lied, and then she looked at Ramsey's face.

"Jesus, Ramsey! Are you OK?"she asked, surprised by Ramsey's red nose and red eyes.

Still sniffling, Ramsey made a face and put on her tough exterior. "I'm good."

"Yeah ... right, you're fine, Ana."

Smiling for the first time in days, she sighed a cleansing breath as she turned her emptiness into a focus, a mission.

"Well, let's go find that slack-jawed maggot and put an end to this shit," Cratty said as she tried to put the emptiness aside.

I guess I don't have to worry about finding a home or something to do...other than find and terminate Daniels and his command.' She was surprised by both her relief and conviction.

"Yeah," Ramsey said in a low tone. "Let's find that bastard."

Looks like we're both on the same page.

~

Dillon was pulling together more data on Colonel Timothy Carter and Eric Daniels when she got the call in the control room from INTERPOL. After a minute of trying to understand who was calling and why, she finally understood that the foreign agent was reporting that Jeffrey Glenn had escaped from custody while at the hospital and was on the loose. After five minutes of asking clarifying questions, the only thing she learned was that while he was being treated for lacerations at the hospital, Glenn had managed to create a diversion, and escaped without detection.

"So you guys bring him to the hospital, let him be treated while covering the door, and with no one in the examination room with him? No officer is present? No one thinks that maybe this guy might have training in evasion? What the hell?" she said as her voice continued to escalate in shock and dismay. By now Johnson and Gilmore had overheard the details, and were already sprinting to their own monitors to see if there was any data, chatter, or information they could glean.

Dillon found herself breathing heavily and was trying not to interrupt the agent as he explained the limited resources of INTERPOL, hospital policy, and patient privacy, and that they were still not sure how Glenn left. It took an additional five minutes for her to deduce that he had escaped an hour ago, and that local police were already looking for him. After she had the time of escape, she hung up on the agent and conferred with Gilmore and Johnson.

"Please tell me you guys got something."

Johnson shook his head, while Gilmore had little more to report.

"Local police have his name and picture, but they had no luck locking the hospital down, and it's still admitting and discharging patients. One of the INTERPOL agents was found unconscious, with missing wallet, weapon, and cell phone. Sorry Christine, but that's all I got."

Releasing and clenching her fists, she took in a deep breath and released it slowly.

"Forget about it, Gilmore. I got more from you than the agents on site," she said.

Dillon rubbed her temples first and then she rubbed her hands together while thinking of the next steps. Taking in another breath, she prioritized her next steps.

"Okay, guys. You tell Helms and Janeson. I'll bring Davis, Welch, and Cratty up to speed. Anybody have connections in Tangiers?" she said, looking around the control room.

Soon it was evident there were none.

"All right. Looks like we need the bosses to pull some strings."

While Johnson picked up his phone to call Janeson and Gilmore went to call Helms, she found herself feeling a pit in her stomach as she went to make her own calls.

This can't be happening.

Chapter 15

"Hodie mihi, cras tib" – "Today for me, tomorrow for you"

Davis was reading her text from Dillon about Glenn's escape as she saw Burns's truck coming down the road.

Just great. Glenn is on the loose, Burns is back, and I bet "Brown Eyes" is going to make her move.

She had been waiting in the restaurant since her target, Alica Wise, and two men had been waiting in a car for Burns to arrive. Nine and Ice were deployed in the field with rifles, as she was designated to take out Wise.

As she watched all the players coming together in the parking lot, she heard Nine's commentary.

"Looks like we are going to have a showdown, Davis? I'm guessing you will take out Wise while we take care of her protection?"

"Yup. I need to take her in alive. If you and Ice could wing the guys, that would be nice," she said as she formulated her plan of attack.

"No promises," Ice responded.

Pulling her hair into a ponytail, Davis looked out over the parking lot, measuring the distance between Burns, the entrance, and Wise's car. Pushing her semi-automatic weapon firmly on her hip, she pulled her blouse out to cover the bulge, and took her watch off. Even though it was dusk, and the solar glare was peering through the partially bare trees, she opted to forgo the sunglasses, as she anticipated a fight.

She first surveyed the entire area and watched Burns closely as he seemed to hobble and move slowly to the entrance. Looking beyond Burns, she saw Alica Wise exiting her car as two large, nondescript men seemed to have difficulty getting out of the small sedan. Without discussion, the two men headed around the sides of the building as Alica followed Burns.

Is he adding drama, or is his ass really hurting that much?

By now, the story of the legendary Alexander J. Burns being shot in the ass was spreading like wildfire throughout the intelligence community.

Now you know what's it like to be embarrassed ... like being called "Cougar."

Davis moved away from the window and spoke into her headset as she made her way to the restaurant's entrance where Burns and Wise were headed.

"Nine? Ice? This is it. Take care of the guys. I'll take care of Brown Eyes."

While she circled the bar, she heard both men's confirmations as she took one of the patron's drinks and poured it on her own blouse. Shocked, the patron was going to complain until he saw she was showing more cleavage than he anticipated, and he gawked.

"Well hello, little lady," he slurred out.

Smelling the alcohol on his breath, she gave her best smile.

"Well hello to you," she said, and then she pushed him off the bar stool. As he went crashing to the ground, she moved to two young women sitting just in front of the door. Just before exiting, she made sure to bang into one woman holding her drink, hard enough to send her falling over the table to hit her friend.

"Sorry! Passing through!"

As she moved onto the porch, there was a ruckus inside of angry patrons and loud shouts yelling for where she exited. As Burns was navigating his last step, Davis seemed to stagger and fall into him.

"Sorry, honey," she said loudly as she grabbed his ass.

Hearing him grimace in pain, she responded in a drunk fashion, "What? You don't like girls?"

"Oh ... you are a woman?" Burns responded through clenched teeth of real pain.

Oh ... burying yourself in the role, I see.

Pushing herself from him with force, as if she was angry, she yelled at him as she nearly stumbled down the three stairs.

"Screw you, Scar-face!"

As she ambled away, there were at least three angry patrons yelling at her; the bartender and waitress were assisting Burns as they yelled back at her.

With an eye on Wise, she could see she was solidly focused on catching up with Burns.

Looks like you got murder on your mind.

Davis used a truck to ostensibly support her drunken stance and allow Wise to get closer.

"Hey, Baby? You gotta a cigarette?" she asked with a noticeable slur. As the gap between them shortened and the patrons' noise continued to yell at her, Davis was impressed by Wise's focus on her prey.

"Hey! Brown Eyes! What the hell? You too good for us townies?"

Wise shifted her gaze away from Burns as she slowed her pace to look at her, but continued walking toward the porch where Burns and people were watching.

"I don't have time for you," she hissed out as she turned back to look at Burns. Suddenly, Wise stopped and looked at the porch, and then the sides of the building and the cars. It was obvious to Davis that Burns had done one of his famous disappearing acts to distract Wise.

"What? Where the hell ...."

"I know, Alica. Burns does that a lot," Davis said calmly. She enjoyed that in the brief second she was now standing within three feet of Wise.

Although initially still, Wise's head snapped in her direction and her hands were moving to her side.

She was impressed with Wise's speed as she produced her weapon and drew it in Davis's direction. Burns's distraction allowed Davis to shorten the gap to catch Wise's hand with both of hers, and hold it as Wise squeezed off three rounds that went wide.

Screams and yells were now emanating from the porch and inside the restaurant as the shots rang out.

With one hand firmly holding Wise's wrist, she was able to strip her hand of the weapon. Wise didn't give up easily; she head butted her and slapped her with her free hand.

Did you just bitch slap me?

Surprised but not deterred, Davis regained her footing in time to see a retractable baton being raised to strike her head as Wise gave a guttural cry.

"Screw you," Wise said as she put her entire body behind the strike.

Stepping out of the way, Davis continued moving out of the baton's strike zone as Wise attempted a follow-up to strike her torso.

"Alica? For a sex vixen, you are pretty good with weapons."

Eyes narrowed and seething with hate, she could see that the taunting was having the desired effect of making Wise more angry and as a result, more reckless and careless.

Wait for it...

Davis avoided yet another wild strike.

With her back now against a utility truck, Wise turned on Davis and started to move, but her attention was distracted by a distant but clear rifle report that came from behind the truck.

There's the opening! Enough of this bullshit!

Davis shortened the gap while Wise looked for the source of gunfire.

With two fists tightly chambered from her waist, Davis rapidly extended the two-fist punch as she stepped well within Wise's strike zone, simultaneously connecting with both her sternum and stomach. As it was Davis's intent for the strike to go through Wise's body, she was pleased with the crunching of bone and the strong exhalation of air.

Surprised by the dual strike, Wise visibly lost her breath and strength as she fell back hard into truck's side, only to bounce back toward Davis while her baton fell useless to the ground.

While she was clearly dizzy, hurting, and seemingly nauseous from both the strike and the collision with the parked truck, Davis swooped down low, firmly grabbing the hem of Wise's pants, and in a wide, high-raising arc, lifted Wise's leg well above her own head, making Wise fall hard on her back. Davis heard another rifle report, but this time it was to her left. Not looking to see, she focused on Wise, who was still dazed, but not out. Not wanting to take any chances, she kicked her in the ribs. After hearing another satisfying crack and seeing Wise put both hands on her torso, Davis dropped to her knee, pulled Wise up by the collar, and punched her in the jaw.

Feeling her body go limp, and satisfied that she was down for now, Davis sighed, pulled out her handcuffs, and pulled Wise's hands together to secure them. Sensing that someone was above her, she looked up suddenly to see that Burns was watching casually.

"Davis. It kind of took you long enough. I expected a bit more, with you being about two feet taller and with more field experience," Burns said without criticism or judgment.

"I do have to say I liked your kenpo move. Not really economical, and pretty flashy--but then, Wise was over her head."

Compliment? Probably not.

Returning to handcuffing Wise, Davis called into Nine and Ice.

"Status on her friends."

"Goon on the north is down. He won't be getting up," Nice said.

"Goon due west is down. Notify next of kin," Ice responded.

So much for taking prisoners.

"Stay in position until authorities arrive. Nice job."

Taking in a deep breath, Davis busied herself with going through Wise's pockets.

"Do you think calling her a 'sex vixen' was really fair?" Burns asked as he stretched his legs.

Ignoring him, Davis continued her search of Wise's clothes, which yielded a knife, wallet, two clips of ammunition, a roll of cash, and two cell phones.

"You know, Burns, you of all people shouldn't question tactics of deception, distraction, and acting. And for the record, you used that same kenpo move on me a couple of years back. How's your ass, by the way? Sorry for improvising and using it as a prop."

She spoke while she went through prisoner's personal effects.

Hearing multiple sirens arriving, Burns's response was again without judgment.

"I must say your use of name-calling, 'Scar-face,' I found particularly compelling."

Man ... that was an asshole thing to do.

"Sorry," Davis said sheepishly. "I buried myself in the 'drunk, angry woman' mode."

Looking at Davis askance as multiple state troopers and local police arrived and spread out to contain the crime scene, his following comment was audible, matter-of-fact but low.

"I actually expected you to find your inspiration from medication intoxication rather than alcohol."

Davis's head snapped up to look at him walking away as she remembered clear as day how Burns had witnessed her medication-induced behaviors and sexual advances in her own house.

Damn it! I just can't catch a break here.

As state and local officers swarmed around the parking lot, Davis didn't have time to respond as she watched Burns walking to Helms and Andersen, who had also arrived.

Shaking her head, she watched Helms talk to Burns as Andersen came directly to her.

"You okay, Davis?" Andersen asked as he pulled out a handkerchief.

"Yup! Little Miss Kitten here was a tough nut to crack, but we were rewarded with SIM cards and cell phones." Davis traded the cell phones for the handkerchief.

Wow! I'm really sweating.

Taking another look at the cloth, she wondered, *Who still uses these things?*

She was surprised that he seemed to anticipate the question.

"It's a gift from my daughter," he said as he looked at the phones and then looked at Wise.

She was grateful for the large, dry white cloth as she wiped her face, the front and back of her neck, and her hands as she listened.

"So, do you think she knows where Daniels is?"

Davis shook her head.

"I'm guessing she had contact with him, but probably no idea about his location," she said while recalling her own training at the Foreign Intelligence Agency.

Helms joined them and was looking down at Wise as well.

"Kind of roughed her up a bit, didn't you, Davis?" he asked.

Looking dead on, Davis put her hands on her hips as she pushed Wise's unconscious body with her foot.

"Well, Brown Eyes here was well-armed and clearly had murder on her mind. I guess with everything going south for Daniels, he must have given the order to just kill Burns. Honestly, I can understand Daniels's frustration and Wise's motivation to kill him--from a professional perspective, of course'.,"

Davis finished up with rubbing her face with the handkerchief and handed the drenched, gray cloth back to Andersen, whose smiling changed to a grimace. Looking at the handkerchief, Andersen waved his hand.

"You keep it, Davis," he said. He next turned to Helms for his next question.

"Any word on Glenn's escape?"

Shaking his head, Helms continued, though his mind appeared to be elsewhere.

"No. This may be a problem, with him MIA...and the French and Israelis looking for Daniels doesn't help. The French I'm not worried about, but the Israelis don't recognize local law enforcement when they're pissed and have a target in mind. I think Burns is right. If I were Glenn and felt screwed, I'd find the 'enemy of my enemy,' and either dig in deep, or ally with a new group for protection."

Davis was about to ask another question when Nine came over her headset.

"Davis? I lost track of Burns. Too many people. Do you have eyes on?"

Davis looked beyond Helms and then all around.

"Negative. Ice? Do you have eyes on Burns?" Davis asked.

Helms and Andersen picked up on the conversation and started to look around among the local police, state troopers, and civilians all cluttering the parking lot.

"Nope. Lost him among all the activity. He's a ghost," Ice said.

Damn it! How does he do that?

"Forget about it, Davis," Helms started. "It's all part of the plan. Burns has to go rogue and off grid to appear to be looking for Daniels."

"I don't know. I just don't like it when he disappears like that," Andersen added.

Shaking her head, she said nothing as she looked around the crowd.

How does he do that?

~

With butterfly stitches still holding his cheek together, Glenn was quietly standing in the darkened recesses of the doorway waiting for his target to emerge from the bar. Still feeling the residual bruise from his hands being bound, and swelling in his face, he felt more than content being a free man.

Looking back, he found it comical that the INTERPOL agents successfully covered the patient entrance and exits, but not the medical doctor's office door into the patient's room. He smiled as he still replayed in his head how the busy doctor casually opened his door and walked through while reading a chart. He had waited for him to pass from behind the door and then simply walked out. With luck on his side he caught the waiting agent smoking by the car off guard. He was an easy target.

But now, he was holding his newly acquired gun waiting quietly in the dark as his breathing remained level, palms dry. He had been to this particular drinking establishment before when he had first met his crew for drinks. He hated meeting there, since the area was not secure and people drifted in and out, making secrecy a problem.

But Smiley and the monkeys loved it here.

Shifting from one foot to the other, Glenn put his fatigue aside as he patiently waited. The drive back to Torrox was uneventful but tiring, and waiting made it worse. He had already contacted his old connections in the Israeli Special Forces to broker a deal: protection and money in exchange for finding and killing Daniels.

Sounds fair to me. Looks like the Israelis were already on the move. They sure are efficient.

He focused on the present mission and saw the door to the bar open, and a pretty drunk man in a makeshift leg splint, two mismatched crutches and arm sling slowly walking away.

Huh? I thought they had socialized medicine here?

Looking around in the dark to make sure there were no witnesses, Glenn quietly walked up behind the injured figure and closed the distance to three feet before he spoke.

"Hey Smiley? How you feeling? No te ves muy bien. Tener un mal dia?" Glenn asked.

Initially startled and nearly losing his balance, the former team member turned around and knew immediately who had called him.

"Mr. Glenn? Is that you?"

In response to the question, he squeezed the trigger of his semi-automatic weapon three times. While the loud gunshots stirred a number of dogs to bark and people to yell, it was Smiley's body crashing into metal garbage cans as he took each bullet in the torso that made the largest racket. Stepping over Smiley's body, he casually walked away.

"Have a good day, Smiley. I know I'm going to."

Glenn holstered his weapon and disappeared into the night.

Chapter 16

"Habetis bona deum" – "Have a nice day"

Diane Welch had reviewed a number of index cards with some important information she wanted to convey to Daniels. When the number of cards jumped to twelve, she decided to just look at what she had and wing it. The primary thing she wanted to do was bait him, and attack his narcissism. Both Janeson and Dillon had each come to the same conclusion: take control away from him and mock him. With Daniels's phone numbers obtained from Glenn and Wise's cell phone, she had two shots at making her points. With Janeson, Dillon, Gilmore and everyone in place, she gave them the nod to place the call. Once he picked up, they would start the trace.

Well ... here it goes.

With the control room absolutely quiet with more than twenty people manning their monitors and listening, Welch had never felt so much onstage as she did now.

So this is what actors feel like on opening night. I should have got pointers from Martin.

After the fifth ring, Welch wondered if they had the wrong number or if he was going to pick up at all. Then, a low, commanding voice broke over the intercom.

"Report!"

Letting the silence sit for a moment, not wanting to jump at his command, Welch counted to five and then spoke.

"Eric? I'm sorry, Eric. I dropped something and had to pick it up before someone tripped on it. How you doing? We missed you at the last Senate meeting. Are you on vacation?" she asked. Welch made sure to speak in a casual manner, like talking to an old girlfriend she had not seen in years.

After a moment Daniels's response was short: "Diane Welch."

"You could tell it was me? I'm impressed. I'm never good at putting voices to names over the phone. But I know you're going to hang up before we can complete the trace, so I'll be brief. Mr. Tombs at the Secret Service passes along his regards and a note from Vladimir, Liang, and Seo-yeon that all your foreign assets in their respective countries are frozen. Please feel free to check so that we can try to trace you again. Also, Glenn is MIA, but we have his sister and niece, so I'm less worried about us and more worried about you. Ms. Wise is in custody, but will probably be going to Gitmo. And Eric ... I don't know what you did to piss off the Israelis, but Yitzak made it clear that he doesn't care if you're in Canada or the US, he's going to find you and kill you. And don't get me started about the French. What's their story?"

Well? What do you have to say about all that?

With more than a minute to go to complete the trace, Daniels hung up the phone.

Welch looked over at Dillon and she gave the thumbs up.

Janeson nodded approvingly with the comment that "your presentation was superior without being obnoxious."

"I'll work on that," she said as she fished in her sweater pocket.

After some searching, Welch took out Angelo Panelli's confiscated cell phone. There were three numbers that were potential connections to reach Daniels. While the first call went into a woman's voice mail, the second number led to Daniels. With the same silence that started the first call, Daniels's response was a bit more tired.

"Hello?"

"Oh, Eric? I forgot. The Panellis seem to be under the impression that you sold them out on the Spain deal. Word on the street is that they are considering reaching out to the French and Israelis to share resources after they make peace with John Murphy and friends. I guess they all plan to find and kill you. So you may want to hold on to this number in case you want to come in from the cold."

After a moment of silence, Daniels asked his only question.

"Where's Burns?"

That tone sounds either tired or pissed. Maybe both.

"Excellent question, Eric," Welch said as if praising a six-year-old for getting a hard math problem right.

"He's gone rogue again. Something about wanting to make your skull his coffee cup, or something. He's more imaginative than he used to be ... but you know that by now. Anyway, hold onto this number but don't call after 10:00 p.m. Have a great day."

This time it was Welch who closed the line and looked back at the team, who were all smiling and giving each others high-fives, with the exception of Janeson who was already walking toward her with the next steps.

"Well, Mrs. Welch, I suspect that your closing the line on Mr. Daniels will undoubtedly anger him ..." Janeson started to say, until she noticed her cell phone already vibrating.

She reverted to her old warrant-officer days and belted out a whistle to the staff, who were still celebrating. With Janeson running to her post, pointing to Dillon, Gilmore, and Johnson to ready themselves, Welch had a rush of the old days of shouting commands.

"Quiet, people!" she barked while raising her clinched fist in the air, the visual command to be silent and ready.

After about six rings, she answered.

"Hi, Eric. Could you hold a minute ... actually, no. Ah, what can I do for you?"

More silence until a more contained angry voice came over the intercom.

"I'm not done," he said with venom.

"Oh, Eric ... I was really hoping you'd come in. But we'll do it your way. Again, don't call after 10:00 p.m. nor before 6:00 a.m. Talk to you later--or as the French say, and I hope to get this right, 'Passez une bonne journée et bien dormir.'"

Welch hung up again.

That's really gotta piss him off.

Looking at Janeson, she gave the thumbs up and looked at Gilmore, who nodded his head affirmatively.

"Confirmed. He's in Canada. British Columbia region. He's got elevation, so I bet he's in the mountains. That's as close as we got," she said.

"Yes!" Dillon blurted out as shouts of joy erupted from the team. Smiling, Welch nodded approvingly and waved Janeson and Dillon over.

Pulling them aside, she found herself almost excited to be issuing orders again.

"Dillon, we need to train our new insertion team so that we can mobilize within a two-hour notice. We have only six to seven weeks to train before he has enough resources to mobilize another attack or to dig in deep. Janeson, confer with Helms, but I recommend that in addition to notifying border patrols on both sides, we talk to our Canadian friends to ask if they would be opposed to us informing the Canadian public about Eric Daniels as a wanted fugitive."

Looking perplexed, she explained, before Janeson asked:

"I want some pressure from the public on Daniels so that he will have to duck and cover rather than walking through borders and eating at diners in peace. I want him to know we are getting close. Also ask Helms if he thinks it's a good idea to inform various embassies of Daniels and Glenn's last locations."

She watched as Janeson's head tilted in understanding as Dillon smiled.

"Mrs. Welch? If we do that, the Israelis will have a jump on finding Daniels. Is that your plan? They are very likely to shoot first and ask questions, if at all, later," Janeson asked.

"Yes ... Swat Valley, 2006. It's about time that Parks, Grimm, and everyone else rest in peace," Welch said with little happiness in her heart, thinning lips, and downcast stare. Pulling herself out of herself, she returned to business.

"Those are my biased recommendations. I'll let Helms and the Bureau make that call," she said, looking Janeson in the eyes.

"Will do, ma'am," Janeson said as she took the main headset to contact Helms.

"One other question? Why did you tell Daniels 'Have a great day and sleep well,' in French?" Janeson asked.

"No reason. I just wanted to close the loop that even the French don't care for him." she smiled as she walked away.

She was about to head out of the control room to an outer office to make her own calls when Dillon asked her an important question.

"Mrs. Welch?"

Jesus. Why do they all call me "Mrs. Welch?"

Visions of her young boys and neighborhood children running in and out of her house, all asking for cookies, flooded her mind as she turned to respond.

"The team I put together is comprised of people who are biased to kill Daniels rather than to capture. What are the rules of engagement? Is this a capture or kill mission?"

Taking in a deep sigh, she moved closer to give her best answer.

"I don't know. We'll train for both. Helms will set the rules and I'll be in command on the field. I guess we'll have to see" she said in a soft tone.

Thank God Helms will make that call.

"Sounds like a plan. Thank you," Dillon said as she returned to her console.

Looking around the entire control room, taking in the energy and the enthusiasm of maybe turning the tide to offense, Welch smiled and exited.

~

Daniels remained standing with the closed phone in his hand as he looked out over the vista. It was still warm, but he was feeling both hot and cold at the same time. He was angry at himself for letting Welch push the conversation in her direction. As he wound up to throw the cell phone into the ravine with the other one, he thought twice about it.

If she's not lying and all offshore assets are dried up, that means all I have is what's in my truck. Israelis? They are going to be a problem.

He replaced the phone in his vest pocket. As he thought back he suddenly remembered why the Israelis were pissed.

"Oh yeah," he said to himself as he smiled.

I guess the Prime Minister is still pissed about me outing him. I guess his people aren't as progressive on gay rights as he had hoped, especially his wife and family.

Sighing, he resolved that getting angry at Welch was stupid, and now he had to move as soon as possible.

"That little outburst probably gave them a lead on where I might be at."

He walked back to his already packed SUV.

My skull as a coffee cup?! That wasn't Burns. He's not that creative. It's got to be another jab from Welch. Screw her.

Stepping into his SUV, he took his revolver out and put it on the passenger's seat. He retrieved a map from the cluttered glove compartment, and began to think in terms of the fastest way north, and then he would head south once he was sure he was out of their search pattern.

Vladimir of Russia, Liang of China, and Seo-yeon, North Korea. You really did your homework, Tombs. What the hell did I do to you?

He tried pushing his angry thoughts out as he started up his SUV. After an hour ruminating on how he was feeling stupid for getting angry, he recommitted himself to a new plan. With no one on the road, he drove in peace, half- listening to the radio until a news report came on that caught his attention, as a female announcer with a French-Canadian accent mentioned his name.

"... It is believed that Eric Icarus Daniels, former Chairman of the Foreign Intelligence Agency, responsible for years of black operations against allied nations, is now on the run after refusing to attend a number of US Senate and judicial hearings. FBI Headquarters in Washington, DC, has issued an apprehend mandate to detain and capture Daniels. Recent assassination attempts coordinated by Daniels in New Hampshire, and Boston, Massachusetts, America, and Torrox Costa, Spain, were foiled by local and national authorities. All citizens in the British Columbia area, be on the lookout ...."

Daniels felt his blood pressure boiling as his nose burst with blood.

"Fuck!" he said. Blood poured down his lip and he started driving with one hand so he could search for napkins to stop the blood flow.

"You fucking people put an all-points bulletin on me? You fuckers!"

It took handfuls of napkins just to slow the flood of blood.

Focusing on his breathing, he pulled over and slammed the radio button off. Holding his nose up and trying to be patient, he had to think of another plan. After fifteen minutes of waiting for his blood to clot, he was finally able to move and look for a map.

"Okay. Major cities, highways, tolls, and borders are off limits, now," he said to himself. Taking a mental inventory, he listed what he could leave behind and what he could carry on his back when he abandoned his SUV to cross the border back into the US. With the blood stopped, he reviewed his mental list again, and his limited financial resources. After listening to silence, and consolidating his plan, Daniels reviewed the map again and altered course to head south, away from cities and major roads.

"So ... you think you can get the public to help you?"

"I've got friends, too. They're patriots. They'll make Burns pay. They'll make all of you pay."

After five minutes, he noticed that his knuckles seemed to be turning white from his grip on the steering wheel. With concerted effort, he released the pressure.

"God, I hate them! And when the fuck did Welch learn French? 'Have a great day and sleep well!?' Damn it!" he said angrily as he drove at the speed limit.

~

Becky was still holding Burns's handwritten note as she listened to Emma talking to Deputy Director Janeson. The woman was odd, she thought, but seemed to be genuinely interested in Emma's knowledge of starfish and sharks. Looking back at Burns's note again, she wanted to make sure that her emotions were not blinding her as she sat outside the door where Emma's half-sister and paternal grandfather were waiting.

"There are no words that can capture the loss of both Samantha and David; your sister and husband, my love and dear friend, the ones that saved me from death and worse. I am fortunate to have you and Emma. I wish I could be there, but I need to find Daniels, and finish this. I promise. I met Rosemarie. She's like Emma, but older. She had a hard day today--she was kidnapped, bound, and was only ten minutes away from being killed. And now, if all goes well, she will have to leave her mother, family, and life to be safe. But then, sisters should be together. Don't you think? Take care. Alex."

Becky closed the note and took in a deep breath as she stood up and faced the door.

The father of the man who killed my brother is in there. Emma's half-sister is in there. Her father, Emma's father, killed my brother, my Tony.

Conflicted, she read the note again and focused on one part of the letter.

But then, sisters should be together. Don't you think?

Closing the note, still not sure of what she was going to do, Becky opened the door and entered to see an older man starting to stand up as a taller version of Emma was hugging him, still holding him and apparently still crying.

As she walked toward the man named John Murphy, she found herself devoid of past hate and desire to kill him.

What's to be gained? More misery for someone else? It won't bring back Tony. It won't bring back Samantha ... or David.

As she stood silently behind Rosemarie's back, she took a moment to choose her words carefully. Finding her voice was the most difficult, as her thoughts drifted to how David would deal with this.

"What was it that Burns and David would say? 'For what shall it profit a man, if he shall gain the whole world, and lose his own soul?'"

It became a bit clearer...not crystal yet, but clearer.

"John Murphy? My name is Rebecca Littleton. Emma is my daughter. She is also your granddaughter." She took another moment and then continued.

"Emma and Rosemarie are sisters, and it's unsafe for both of them to be here." Still having more to say, she needed a minute more to think of the right words.

"Ms. Littleton. I am very sorry for your recent loss, and you are right. It's going to get pretty bad around here, and I need to make sure Rosemarie and Emma are safe. I can think of no better person to take care of her, than you," he said through tear-filled eyes.

My God .... He's an old man. A grandfather. Emma's grandfather.

Becky turned unexpectedly to the door. She was sure Murphy must have thought that she was angry and leaving. As she opened the door, she called out for Emma to come in.

"Emma? Come in here and meet your grandfather and sister."

I never thought I would say that.

Emma sheepishly entered the room to meet her paternal family.

Becky watched as Rosemarie finally turned around with tear tracks on her cheeks, eyes red from crying.

My God! Burns is right. She's an older version of Emma.

Then Becky felt her heart break as she listened to Murphy say to Rosemarie, "It's okay, Pumpkin. Ms. Littleton will take care of you, and she will be able to find me in case you need me. You know that, love."

"Pumpkin"? I called Samantha "Pumpkin."

Rosemarie remained still, attached to her grandfather's side; it was Emma's turn to walk slowly to her and carefully extend her arms to hug.

Becky's eyes looked down to the floor as tears began to form.

David would have been so proud of you.

Trying to be brave, Becky looked up and saw that Rosemarie had moved to embrace little Emma, and hugged her.

Becky looked at Murphy to see that he was less concerned with looking brave as tears ran freely down his face.

After an uncomfortable minute, she walked directly to him and spoke softly but clearly, in her business voice.

"Mr. Murphy. I need contact information of different ways to get a hold of you if all this goes to shit and I have to go off grid. I have resources and supplies to be underground forever if I have to, but Rosemarie will need to get a hold of you, and Emma may want to as well. I need that information now. The marshals are going to relocate us now and I have to be prepared to move, keep the girls safe, and not be found. Okay?"

If he was surprised and angry, he hid it well, and sat down to give numbers and locations.

As Emma and Rosemarie were talking while Becky was watching them, Murphy finished his note and handed it to her.

As she was about to take it, Murphy took a moment to say something that had to be important.

"Ms. Littleton. Thank you for taking care of Emma, and now Rosemarie. I wish I could change the past and undo my son's actions, but I can't. I'm sorry. If you, Emma, or Rosemarie needs anything, you know where to find me."

Becky was slow in responding as she recalled that David often said, "You know where to find me," especially when saying goodbye.

He always said that to Sam and Burns....

Feeling crushing pain in her heart, Becky croaked only one sentence.

"Thank you," she said, as she put the note in her pocket with Burns's letter.

Becky walked to the door as the deputy director and the marshals walked in to move the family to a new life. Turning, she saw Murphy gently hugging Emma and then Rosemarie, until he let her go and ushered both of them to her.

Sisters should be together.

She thought about how difficult it had to be for Murphy; both his grand daughters were leaving their grandfather, an old man who lost a son and saw too much in life, alone in the room.

Chapter 17

"Flamma fumo est proxima" – "Flame follows smoke"

Andersen was happy to be driving to work for the first time in weeks. Until two days ago, he had either been in DC, New Hampshire, or FBI Regional in Boston. Taking his favorite route through the winding roads of town with colonial homes, he was glad to get back to his own office and catch up in his own work. His plan was really simple--do all the paperwork, catch up on news, and then get back home to spend a couple of days with the family.

Laura's got to hate this, me chasing Daniels.

The familiar roads, sights and people were great to see. He was just happy to be at the station and enjoyed pulling into the "police only" parking lot. He really never thought he would enjoy coming to work.

First it was Burns, and now it's Daniels. But she does love hearing the stories.

Still in his thoughts he casually walked to the "police entrance only," juggling his briefcase and coffee. As he approached he noticed two people: a tall, thin but muscular man and an athletically built woman of average height. He first noticed the young man's hair, which seemed so dark brown that it looked red, while his partner's jet-black hair was pulled so tight in a pony tail that it hurt just to look at her. Taking in their youthful, healthy complexions, Andersen was also struck by how they were motionless and appeared relaxed but still focused on everything around him.

Something familiar about these two, he thought as he slowed his pace.

Maybe new recruits from the army. More likely from special forces. That's it! They look like Davis, Burns, Cratty ... shit.

"Damn...military, intelligence or law enforcement."

He watched their gait, efficient movement and constant surveillance of the scene even as the woman approached him with her male companion in tow.

"Lt. Steven Andersen?" the woman asked with some strange accent, in perfectly fluent English.

Nodding his head as he came to a full stop, he decided to dispense with the typical greetings and get down to brass tacks.

"By the way you're both dressed and hypervigilant, I take it you are from some kind of Special Forces group or intelligence agency," he said with a certain degree of resignation.

Helms had warned him and the team that both the Israelis and French had been asking a lot of questions, and that the CIA were following up a number of leads regarding their entrance into both Canada and the US.

The woman tilted her head slightly as she smiled and introduced her partner before herself.

"This is my colleague John, and you can call me Ruth," she said.

"Bonjour," the young man said as he watched Andersen closely.

"I can call you 'Ruth'? And this is 'John'?"

"Yes" she said.

"Oui," the French man said.

Andersen waited for more information. None came.

"So I just call you Ruth and John. No last names, no titles, no agencies mentioned, no bosses, no national affiliations...just Ruth and John?"

The pair looked at each other and then back to him."

"Yes," Ruth said in a pleasant voice, as she did her best to smile and keep things low-key.

Andersen looked closely at both of them and noticed identifying features in addition to their physiques, dialects, and their keen awareness.

In addition to the woman's hands being weathered as if she used them a great deal, a gold Star of David symbol hung on a necklace, prominently showing in contrast to the woman's dark skin and black hair. The man's clothes were impeccably tailored and seemed consistent with his own obvious physical prowess.

A tailored and cleaned-up version of Davis and Burns.

Sighing, he decided to be blunt.

"Okay. What does the Mossad and French Intelligence want with me?"

Andersen put his briefcase down as he took a sip of his coffee and watched for any reaction. Their response was telling--their behaviors did not confirm or deny, but the man named John, talking in French, did say something.

"Il possède des competences," John said eloquently from behind Ruth.

Smiling, the woman continued as if her partner had said nothing.

"Lieutenant, we wish only to offer our assistance and join the team you are training to pursue Eric Icarus Daniels."

"What makes you think I have a team? Daniels is a national threat and falls under the purview of Homeland Security and CIA. A North Reading police officer has more local authority."

Andersen watched the couple as the woman smiled yet again and the man raised an eyebrow as he spoke again to Ruth.

"Il doit penser que nous sommes stupides."

While keeping her eyes on Andersen, she spoke harshly to her colleague, and then turned back to Andersen as if she were asking him to tea.

"Soyez calme et laissez-moi parler. Il est l'une des personnes clés, nous pouvons et je ne veux pas que tu de cette place! Please excuse my partner's manners," she said, and then continued with her point.

"Under normal circumstances that is what your government would usually do. However, since you and FBI Director John Helms, Warrant Officer Diane Welch, and former FIA agent Jillian T. Davis have been involved in the Burns and Daniels's case for years, I am positive your President and Secret Service have given you authority to pursue outside the chain of command."

Hmmm. I wonder if they know what the "T" stands for in Davis's name? Maybe something like Tabitha?

Andersen became uncomfortable as the woman closed the gap between them.

Taking a step closer, she added quietly, "Mr. Daniels is a threat to us all, and has caused all of us hardships. We offer our services to help find him ...."

"And kill him?" he finished for her.

"Welch, Helms, Davis, tout le monde veut Daniels morts," John added as he scanned the area as casually as possible.

If it wasn't for the red hair, you'd look much more threatening.

Though he did not know French, Andersen did know that "Daniels's death" was at the end of a sentence that had a list of people who might want him dead.

"Well, I don't want him dead," he smoothly answered, as if he understood John all along, and watched for another response.

Returning his gaze back to Andersen, he raised another eyebrow before he finally asked a question.

How does he do that? Raises each eyebrow individually? he thought as a smell of perfume filled his nose. *Is she wearing musk?*

"Son dossier ne mentionne rien lui connaître le français?"

"That is because he could figure out what you are saying, espèce d'idiot!" Ruth answered without looking back at him.

"Please forgive John, and please take my card in case you need to get a hold of me. Our offer to help is time-limited, so this is my direct line and I will always answer for you."

She handed him her business card, and stepped back to walk away.

Looking at the card he saw that it was one of the more expensive cards he had received, with probably the least amount of information he had ever seen. With a gold border and cream color, the card held one name, "Ruth," written in fancy calligraphy, and a phone number.

Pretty expensive card for a name and number only.

Without another word, both Ruth and John walked away, scanning all around them to make sure that if they were being watched, they would find a way to disappear.

Still standing with his coffee getting cold, Andersen watched as he fingered her card again to see if there was anything on the back.

"Maybe if I apply heat, the invisible ink will be readable," he said to himself.

He took another breath, picked up his briefcase and continued to walk into the police station.

Great! Helms is going to love this.

~

"Yeah. That's just great. Talk to you later," Helms said. He hung the phone up and looked back at his guests. Janeson and Davis had been reviewing tactical strategies and training in his office when Helms got the call from Andersen about his encounter with Ruth and John.

"Bad news, Boss?" Janeson asked.

"Yes," he said, resisting a sarcastic remark, knowing that "Janeson doesn't do sarcasm."

Smiling more at his thoughts than at the bad news, he consciously changed his expression so as to give a token of how he felt about the bad news.

"It looks like the Israelis and French have asked to join our team. And they had intelligence on who all are involved in the task force." He leaned forward on his elbows.

"That's bad news, John. With them teamed up, that could create a problem with finding Daniels and then keeping him alive," Davis said.

"How is the schedule looking for the insertion team?" he asked, deciding to talk about something he could control.

Davis nodded her head positively as she shifted in her seat to read and summarize the report.

Half-listening, Helms watched Janeson as she was sitting quietly, looking intently at two tablets as she shifted from one to the other with great interest. Unable to take it anymore, Helms stopped Davis with his raised hand and waited a minute to see if Janeson even noticed. As a minute was about to turn into two, Janeson stopped and looked at him staring at her.

"Sorry, Boss. Did you want the report on resource breakdown?"

Hmmm. What are you doing, young lady?

"Without touching your screen, missy, hand me your tablets."

He held his hand out and waited for her to deposit her tablets in his hand.

Slowly and cautiously, Janeson reluctantly surrendered her tablets.

Narrowing his eyes at her before he looked down to see what she had been intently reviewing, Helms was surprised to see that either guilt or shame had registered on her face.

What is going on with you?

The larger tablet had a resource report, cash distribution, and a list of mortuaries and grave sites in Spain, Kea, Virginia, and Boston. The smaller tablet was far more provocative and a genuine surprise to him.

He looked up to ask her a question, he was again surprised to see that she looked as if she were blushing.

Okay. This is serious.

Taking in a deep breath, he suddenly turned to Davis and cocked his head to the door.

"Davis? Could you give me a minute with Rachael here? And close the door on the way out," Helms asked as casually as he could.

Davis's eyes widened at first, and then she quickly collected her material as if the room was on fire, without even uttering another word.

With just the two of them in the office, Helms took on his avuncular demeanor, difficult for a Marine, but then, Rachael was like a daughter to him.

"Okay, Rachael. I understand some of this," he said as he held the larger tablet.

"But this? Edgar Allen Poe's *Annabel Lee?* Poetry?"

He raised the smaller tablet to make his point.

"Boss, I'm working an angle. An unlikely, small angle, but an angle to locate Burns," she said.

While her words said one thing, her body language said another. She corrected her back and sat perfectly erect in her chair.

Before looking down at her confiscated tablet, he narrowed his eyes to see if he was actually seeing a slowly forming blush on Janeson's neck.

Embarrassment? That would mean she would know she should be embarrassed.

He looked back down at the passage. He remembered how he thought Poe's work was morbid as he read the last stanza to himself.

"... And the stars never rise but I feel the bright eyes

Of the beautiful Annabel Lee;

And so, all the night side, I lie down by the side

Of my darling–my darling-my wife and my bride,

In the sepulchre there by the sea -

In her tomb by the sounding sea."

Looking back up at Janeson, who did her best imitation of stone while the blush slowly encroached on her face, he formed a question to keep her talking so that he could figure out what was going on with his deputy.

See, Steve, you would be helpful right about now.

Helm wished he had Andersen's skills as an interrogator.

"Burns will find us. He has to go dark so that it looks real. Then he'll get a hold of us. So why are you looking at mortuaries and Poe's poetry?"

Helms watched as it was clear that Janeson's approach, though typically logical, had some emotion involved.

Picking up on a lot of social cues that she used to miss. Is it that damn dog she's watching for Burns?

Helms recounted a number of social interactions he witnessed that Janeson had handled well over the course of the last several weeks.

"Boss, I'm talking about finding Alex when it is over. When we find Daniels. Alex has a history of disappearing without a trace. But when we checked to see where Samantha Littleton's body was buried, we had to go to three different places. All were where she was supposed to be, but was not. Alex or one of his team made that arrangement. With Dr. Caulfield's death, his body was shipped and sent to a mortuary in Kea. The problem is we checked and there is an empty grave there with a similar name but nobody within. Another clear lead had his body moved to Virginia to be with his first wife. I am waiting for the body to arrive. I am convinced it never will. I am convinced it will go to wherever Samantha Littleton's final resting place is."

Eyes narrowed, Helms made an inference based on his knowledge of Burns's love of Samantha Littleton and Poe's love story of his deceased love. But his thought jumped to something far more telling: *She called Burns "Alex."*

"You mean 'Annabel Lee's' final resting place?"

He waited for a reaction.

As the blush on her face was both clear and uncomfortable for him to watch, he was struck by her overt aversion to making eye contact as she spoke next.

"I am trying to get insight from an authority on someone's heart getting broken and what ends they would go to."

Helms noticed she spoke with a slight edge to her voice.

Hmmm. "Insights," my ass. More emotions these days. Ever since her time with Burns.

Helms decided to change from a frontal assault to a more subtle approach.

"Any insights?" he asked as innocently as he could.

Janeson's tone and expression shifted abruptly to bright and almost cheery.

Hmmm. Mid-thirties, attractive woman, works a lot of hours and is constantly watching an intelligent rogue spy we're using for bait as she watches his dog ... yeah. She's gotta a thing for Burns. But she's smart, damn it! Shouldn't she know better?

"Yes. Ever since Alex's head injury and his treatment with Dr. Caulfield, he has significantly changed. When Ms. Littleton died, he became more maudlin. He holds onto the crucifix and necklace that she held when she died, implying a romantic motive to hold on to her by proxy. I suspect that whether it be through emotion, affection, or ritual, he would visit her grave. With Dr. Caulfield's death I suspect that it might lead to her actual site as well."

"You think they are both buried in the same place?"

Not very spy-like. Would Burns really make that mistake?

"I think that both Ms. Littleton and Dr. Caulfield saved Alex's life. Alex could have left them early on, but he didn't. They worked as a team together for nearly five years and then paired off to live together and protect each other. I think they became a family in life and now in death."

With his eyes still locked on her and getting narrower, he handed her tablets back.

Okay, Rachael. You're a watch.

He watched her blush fade slowly.

"Well, there is logic to that. Keep searching. But watch yourself. I don't want you get emotionally invested in Burns."

Averting her eyes from him, Janeson extended her hands to receive the tablets as she said, "Yes, Boss."

He watched her as she quickly slipped the smaller tablet back in her sweater pocket and looked down at her tablet, and then looked at the door. Without looking back at him she said, "I'll get Davis, Boss," and exited into the corridor to find her.

Alone in his office, Helms listened to Janeson's footsteps recede in the distance as he shook his head.

"Damn it! She's fallen for the bastard. Hard, too. How the hell does that happen?"

He shook his head and made a mental note to ask his wife and Welch on the best strategy to deal with this before it got worse.

"I don't need this."

He reached for one of his many color-coded files, all of which dealt with Daniels and Burns.

After five minutes of not being able to focus, Helms called his wife rather than wasting time as he waited for Davis and Janeson to return.

~

Burns was very tired as he waited outside the mausoleum in Cumberland Hill's oldest cemetery in Rhode Island. It had taken him longer to come see Sam since he had to stop at two offsite storage containers to replace various fuels, ammunition, and cash for the future in case Becky or he needed it later. He thought he had timed his arrival after the groundskeepers had refreshed the flowers and candles, but since it was misting and raining torrents periodically, they were obviously running behind. After ten more minutes, he was greatly relieved when two men emerged from the crypt with old flowers and cleaning gear, put them in the truck, and then drove away.

After another minute, he walked through the light misting rain to the entrance, but stopped in front of the door to read a small inscription recently completed in dark marble above the door. He rubbed his temples and pulled on his old training. It took him a few minutes to decipher the German.

"Hier liegen die Leichen der Albatross Familie durch Liebe und Feuer geschmiedet."

After he repeated it twice he knew it sounded like something David would say.

"Here lie the bodies of the Albatross family forged through love and fire." You were always good with words, David. Hiding in plain sight, as always. He smiled as he entered. Stepping into the crypt, he quietly enjoyed the thought that once again someone would have to know exactly where to look to find him and his crew, hiding in plain view.

The combination of incense, fresh flowers, and polish filling his senses made the mist and cold elements fade away. He found his seat in front of Samantha's tomb. It was very difficult to sit down, so he decided to stand instead. Not wanting to look to his left, he forced himself to see that recently arrived pictures were in place in front of David's tomb, which was open as if ready to receive a body. Looking away quickly, he closed his eyes and focused on Samantha's pictures.

"I'm sorry, Sam. I couldn't save him. He and Emma were ambushed in Spain while I was looking for Daniels here."

Taking in a deep breath, Burns explained as if she were alive.

"I know I can't be everywhere, but I should have been there. Half of Cratty's people were wiped out, but they managed to get Becky and Emma out, and find leads to Daniels. Still. It won't bring David back. This has to be killing Becky ... I'm sorry."

He stopped and moved a bit slower than usual. The thought to bring Samantha up to date popped into his head.

"Yeah. I was shot in the ass. Not exactly heroic, but it kept Murphy and Rosemarie from being hit. Oh yeah, I met Rosemarie, Emma's half-sister. It's eerie how she looks just like Emma."

As Burns paced, he started to feel more tired, and decided that instead of trying to sit, he would lie down on the marble bench. He heard the rain pick up outside and found the warmth of the crypt and low candlelight relaxing. He pulled at his necklace. It was more comfortable to lie down without pain, but then he felt more and more tired suddenly. Days of not sleeping were catching up with him finally.

"I'm going to have to leave for a while, Sam. I have to track down Daniels and take a more aggressive approach in finding him. It seems I've got Welch, the FBI, and Secret Service on my team. Not bad for a rogue former agent. Still, I'm sorry. I'll be gone for a while. And I found someone to take care of Roxie. She's kind of odd, but likeable and smart. She'll take good care of her."

Feeling the cross on his necklace, he became acutely aware that at some point he would be taken, and more likely he would be separated from his cross--the same cross that Sam had held when she died. After another moment of reflection, he rolled to his side to get up and start his search. He took his necklace off for the first time in years and held it firmly in his hand as he looked around for a hiding place. Feeling suddenly guilty, he looked at the tomb and spoke.

"I know. I just don't want to lose it--and if it comes with me, Daniels will take it as a souvenir," he said to Samantha's tomb as if she were watching him.

He looked around the base of the tomb toward the back of the cryptand found a crevice to put his necklace for safekeeping.

"There. You can watch it for now. But I want it back," he said with a tired smile.

As if fatigued from bending over and securing the necklace, a wave of exhaustion seemed to overcome him. Feeling better that it was now safe, he made his way back to the marble bench to lie down again. The pace of the rain had picked up and the crypt felt warmer than usual.

Yawning and eyes drooping, he found himself drifting off for the first time in three days.

"I'm just going to rest awhile, Sam."

He closed his eyes and felt his body drift as his breathing deepened.

"I love you," he said quietly

Sleep enveloped him with the sound of rain and running water from the roof still resonating in his ears. Images of rain falling into the sea filled his thoughts as he heard his breathing deepen and his pain recede.

Finally ... rest.

Epilogue

"Frustra laborant quotquot se calculationibus fatigant pro inventione quadraturae circuli" – "Futile is the labor of those who fatigue themselves with calculations to square the circle" Michael Stifel, 1544

Dillon walked into the quiet, dark control room half expecting five or six people covering the evening shift. To her surprise, Gilmore, Johnson, and Janeson were still there from the shift earlier that day. Feeling a bit grumpy that she had to cover for Davis while she went looking for Ramsey and Cratty, she walked slowly with a cup of coffee in her hand to get an update from Janeson.

After four months of preparation, trainings, briefings, and searching, Dillon was itching to get back in the fight. By all analysis, Daniels had no resources at hand except for "end-of-days-peppers" called the Republican Citizens Army, in Colorado and Maine.

Man, I hate those vigilante groups.

She saw Janeson pacing the width of the control room. She was in rare form of late. Presently she was wearing her headset while looking at one tablet and balancing a smaller, lighter tablet in and out of her sweater pocket. What was different about Janeson was that she was talking in a low yet animated fashion into her headset microphone as she paced with all of her electronics gadgets, going in concentric circles. With the floor-to-ceiling screens off, and the low light of all the smaller screens glowing, Dillon could have found a corner and easily have gone to sleep until Gilmore waved her over.

So much for a nap.

Walking over, she could see that Gilmore had something to say, while Johnson came over as well with his own tablet.

"Christine, you gotta talk to Janeson about Burns," Gilmore started.

Oh no. Not again.

Over the past several weeks, Gilmore and Johnson had been taking turns talking to her and Davis about what they thought was a crush Janeson had on Burns. Conceptually, the idea of Janeson being romantic and having a crush was simply too farfetched to get her head around it. Add that she had a crush on Burns, and the idea moved from conceptual to impossible.

"My God. Janeson? Burns? Why would you two even think of such a thing?" she asked.

As Gilmore and Johnson exchanged looks, she suddenly became uncomfortable.

"Okay, you two. What's up?"

Okay. Fine. If you're going to come up with something that crazy, you better have proof.

As Janeson's pacing brought her a bit closer to Dillon, she overheard her part of the conversation.

"... but we are all mammals, and mammals mate. Humans are the only mammals that ascribe emotion to sex and mating. Having sex can be easily done without emotion. Typically it is. But to be in love with someone without sex does seem unlikely, improbable though not impossible ...."

I really don't want to deal with this ....

Gilmore and Johnson looked at Dillon as she tried to think of some reason such a conversation would happen in the FBI Control Room, while averting their stare.

Taking a sip of coffee, Dillon asked her question even though she knew the answer.

"Is that her check-in with Burns?"

Johnson sighed before he answered.

"Yes," he said simply, but then he shook his finger and gave a sarcastic laugh as he continued what Dillon was sure was going to be an extensive list of what was wrong with how Janeson and Burns "check in."

Here we go ... I hate it when he starts.

"Funny thing, though. When I check in with Burns I get three minutes at the most. When anyone checks in with him it's about three minutes. Davis, he'll talk to for about ten minutes, mostly to give her shit. But when Janeson checks in, well ... it's about an hour. Then two hours later he's checking in again for another hour. When he doesn't check in, she starts pacing, brings up satellite thermal imaging, and then runs diagnostics on the satellite to make sure it's working. When he finally does check in, he's all apologetic and she moves from pouting to happy in minutes ... if you remember our 'old Janeson,' she doesn't do 'pouting,' or at least she never did. Except when the boss figured out what May 2nd meant before she did, but that's not important. Worst of all ... she giggles sometimes when she talks to him. To Burns! Do you have any idea what it's like to have Janeson giggle?"

Shit ... this is bad.

"Jesus, Johnson, take it easy. I'm sure there's a good reason ...."

Dillon trailed off as Janeson's orbit brought her close to earshot again.

"... no. All my boyfriends ... I found that aspect of our relationship unsatisfying but they were quite satisfied ... I guess their consistent returning for years at a time would imply they enjoyed the acts. I also experimented with a number of different venues ...."

Oh, my God!

Feeling two sets of eyes burning in the back of her head, Dillon felt the walls closing in. In an attempt to delay engaging them, she took another sip of coffee.

Closing her eyes, Dillon turned to both men.

"Okay. It's just talk. Inappropriate talk--but then, that is Janeson. She misses social cues and conventions."

Both men looked blankly at her until Gilmore waved her to his laptop.

Reluctantly, she followed.

"Okay, then. Check this out. For the last six weeks I have seen a steady rise in Janeson's use of RAM, and the cache history of what she is researching is pretty interesting," he said as he pointed to different sites, time indexing and megabytes of memory used.

Dillon's eyes widened at the array and amount of data collected. Mathematics, love poems, erotica, human sexuality and autism, biology, physics, women and male physiology, the psychology of love and sex, biochemistry ... the list seemed endless.

Standing straight and taking another long sip of coffee, she attempted to go on the offensive.

"Wait a minute. Are you spying on her?"

Johnson smiled before he answered.

"Sorry, Dillon. That won't work. 'Spying' would suggest we needed to dig and break into her computer. All of her research is on her laptop and that smaller tablet she carries around with her all the time. Both were issued by the Bureau, and she has no problem leaving the screens up for anyone to see. Fortunately, she has taken our suggestions about keeping a lower profile, lest she give others the wrong impression."

Dillon took another long sip as she tried to generate some other possible reason that Janeson might have this information on a federal, public server.

"If it were megabytes on 'stress fractures effects on long-range shooting,' or 'global warming effects on wind velocity and sniper fire,' then it would be understandable. But Janeson learning about erotica, psychology, human sex organs ... that's just not the Janeson we all know," Johnson added.

As Dillon struggled to think of any reason, Janeson unwittingly proved Johnson's point in her next pass.

"... Alex. Just because you have had sex and loved one person, and had sex and not cared about another person doesn't mean you are a sociopath one day and a sweetie the next. It doesn't work that way. My experience is that true love making, if there is such a thing, has an animal quality to it. A roughness ...."

"Sweetie?" "Roughness?" This is worse than I thought. Nice, Davis! "Had to go help out Ramsey," my ass! Now I'm stuck dealing with this!

Taking another sip, Dillon looked over her cup to see both men looking at her.

"Damn it, guys! Why can't you talk to her?"

"Is that vodka in that cup, Dillon?" Johnson snapped back emphatically.

With a more conciliatory tone, Gilmore articulated what Dillon already knew.

"Christine. We're like brothers to her. We're her pals and we love her like a sister. We can't talk to her about girl stuff. We're men. Helms can't talk to her about it. He's a guy and the boss. Davis and Mrs. Welch said they would, but they haven't worked with her like you have. She needs to have someone who is a peer to talk to her about men, crushes, and having a relationship with a guy like Burns that could really hurt her."

Dillon could easily hear the protective and caring tone in Gilmore's voice. *I hate to admit it, but it's very nice of you, you bums. She really couldn't find a nicer group of guys.*

She drained her cup of coffee and tossed it in the basket as she started to walk away.

"I hate both of you," she said without turning around to look at them.

"Love you," Johnson said as he returned to his post and Gilmore cleared his board.

As Dillon approached, she heard more of the one-sided conversation.

"... I had thought of being a nun but I don't believe in God .... Yes Alex ....Yes, I am aware of the logical argument for why there must be a God ...."

As she approached she made a gesture for Janeson to put Burns on mute.

"Alex, hold on. Ms. Dillon needs me for a minute. One moment please." As Janeson pulled the headset off, she shook her hair out to giving her the just-fallen-out-of-bed look. But it was the smile that Janeson sported that really threw Dillon off.

Oh Christ ... the smile of "my boyfriend likes me"

"Yes, Christine? What can I do for you?"

Janeson mood was cheery which was unheard-of.

Who the hell are you? What have you done with Janeson?

"Okay. Okay, Janeson. I have to talk to you about a personal matter ...." Dillon started.

"Absolutely. What's on your mind?" Janeson asked as she looked down at some beeping on her larger tablet.

Taking in a deep breath and looking around the control room to make sure no one was listening, Dillon found herself trying to formulate a starting point.

Okay ... same conversation I had with Lucy ... when she was ten. No difference except this one is thirty-six, with an IQ of a thousand and proficient in three weapons ....

She took another deep breath and pushed out the massive age discrepancy between her niece and Janeson.

"Janeson ... in the course of a young woman's life ... emotions and urges start to ... emerge .... Sometimes we have strong feelings for boys, I mean, men ..." she started.

"Uh ha," Janeson said. She might have been listening but looked distracted.

Embarrassed to have to say anything Dillon continued to get the job done.

"So when a girl, I mean woman feels she's really likes a guy, it's really hard to figure out these emotions. Ah, sometimes we like boys and girls but it's not the same,"

Dillon had a thought that maybe Janeson could be bisexual. It made sense. Janeson being logical would lend itself to have more options than less.

Why relegate to one gender? Maybe transgender too? Okay...just pick one for now. No, pick two. Crap!

"Sometimes we do like boys and girls the same way and that's confusing too...ah Janeson?"

She looked closely at her, she saw that her newly acquired, carefree smile had disappeared, and she was now stabbing at her tablet. Suddenly, Janeson's head shot up, looking behind Dillon as the floor-to-ceiling monitors came to life, displaying thermal images from orbit. All was dark except for ostensibly a person near some kind of fire. At the very edges, coming in from all sides, were a series of five clusters of thermal images slowly encroaching on the one in the middle.

When she hit another button, the lights in the control room increased while previously sleeping monitors miraculously turned on.

"Gilmore! Johnson! Get everyone to their posts! This is it!" Janeson yelled.

"Dillon! Scramble insertion team. Crepes! Contact the boss and Mrs. Welch!

Within seconds, the control room sprang to life from a deep sleep and Janeson was back on the line as a completely different person. This time, she had their conversation on loudspeakers as everyone went about their tasks.

"Alex. There are five clusters of heat signatures moving from all directions. The smallest one is due south if you want to evade. Closing at thirty yards," she said as she consulted her tablet again.

Dillon was texting Ramsey, knowing that Davis and Cratty were probably with her.

"No, Rachael. This is what we've been waiting for. I'm going to leave the line open on the phone in the tent. The LEDs are off so it looks off. Wish me luck," Burns said.

"Be safe, Alex," was all she said.

Dillon heard a lot of weight and depth in those three words. More emotion she had heard in a long time. The same depth as "I love you" would have.

It was strange to see a glowing image on the screen move into something that dimmed it and then return to the same spot just as the five clusters were within several feet of his position.

As low voices within the control room were talking to others and making arrangements, the silence over the intercom was unnerving. Then, a series of smaller thermal images seemed to break off the larger groups, and muffled sounds could be heard.

"Hey! Can I help you?" Burns said pretty loudly as if he were pissed off.

Then the smaller images broke from the larger clusters and jumped on the one image. Dillon watched as she saw the smaller images, while many were being thrown off.

"Wow," she said as she wondered if Burns was actually going to successfully defeat the group. That hope vanished as the larger groups joined in en masse, with a corresponding cacophony of men's voices filling the intercom. As the sounds died down and the movement subsided on the screen, it became evident that one thermal image was motionless, though still glowing. After a minute, there was a loud ripping of fabric and a conversation became clear as day.

"... maps, anything. Is Wise here?"

"Are you sure it's Burns? I'd hate to bring the wrong guy."

"Shut up, Harry! Is Wise here?"

"No! Bob's back with the colonel and the new guy."

Noise of things being thrown around could be clearly heard.

"Looky here ...."

"Wow ...."

"Leave it. That money could be laced with fibers that can be tracked."

"No way! The government is too stupid to do that."

"That's how they track us, Dan!"

"How about this? It's probably about two hundred bucks, small denominations."

"Probably okay ...."

The sound had a jarring noise and became very loud.

"Is that on? Was he talking to someone?"

"Naw ... it looks like it's off."

"Well, let's make sure ...."

A loud cracking sound and the control room fell silent, with the exception of staff's low tones scrambling the teams.

Having sent her message, Dillon walked to Janeson who watched the thermal images moving in five separate directions, with watery eyes.

"Are you okay?" she asked quietly.

Tears? This is bad.

Answering more slowly than expected, Janeson nodded her head.

"Yes. It's all part of the plan," she and returned to her tablet, and then re-engaged her staff.

"All right, people. Daniels has taken the bait. Time to end this once and for all. There is no tomorrow--only now. We find him, take him, and put this behind us and live free again. Ready?"

A series of "yes" and "yeahs" went up in the near vacant control room.

"Good. Keep an eye on west group. See if they took the money. "Let's get them."

Acting. Excellent leadership.

Turning toward Davenport, Janeson added, "Call Martin tonight after you call your list and have him head down to Connecticut to talk to Alica Wise. It's time to rattle her cage."

That was a whole lot of emotion ... a whole lot of hate.

Janeson looked back up at the screen and then muttered something unintelligible to herself as she walked to her own console.

Surprised, she was about to turn away until she saw Janeson bending over, under her desk. She stayed there for a moment with her hand extended underneath, and then took her chair to sit down as she pulled her small tablet out to read. Dillon was then able to see Burns's small dog lying down in her bed, under the desk at Janeson's feet. Months ago the creature had refused to be touched by anyone. Janeson was the only one she was friendly to.

Looking back at Janeson, she shook her head.

Poor things, she thought for both of them.

~

"Damn it, Steve! All I wanted to do was go home and sleep. Instead, I have to be entertained for a couple of hours and then go to my birthday party? Couldn't you just give me my present early and drive me home so that I can go to bed?"

Welch complaints went unanswered.

Fifty-three years old, and all I want to do is sleep. It's kind of sad, I suppose. But these trainings and scenarios are killing me, and the four-hour airplane ride and two-hour drive from camp doesn't help. North Carolina? What was I thinking, having the team train there? I really have no business being out there with such a young group.

With Steve Andersen behind the wheel and John Helms riding in the front seat, she had the entire back seat of a very late model Crown Victoria sedan.

"And didn't they discontinue this model thirty years ago?"

Welch could see that her complaining might be having an effect, as Andersen's sighs were increasing in frequency and depth, and Helms's interest in his smart phone significantly increased.

Maybe if I just keep at it, they'll give up.

"Diane, forget about it. Darlene and Laura had planned this months ago, and Helms's wife made her famous chocolate cake for your surprise birthday. So remember to be surprised and enjoy yourself, because if you don't, both Darlene and Laura will be up my ass about it."

Andersen looked at helms for support.

"Anything you want to add?"

Helms took his time and then articulated his thought.

"Why are you such a baby-ass about your birthday? Is Cratty and Davis driving you shithouse, or are you just antisocial?"

Welch watched Andersen's shoulder slump as he shook his head.

Hmm. Actually that's not a bad question for a Jar-Head, Welch thought. *Cratty has been pushing herself and Davis has been actually looking out for her. Still, these young people are tiring.*

Sitting back in the comfortable back seat, she took her time to organize her thoughts and wrap, and was about to say something when Andersen stepped in.

"Nice job, John! Now you just pissed her off, so now we have to listen for the next ten minutes to an unending, exacting diatribe on why she's right. Don't you get enough of that at home? You'd think after being married to Ellen for thirty-plus years, that she would have taught you a little something about not pissing off women."

Helms shook his head and started to stare out his window.

She smiled and was again going to start when she felt her phone vibrate in her purse. As she fished around in her clutch, she heard Andersen's phone chime and Helms's phone light up.

All three of us called at the same time? It's gotta be Daniels.

The car fell silent as all of them read their texts, though Andersen's focus seemed still to be on driving.

"Burns was snatched three minutes ago. Satellite still has him with about twenty-plus attackers. Sending out the call to mobilize insertion team. Martin called to set up office for three-day continuous operation. Insertion team briefing in one hour. Tactical in two. Leave in four to staging area from private airport. Regional and local authorities to be mobilized in twenty-four hours. Mission is green."

"Damn it! Darlene and Laura just won't believe this!"

Andersen looked for an off-ramp to head back to the FBI regional office.

Helms looked back at her with a small smile on his face.

"Happy birthday, Diane."

"Thank you, guys. And don't worry, Steve. I'll talk to the girls later about this."

Shaking his head, Welch heard Andersen muttering, "Act of God, right?"

~

"God damn it! Why did you wake me?" Alica Wise complained. She was roused from her sound sleep by banging outside her cell. Being in isolation at the Federal Correction Institute Bradbury in Connecticut had the advantage of twenty-three hours alone and away from the other inmates. That meant plenty of time to sleep, read, do push-ups, and repeat.

It also means no contact with the real world, no visitors, no family ... except for those fucking guards.

Nearly all the female federal prisons tended to be minimum security but at FCI Danbury, there was an entire new block of high security cells typically left for serial killers, sex offenders, and terrorists. After months of detention under the charges of domestic terrorism, conspiracy to commit murder, assault and battery of a federal agent, obstruction of an ongoing federal investigation, refusing arrest, and obstruction of justice, Wise's only total escape was sleeping. That is, until Officer Janet Tate woke her up in the middle of the night.

"Hey, convict! Don't bitch at me! I had some news for you and I thought you would like to know since you asked to be notified when you were going to have a visitor, but screw you, girly!" Tate said from behind the steel door, through a thin grill.

That bitch! She waited until now to tell me?

Jumping up from her cot, she was at the door in seconds with her hands pressed flat against it and her mouth close to the grill.

"I'm sorry. I was sleeping and I was startled. I didn't know it was you," she said as sweetly as she could. After a moment of silence, she felt her mouth tremble a bit before she spoke again.

"Officer Tate? I said I was sorry. Please?"

After some more silence, it was obvious to her that Officer Tate was going to make her suffer.

She closed her eyes and thought of a plan to get Tate to talk.

"Please, Officer Tate. Maybe ... maybe we can do that thing you like after my visit?"

"Hey! Keep it down, Wise."

Just wait, Alica. Just give her a minute.

"Okay, Wise," the disembodied female voice said harshly. "Special Agent Martin from the Boston FBI will be down tomorrow morning. Looks like he wants to talk to you about your situation, your brother, and those preppers you were hanging out with. So you better be on your best behavior and don't fuck up! Got it?"

Breathe. Breathe.

Wise continued to press up against the door and close her eyes.

Finally, a visitor.

Because of the terrorism charges, and her status as an enemy combatant against the United States, she was not entitled to the 6th

Amendment's Right to Counsel, let alone visitors. Almost overnight her loyalty to Daniels had cost her rights as a United States citizen.

"Thank you, Officer Tate. I will be good, okay?"

After a moment of silence, she waited to hear Tate say something more.

"After your visit you can make things right with me, okay?" Tate said in a lower. She had a less hostile tone, as if she were close to the door.

Smiling, Wise let her voice drop to a more even, almost seductive tone.

"Sure can. Just like last time."

As silence fell and she walked the short distance to her cot, she wondered who Special Agent Martin was and why he was visiting tomorrow.

Turning on her side, she found herself thinking about getting her hands around Tate's throat and squeezing the life out of her.

Yeah...you'll be first. You and your family.

That thought, however, was not as gratifying as her fondest of wishes of late. Feeling the corners of her mouth pull up and her eyes narrow, she sighed at her most recent obsession.

Eric Daniels. You set me up. I'm going to find you. I'm going to track you down and going to find you. And when I find you, I'm going to kill you very slowly.

Wise heard a familiar noise in the corner of her cell. She looked to see that her favorite field mouse had returned. Sitting back up, she carefully removed a small piece of bread from a napkin she saved from dinner, and placed it carefully at the other end of the cell. Sitting cross legged on her cot, she anxiously watched the mouse slowly approach the morsel of food.

"It's all right. It's food."

After a moment, she felt relief when the mouse took a small piece with it as it returned to the hole it came through. Sighing, Wise retrieved the remainder for the mouse later, and to keep the larger rats away. Lying back on her cot, Wise just couldn't wait until tomorrow.

A visitor. Finally, a visitor.

~

Glenn found himself sitting comfortably in the back seat of a luxury SUV as it maneuvered deftly around two cars as it followed at a distance from its prey.

Not exactly low-key, but it sure has comfort and style on its side.

John was being unusually quiet as Ruth continued the professional driving of following a car while appearing to be invisible to the targets she was pursuing. he was feeling his newly formed crooked though healed scar above his cheek when he was pulled back from his daydreaming by Ruth's protesting.

It's a shame I left before the doctor stitched this up.

While it was commonplace for John to complain endlessly in French, it was out of the ordinary for Ruth to be the source of complaining.

"How can you be sure following this piece of shit will bring us to Daniels? The FBI and our counterparts have been scrambled in the opposite direction?" she said in her heavy Jewish accent.

Glenn shook his head. He had gone over the subject and the same objections repeatedly for days. He rubbed his head with both hands for a moment before answering.

"Ruth? Following Burns and the others will be just distraction. Following Robert Wise as he hunts for his sister will, without a doubt, bring him and us to Daniels. Wise will blindly go and find her and will in his travels come along to Daniels. She's his family. Only family. Wouldn't you do the same if it were your sibling?"

He watched as Ruth seemed to think the scenario through before John looked at her askance and answered for her.

"Bien sûr, vous, Ruth. Se souvenir de Terran?" he said quietly.

"Tais-toi, John!" Ruth said with hot anger while still transfixed on her target several cars ahead of them.

Well, that sure hit a nerve.

After a moment of composing herself and stretching her fingers, which had been clenched on the steering wheel, Ruth asked another question.

"So why is Wise heading to New England when everyone else is in the midwest?"

"Excellent question," he said, as if he were proud of a leading question he was about to answer.

"I have no idea," he continued calmly as he looked out the window.

"It doesn't matter. He is looking for his sister. He will find Daniels faster because he is more motivated than anyone right now. He will be more careless as a result. That's when we move in and kill Daniels."

Glenn caught Ruth's head moving up and down in agreement as John verbally agreed.

"Il a raison."

"Je sais," Ruth responded in perfect French.

I really have to bone up on my French.

He touched his scar again and continued to look out the window. As an afterthought, he suddenly fished through his pocket and found a tube of sunscreen. He resisted the urge to put it on; just knowing that it was there was good enough for now.

Maybe when we get out, I'll put some on.

He held on to the tube while he looked back out the window again.

~

Ramsey found herself feeling very uncomfortable. She sat near the bar's entrance waiting for Davis to finally arrive. She looked at her smart phone for the tenth time in ten minutes and couldn't understand why it was taking more than an hour and a half for her to show up.

Jesus! What's taking her so long?

Ramsey felt someone looking at her. She returned a nervous smile back at a woman sitting alone for the moment as her date went to get refills at the bar.

I got lost and had to do a bar search and found it in an hour. I gave her the address and she's taking longer? Jesus, Mary, and Joseph!

Regretting her actions, she understood the meaning of the adage that "no good deed goes unpunished."

She took her time working on her third unfinished drink., She looked back at the bar hoping that no one else would send her another drink as a "friendly gesture." The *Purple Sierras* was not her first choice in bars. In fact, if her parents ever saw her in a lesbian bar, they would probably have dragged her to confession and hold a whole week vigil.

"So how you doin there, hun," the waitress said, a bit too friendly.

"Okay," Ramsey said. She looked briefly up to make eye contact, do a quick smile, and pray she would leave.

"Oh yeah. You are doing pretty well," the waitress said, leaning a bit closer to collect two of the half-filled glasses. "You know it would be easier if I knew what you liked. There's another woman, redhead, asking what you're drinking."

Ramsey reached her limit of discomfort. Her reaction more brittle than she wanted.

"Please! No more ... I ... I ... just got back from overseas and I lost some friends. I'm just trying to relax."

It was all true, she thought. Instinctively her hand went to her blouse pocket to make sure her group picture was still there.

Suddenly embarrassed and apologetic, the waitress dipped closer and spoke very softly.

Ramsey didn't want to draw attention to herself and fearful that her personal space was about to be intruded upon. She froze and held her ground as if she were defending her last living relative to the end.

"I'm sorry, honey. I'll pass the word that you're not interested. And thank you for your service."

Ramsey was relieved when the waitress left and began to breathe again. She looked at her phone one more time and cursed again and then cocked her ear up to hear the song playing.

Damn it!

An all too familiar song came on - Carrie Underwood's "Next Time He Cheats" was playing for the third time. *My parents listened to that.*

Spying a look up near the back of the bar at a closed-in booth, she saw a very attractively dressed Denise Cratty emerging holding a drink in on hand and a very young woman's hand in the other as they walked to the dance floor.

"Hair and skirt length's pretty good, Boss, but the cleavage? Glitter? Heels are pretty high"

With only five other couples on the large floor, it was easy to watch her boss unobtrusively from a distance.

"Jesus Christ," Ramsey said. Looking back down, she continued to wonder why she was there. *Oh ... I was worried*

She fiddled with her high school ring. She did that when she felt nervous and she felt some guilt in following her boss to this getaway. Over the past four months of near daily, rigorous training, Cratty had been pushing herself harder than any of them in the various insertion scenarios. Even the boss, Mrs. Welch, spoke to her to ease her back a bit so as not to hurt herself. Then, no matter where they were training, Wyoming, Kansas, Texas, and presently North Carolina, Cratty would disappear for hours after training and return a couple of hours before dawn. She would leave wearing civilian clothes that were invariably more feminine than Ramsey was used to seeing on her boss. When she came back she was still put together but a bit disheveled. Still, she was looking terrible. And then there was her perspiration and breath that smelled like old alcohol. After seven disappearances, Ramsey told Dillon and Dillon brought Davis into the loop to deal with it internally. Davis made it clear that if it happened again, she was to follow her and call her as soon as she had a location.

"Speaking of Davis ..."

A sigh of relief came in the form of Davis casually walking into the bar, looking around as if she was a regular. Ramsey was relieved to finally have some company.

"What took you so long?" Ramsey asked as calmly as possible. Davis was scanning the entire area until she locked in on Cratty on the dance floor with her date.

It was easy to see that Davis assessed the situation and then responded to her initial question.

"It's pretty far out of the city limits and GPS was offline. Then there was the parking, which is anywhere in the woods you can find. I've heard of roadhouses, but this is the real thing."

Sitting down and continuing her scanning, Ramsey wanted to ask if she could leave, but reframed the question to sound less anxious.

"So when do we get Cratty out of here?"

Turning to look Ramsey in the face, Davis gave her a questioning look.

"Has she just been dancing? Kind of hard to make a big deal if she's dancing. Unless of course ...." Davis paused and squinted her eyes at Cratty's partner.

What? Something I missed?

"Unless of course her partner is a minor, which is possible. She does like them young."

Flustered, Ramsey provided more details.

"Well, just so you know, Marge the waitress has been at their booth four times in the last ninety minutes. Fresh mixed drinks, beer, and shots go in, empties come out. And I think she's going slowly, because she laser-ed in on her new friend. If we get called and she's half in the bag, she's grounded."

She liked her boss and it didn't bother her that Cratty was gay. What bothered her was that her boss was in pain with losing her team and she had no one, no family or loved one to be with. She had gotten close to Becky and Emma, but they were gone too. Ramsey had her family, Dillon had her boyfriend, Janeson had Burns and his dog, even Davis had Andersen and his wife. Cratty had no one...except drinking.

"Okay," Davis said, startling her out of her thinking.

She stood up and started messing up her own hair and pulled her blouse out over her pants giving her a somewhat "frumpy" look.

"Give me your ring, stay close, and watch for my signal," Davis said as she rolled up her sleeves.

"My ring? Why?" she asked as she pulled it off her finger and Davis put it with some effort on her left-hand married finger.

"Just follow my lead."

"What? What's going on?"

Davis dipped her fingers in a glass of water and splattered her face.

"What the hell?"

Davis walked to Cratty and her party on the dance floor. Ramsey followed a bit behind her.

Looking to her left, the woman with the date watched and smiled at her as she walked by. Suddenly, the woman's date, a very attractive but athletic-looking woman turned to look at her, and she didn't smile at all.

Ah shit ... I can't get in a fight here.

"Whatever you're going to do, do it fast," Ramsey warned.

She veered to the left of the dance floor as Davis marched on toward Cratty, who was now fully embraced in the young woman's arms.

Standing near the dance floor, she was ill-prepared for the spectacle she was about to witness.

Davis came up behind Cratty, turned her to face her and then tripped her to the ground. This caused her to fall on her ass spilling her drink everwhere as she hit the dance floor. Cratty looked up at Davis with a combination of shock, anger and confusion. Looking up from the floor, dress resting a bit high on the thighs, Cratty's response was what she expected, as Ramsey was also shocked by Davis's behavior.

"Davis! What the hell is wrong with you!?"

With all eyes now turned on them, Davis took center stage.

"I can't believe you left our anniversary party to go out drinking and hooking up with this ... this little girl," Davis said pointing at the young woman.

"Hey! I'm twenty-five," the young woman said. She did a good jobcomposing herself in light of being caught in a love triangle with a woman who was obviously married. All throughout the young woman's hand was placed firmly on her hip and a glass still in her hand.

What's with these chicks? Dancing and drinking at the same time?

Davis started shaking both her hands at her face as if to fan herself and keep from fainting.

Ramsey could see nothing but shock and awe in Cratty's face--the same look she and everyone else undoubtedly had as well.

What the hell are you doing with your hands, Davis? Flapping?

"Twenty-five!?" Davis said with exasperation. Turning back on Cratty, Davis continued with her tirade: "She's twenty-five years old? Are you having a mid-life crisis, or did you think this ring and our commitment to each other was time-limited, Patricia!"

As Cratty was attempting to get up, she stopped at the name Patricia, obviously wondering who "Patricia" was.

"Patricia?" Ramsey asked quietly. "Who the hell is Patricia?"

As the bar's level of noise had initially dropped, there was a sharp intake of air as the patrons realized they were watching a domestic situation with someone caught cheating.

Ramsey was as shocked as Cratty, as they both watched the drama unfold.

Looking hurt and shocked, the young woman looked at Davis, then down at Cratty, and then back to Davis.

"Patricia? I thought she said her name was Denise? She said she was single ..." the young woman said apologetically to Davis and then turned back to glare at Cratty.

Oh shit, Ramsey thought. The look on the young woman's face was very familiar. Ramsey had seen before; it was when her friend caught her boyfriend in the arms of another woman. To punctuate the moment, Elvis Presley's "Suspicious Mind" flowed from the speakers as the crowd gathered, shaking their heads disapprovingly. That was when Ramsey watched Davis ratchet the melodrama even more. Turning to her left, Ramsey saw two bouncers and the bartender, all strong, tall women, moving in to contain the situation.

"Denise? Denise!" Davis said as she seemed to stagger back from weakness.

"You used our daughter's name to get into the young woman's pants? She's half your age! My God ... I ... I can't breathe ... I can't breathe."

To add to the drama, Davis backed away from Cratty and the woman and motioned for Ramsey to help her out.

Delayed for a moment, Ramsey realized that was her cue to take Davis out and let the bouncers and crowd do their job.

"That is okay. Honey. I will help you out," Ramsey said mechanically.

Putting weight on her to make it look more believable, Davis covered her eyes as if she was crying, and stayed close to Ramsey.

"You really suck at acting. Pretend you're helping a friend who caught her boyfriend cheating."

Ramsey conjured up the vision and turned back in time to see the young woman pouring her drink on Cratty's head.

"Slut! She's too good for you! Perra puta!" she added with the appropriate amount of vehemence.

The crowd joined in as two bouncers and the bartender converged on Cratty as she finally regained her footing on her high heels and was trying to escape the crowd's heckling.

Once outside, Davis pulled her clothes and persona back together and gave Ramsey back her ring.

"Do you have any idea how pissed she's going to be?"

Pulling her hair back and rolling down her sleeves, Davis seemed as calm as a yoga instructor.

"Yup. Pretty pissed."

Shocked and amazed by Davis's performance, Ramsey asked how she did it.

"Jesus! You did that well. How'd you think of it?"

As Davis returned to her normal self, she smiled.

"I actually pulled it from the Burns and crew's play book of deception and distraction. Let's see if it worked."

Both women faced the door of the roadhouse just as Cratty was being forcefully pushed out of the bar while the bartender was taking cash out of her purse to pay for the drinks.

"Thank you for your patronage and the tip. And a tip for you--get your home in order and don't come back here. We're a family establishment. We don't want cheaters, liars and home wreckers," the bartender said. To punctuate her point, the bartender threw her purse at her. Turning on her heels with the two bouncers behind her, the bartender closed the door with a loud thud.

Cratty looked as if she were in shock. She stood and stared at the door. At first Cratty took two steps, stood for a moment clutching her purse, and then she yelled,

"She's not my wife! She's not even my type! Damn it!" she said as she repeatedly kicked the door in her high heels. After a minute of frustration subsided, Ramsey could see that Cratty calmed down, at least initially.

As silence fell and the crickets seemed to sound very loud, she was struck by Davis's casual, near-conversational tone of voice as Cratty now stood quietly looking in her purse.

"Yeah, about that. What is your type, Denise? You've always been a little vague on that. I do think your dance partner was at least thirteen years younger than you, so I guess maturity is not on the list," Davis said nonchalantly.

Oh my God! She's going to kill us both! Davis? What the hell are you doing goading her?

Cratty stood on the porch for a minute before she walked to Davis, persona non grata. Ramsey found herself surprised by their physical difference, which went beyond hair color and physique.

Cratty was now within three inches of Davis's personal space, with her index finger pointing at her chest and looking four inches up to look her straight in the eyes, even in her heels. With Davis wearing paramilitary slacks and shirt, and Cratty wearing classy though revealing clothes, Ramsey was dumbstruck at the scene until she felt her phone vibrating.

"I am taking a break! Do I mess with you when you go out, Davis? Damn it! I got booze in my eyes!"

Cratty's eyes kept blinking from the spilled alcohol.

All the while Davis remained serene as she looked impassively back at her.

"I'm just saving you from disappointment. She looked like trouble, anyway, Denise. She'll lead you to an empty relationship of quick romance and then ...."

"That was the plan! I wasn't looking for a long-term relationship, Davis! And what was that crack about her being half my age? And stop calling me by my first name."

Cratty was still blinking and angry as she opened her purse again to search for something to wipe her face.

Ramsey felt a vibration in her pocket where her cell phone was; she pulled herself away from the escalating argument and breathed a sigh of relief when she now had something to do, and that her boss hadn't even asked how she found her.

Opening the phone she read the text once, closed her eyes, and read it again just to make sure she was reading it right:

"Mission is green. Briefing in one hour. Tactical in two. Leave in four to staging area from private airport. Mission is green."

Finally! Time to get that bastard!

Ramsey had to raise her voice as Cratty and Davis were now beginning to get into it.

"Guys! Burns has been taken. Mission is green. Briefing in one hour."

Davis stood for a moment and took her keys out as Cratty looked for her own set.

"I'll drive," Cratty said as she started to feverishly look for her keys through stinging eyes.

"You drive? I don't think so, Denise," Davis said. "I'm driving. Do you have your gear in your car, or did you leave lingerie and morning-after clothes in there instead for your friend?"

Davis didn't wait for an answer and walked away onstensibly to her car.

Finding her keys, Cratty responded by following on her trail, but was having difficulty navigating the uneven ground with her high heels and apparent blurry vision.

"I have my gear, Davis! And don't judge! At least my sexual advances have never been rejected by a coworker in my own house with Burns watching, Cougar!" Cratty yelled as she tried to shorten the gap between them.

Oh man! That's low.

Ever since it had been revealed that Davis was called "Cougar" in Burns's interrogation, Davis had made it her business to hurt anyone who called her that.

"I was medicated from being shot, working a case, while you were shopping in New York, Denise!" she countered while expanding the distance between them.

"Just shut up, Jillian! Just shut the hell up!"

"No! You shut up, Denise!"

Ramsey stood for a moment as she watched the two retreating women arguing.

Not sure which was more dangerous, the mission or being around Cratty and Davis, Ramsey reluctantly followed.

"Unbelievable."

~

Rebecca Lambert was sitting in the last booth near the kitchen of the Chinese restaurant, the *Golden Garden*, with her teenage daughters, Emma and Rosemarie.

At least, that's what our covers are. Not bad really. Lambert from Littleton.

It was Friday night, which meant they would spend a couple of hours getting ready, and then go out to the town for a late dinner.

Late by American standards.

SBecky remembered her dinners with Emma and David in Greece and Spain. Willamette Valley, Oregon, was a very nice place to live, raise children, and have a garden. She remembered that Samantha had a plan for all of them to live in the valley before Burns came into the picture, and before Emma and David arrived. With a bittersweet smile, Becky refocused on Rosemarie's story about what happened at school as Emma listened carefully. She watched with joy as she saw her little girl, now fourteen, listening attentively to her older sister she was just getting to know.

Funny. Rosemarie seems like an older Emma. Sisters should be together. You would have liked Rosemarie, Sam.

Becky reflected on how she had once again made a change. Losing David was crushing for her. But with David and Samantha's deaths, she was now left in charge of taking care of Emma and Rosemarie. In the first few days of feeling depression and anxiety crashing in on her, she found comfort in asking, "What would you want me to do, David?" or "What would Sam say about this?" Between the both of them, she found that digging in deep to protect the girls was not an option, but a necessity.

If I don't, who will? Who will teach them to protect themselves? Who would kill for them? Who would die for them?

Becky smiled as she suddenly felt less alone as she put together a mental list of who would step in and take care of the girls.

Burns and Murphy would be there. Cratty, Ramsey, and Dillon would take a bullet for them. Andersen, Helms, Welch, and Davis would be there too. Not too bad, now that I think about it.

The marshals helped with finding the small house and a job, but Becky changed the plan by moving to a small apartment complex with lots of families, and took a part-time position as a paralegal, a job she used to do a lifetime ago. Four weeks into her new life, she could see that money was going to come up short unless she got an infusion of cash.

If you were here, Sam, you'd get the cash the old-fashioned way. I wish I could do that.

Becky utilized other skills and that meant she needed to go off grid, and return to one of two storage sites she was sure was still unknown to authorities, where new identities and cash would be. As a result, that meant telling the girls about their cross-country trek that needed to be completed in three days, leaving Friday after school and back by Monday. To do this, she needed to tell both Emma and Rosemarie the "whole" story. How Sam met Uncle Alex, and how David and she met. About her brother, Tony, and Emma's biological mother, their murders, and her biological father. Elaboration was required on living in Rhode Island, domestic terrorism, stealing for the Foreign Intelligence Agency, and moving to Kea. How Aunt Samantha was killed and how Becky killed the man who killed her sister, moving to Spain while Denise, Fitzy, Witzy, and the girls lived with them.

Becky knew it was difficult for Emma to hear about her father not being David, but actually Rosemarie's father. While Emma knew she was adopted, in a sense, the fantasy of a caring biological father and princess mother was completely shattered by the truth. The only positive point was Rosemarie's second-hand knowledge of the "nice" stories her grandfather had told her. Still, the deaths, conspiracies, deceptions, and people Emma knew doing these outrageous acts was visibly difficult for Emma to accept.

With Becky telling both of them everything as they traveled by train and bus, night into day, it was their arrival at the still intact, fully stocked storage container that provided hard evidence that the stories were true. Opening the large metal doors of the oversized container, Becky found the lanterns and was happy to see that Burns had obviously been there to replenish them as well as freshen gasoline for the late-model, nondescript compact car. The girls watched quietly, taking in all the things in the storage unit, including an array of weapons ranging from rifles to handguns. She realized that her selecting three sets of semi-automatic weapons and corresponding ammunition as if she were buying earrings had to look crazy to the girls. All of this was evidence that her stories were all true.

Becky slowed down to linger at neatly packed and stored clothes that would have been for David.

I miss you, honey

She closed her eyes to see his smiling face for a moment. After reflecting, she got back to work, sifting through what she needed and what she could leave behind. Taking a minute to put gas in the car, she drove it out into the brightly lit lot just outside of the container.

With two years' salary neatly compacted in a backpack, Becky took four blank birth certificates and two forged passports she had for herself, before locking the container up and returning to her new life in a late-model car.

As she walked to the car, she felt Emma slowing down to a halt.

"It's all true. The police and FBI. The old newspaper reports. That computer virus, 'Albatross.' Those people that killed Aunt Sam ... Uncle Alex being a spy .... Is there anything else you're not telling me?" Emma demanded, looking at Becky.

Hmm. Hurt? Sad? Feeling deceived? The last time I saw that look was from Mom a billion years ago. She thought back on her own childhood.

While David and Becky were always honest about Emma's past, they were both vague on why they were hiding from the authorities, except to say that the government just couldn't be trusted.

Taking her time, Becky thought for a moment and then realized she had left out two crucial details.

"Yes ... when they were coming to kill you and your father, your father set the house to explode, killing about fifteen soldiers. I killed at least four people who killed my sister and were going to kill Alex, you, me, and your father. David and I never hurt anyone before. We never wanted this and we just wanted to be left alone. We never forgot what we did and I never want to do that again. But if anyone tries to hurt either one of you, I will kill again. I don't judge people anymore. People have reasons for what they do. I never believed that until all this happened. I don't expect you to judge me. God and I can do that all by ourselves."

Becky fell silent. She looked deep into Emma's eyes with her own firmness and resolve surprising herself.

It was easy to see that Rosemarie was standing still, looking down and feeling very uncomfortable; Emma's eyes filled up as she closed the gap to hug her mother.

"I'm sorry ... it's just so hard to think of all of this ..." she sniffled out.

"I know, Pumpkin," Becky said as she waved to Rosemarie for a family hug. She had no idea how long they were like that.

The trip home was much easier, and quiet for the most part.

While initially she wondered if she had done the right thing, she ultimately felt that having the girls know the truth would protect them. They could now know why and how to be vigilant while not being paranoid. So when she parked and left the car in an underground, private-paid parking lot, she could see that both children realized that the car was to remain a secret in case they needed to leave quickly.

As the weeks passed, and each of them asked questions, one after another, Becky watched Emma mature and Rosemarie become more protective of Emma. To balance the truth, human drama, and tragedy, Becky made it a point to always reveal a positive, kind, and happy moment. That meant Becky could talk about the fun times and create new memories, new rituals, like going out to a fancy dinner as a family every Friday at 10:00 p.m.

You would have loved this, David. Sam ... I think you would have left. Too boring. Alex would have made you stay. I bet.

It was 10:30 when her phone vibrated, surprising her. She had finished a big job at the firm and they never called, and the marshals had a way of simply showing up. With some anxiety, Becky opened the phone and read a text.

"They took Burns. We are mobilizing. If possible, go dark and off grid. Take care. D.C."

Becky reread the short text and then shook her head, more as a confirmation to herself than a response.

So. It starts.

Becky took a moment before she decided on what she was going to say.

"Off grid in one hour. Destination unknown. Signal when to resurface. Will find you. Good luck and all of you stay safe. Tiny."

After reading it again she pressed the button to send, and thought of her next steps. After another moment, Becky wrote and sent a very short text out to John Murphy.

"Just got word to go off grid. All is already planned and prepared. Will be off line in one hour. RL."

Staring off into space after sending the text, she realized that Emma was talking to her.

"Mommy? Is something wrong?" Emma asked as Rosemarie fell silent, acutely aware of the shift in mood.

"It's Denise. The bad guys took Uncle Alex ...."

"No!" Emma said as her hand went to her mouth, while Rosemarie and Becky both reached out to calm her down.

"Emma. It's part of the plan," Rosemarie reminded her.

Grateful that Rosemarie was there Becky reiterated the plan in a soft, quiet tone.

"Honey, I told you that Uncle Alex, Denise, Ramsey, Davis, and everyone planned this to catch the bad guys."

As Emma composed herself, Becky looked at her watch and noted the time before she outlined her next plan. In an almost playful fashion, a method David would have been proud of, Becky posed her next set of questions to both girls.

"Okay. Do both of you have your travel bags packed?"

"Absolutely," Rosemarie said, with Emma nodding her head.

"All right. We're going to have dinner, but instead of going home, we'll leave them there and buy new clothes and stuff."

Rosemarie's smile spoke volumes at the thought of getting new clothes.

"Once we get the car, we'll drive south and east. Rosemarie? I want you to find the bus schedule that gets us to the car. Emma, I want you to think of someplace you've never been before that would be interesting--fun, but no tourists. It's gotta be in the US ...."

"Does that mean I can pick Alaska or Hawaii?" Emma jumped in.

"Not Hawaii. Can't use planes. Land routes only. Car only."

Becky stopped talking as the waiters brought their food. Once they left, Becky watched as both girls took their prepaid smart phones out. Becky was happy to see that neither girl had the marshal-issued cell phone.

Good girls. No cells, no GPS, no tracking. Burn phones only.

Becky felt her phone vibrate from an incoming text.

"Okay. Take care. Let me know if I can help. You know where to find me. Love to the girls. JM."

Becky nodded to herself, took out her small computer tablet and handed it to Emma to find a location as she dished out the food. Smiling, she thought of how David would have loved to have seen how she had turned distressing news and the need to flee into an adventure that could be fun.

Fake it until you make it.

She was worried for Alex, Denise, and Ramsey. All of them were pissed and wanted to kill Daniels. For Becky, she just couldn't generate that much hate or anger anymore to go hunting herself.

Been there, done that. It won't bring you or Sam back. It won't bring my David back.

As Becky started eating, she stopped the girls' searches and had them focus on dinner. In the silence of eating, Becky wanted to keep things as "normal" as possible as they prepared to embark into the night.

"Evaporate into the night," you used to say, Sam.

"So Rosemarie, what do you want to be when you get older? We have to think of college for you, and I want us to be close to where you go. At some point, your mother and grandparents are going to want to see you, too," Becky said as she took a bite of some spicy noodles. Looking up, Becky wondered why Rosemarie was not responding.

Rosemarie's eyes seemed to water up as she responded.

"I'd like that a lot. For you to be close by. I'd like to commute and live at home," she said.

"Cool!" Emma responded. "So what do you want to be when you grow up?" Emma continued.

Becky smiled as she listened, while moving her hand to her purse under the table. Feeling for her phone, she hunted around until she found the outline of her small semi-automatic weapon and extra clips.

At some point I'll have to teach you both how to shoot, too.

"Live at home or live on campus. Emma and I will always be there with you."

List of Characters

Alexander J. Burns – aka "**Falcon 5**." First seen in *Albatross,* Burns survives a helicopter crash while en route to a black-ops mission to kill the terrorist leader, Oman Sharif Sudani. Brain-injured, he gets treatment that helps him regain his memory, and realizes he is a logistics field operative for the Foreign Intelligence Agency, FIA.

Samantha Littleton – aka "**Raven**." Introduced in *Albatross* and carries into *Raven,* she is the first to find Burns being sedated in the hospital and facilitates his transfer to an outside psychologist who specializes in assisting trauma victims regain their memories.

Dr. David Caulfield – aka "**Samuel Coleridge**." First seen in *Albatross* and carried through to *Raven* and *Eagle,* he is the psychologist who treats Burns and helps him regain his memories. He is also the one who convinces his friends to take the fight to the Eric Daniels' organization, the FIA.

Eric I. Daniels – aka "**Eagle**." Mentioned in *Albatross,* first seen in *Raven,* and fully elaborated on in *Eagle,* he is the Chairman of the FIA, a privately held, clandestine intelligence agency that will work on behalf of the United States government when it aligns with its own interests and objectives.

Becky Littleton – aka "**Tiny**." Introduced in *Albatross* as Samantha's older foster sister as well as Emma Littleton's primary caretaker after her brother, Tony, is killed by the mob. In *Raven,* her lethal skills grow exponentially, as does her role as mother, sister and wife.

Steve Andersen – Lieutenant, North Reading Police Department, MA, is the first to interview the witness "Samuel Coleridge" in *Albatross*. Additionally, he was on the team of Army Intelligence at Guantanamo that connected the dots to locate Oman Sharif Sudani. He is also best friends with Diane Welch who grew up in the same South Boston neighborhood.

John Helms – FBI Director, Boston Regional Office, he is the first to detect the diversions and covert plan in *Albatross,* as well as attempting a negotiation for peace with Burns in *Raven*. He was also Diane Welch's CO briefly in Afghanistan.

Rachael Janeson – aka "**Black Swan.**" Specialist at the FBI Boston Regional Office in *Albatross*, she becomes lead specialist in *Raven* where she exposes a plot to thwart the FBI's attempt to bring Burns into custody, and promoted to Deputy FBI Director in *Eagle* where she manages a rescue operation in Spain and a manhunt in Tangiers.

Diane Welch – Commandant, Massachusetts State Troopers, first mentioned in *Albatross* as Steve Andersen's close friend. In *Raven*, we discover she was a Warrant Officer of a Marine Air Ground Task Force on a covert operation to stem the flow of arms from the Swat Valley, Pakistan. Betrayed by Thomas Webber, member of Daniels' FIA team in *Raven*, her role continues in *Eagle* with her in hot pursuit of Eric Daniels.

Thomas "Steel" Webber – First seen in *Raven* as the "face" of FIA, and Eric Daniels's top man, we learn in *Eagle* that he was the team leader responsible for keeping Burns sedated and monitored in *Albatross*.

Jillian T. Davis – aka "**Cougar.**" First seen in *Albatross,* she is an off-duty manager of the FIA's Operations Center who is recruited to courier top-secret, external hard drives to a secure location. In *Raven*, Davis leaves the FIA and teams up with the FBI to negotiate with

Burns, while in *Eagle*, she is lead field specialist with Thomas "Nine" Williams and Daniel "Ice" Maddox, to disrupt Daniels' plans and take down one of his key players.

Denise Cratty – Introduced in *Albatross,* she is the on-duty manager of the FIA's Operations Center when it is compromised. In *Raven*, Cratty is on probation in the new Operations Center where she is the unlikely peacekeeper to end a dangerous standoff and then becomes lead agent on a VIP protection team in Spain. In *Eagle*, after tragedy strikes, she vows to bring her team back to the US and find the people responsible.

Jeffery Glenn – Seen first in *Raven* as mild-mannered Operations Center boss of Cratty and her team stationed in New York. In *Eagle*, after he is discharged from the FIA, he is paid for one last assignment that puts him on a path that will alter Cratty's and Burns's lives forever.

Emma Littleton – Introduced as a baby in *Albatross*, she is under the care of Becky Littleton and David Caulfield. She is introduced to her half-sister, Rosemarie, in *Eagle*. Their shared biological father is the son of South Boston mob leader, John David Murphy.

Alica Wise – Introduced in *Eagle*, she is a former Foreign Intelligence Agent specialist recruited for the top-secret, deep-cover "Intimate Contact" Branch. Still aligned with Daniels, she plans to carry out her orders no matter what.

Christine Dillon & Ana Ramsey – First seen as part of Cratty's Operations Center team in *Raven*, they later become leaders in their own right in *Eagle*. They are close friends of Cratty and her team members Cindy Belben, Kelly Fitzgerald and Molly Horowitz.

John Daniel Murphy – Leader of organized crime in South Boston, he is the paternal grandfather of both Emma Littleton and her half-sister, Rosemarie Flores. His character is hinted at in *Albatross* and *Raven* as the father of the man who kills Tony Littleton.

Dr. Volkov Volkonoff – aka **"Wolf."** First mentioned in *Falcon*, his late appearance reflects the cloak of mystery that surrounds Rachael Janeson's maternal uncle. His involvement in the Russian intelligence community is well documented though unclear in details. With the sole exception of watching out for his niece, his motivations remain unknown.

About the Author

In addition to creating the *Birds of Flight* series and the other award-winning science fiction stories, *Future Prometheus* and *Intelligent Design*, Erickson holds a BA in psychology and sociology from Boston College and a master's degree in psychiatric social work from the Simmons School of Social Work. Certified in cognitive behavioral treatment and a post-trauma specialist, he is also a senior instructor of psychology and counseling at Cambridge College, visiting lecturer at Salem State University's School of Social Work and a senior therapist in a clinical group practice in the Merrimack Valley, Massachusetts. To learn more about the author, his writing and future projects, please look at the following websites:

Blog – www.jmeindieblog.com
Author's website – www.jmericksonindiewriter.com
Publisher's website – www.jmericksonindiewriter.net